watching
oksana

Also by Emily Meier

Suite Harmonic: A Civil War Novel of Rediscovery
Time Stamp: A Novel
In the Land of the Dinosaur: Ten Stories and a Novella
The Second Magician's Tale

watching oksana *and other stories*

EMILY MEIER

SKY SPINNER PRESS
SAINT PAUL, MINNESOTA

© 2011 by Sky Spinner Press
117 Mackubin Street
St. Paul, MN 55102
skyspinnerpress.com

All rights reserved. No part of this publication may be reproduced, stored in a retrieval system, or transmitted in any form or by any means—electronic, mechanical, photocopying, scanning, or otherwise—without the express written permission of the publisher.

Published in the United States of America
Sky Spinner Press Books Distribution through Itasca Books
itascabooks.com

ISBN 978-0-9838983-0-6

First Sky Spinner Press Printing, 2011

Library of Congress Catalog Control Number: 2011913831

9 8 7 6 5 4 3 2 1

Cover and book design:
Jeenee Lee Design
Cover painting: *Resist IV* © David Cost

In memory of my mother

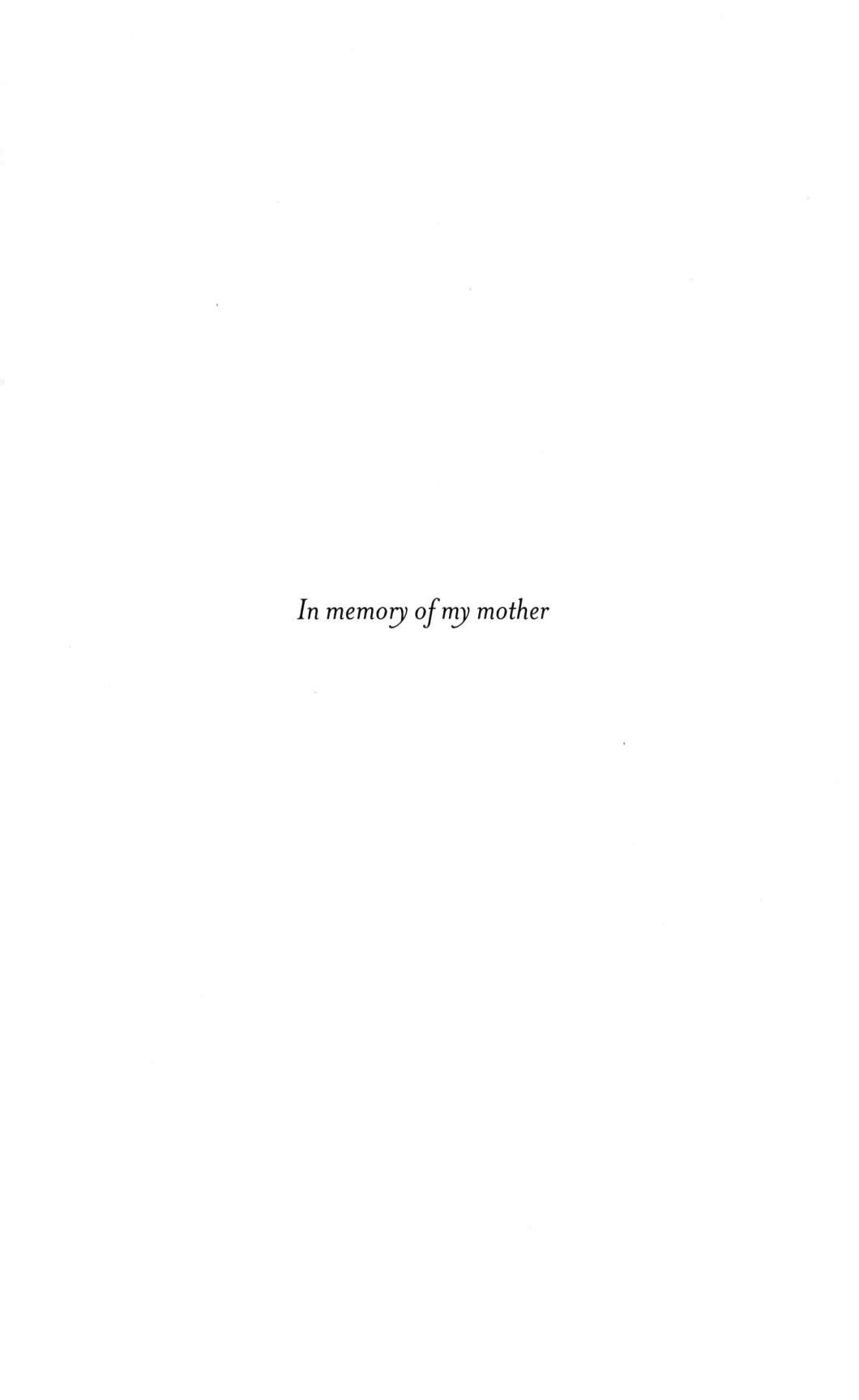

CONTENTS

I WHAT YOU DO FOR LOVE

2   The Temple of Amun
28   Watching Oksana
51   Mother Tongue
77   The Fields of Flanders
87   Moving
95   Eleven Days to China
103 Treasures

II AMERICAN SNAPSHOT

114 American Snapshot, 1993

III LAURA

124 Birdman
139 Journeys in the Hidden World
148 Floating
168 Things

IV SWIMMING

178 Swimming

203 *Acknowledgments*

I

WHAT YOU DO FOR LOVE

The Temple of Amun

Elena has made dinner. Fresh pasta and a green salad, a Stilton she bought on East Houston Street on her way home. Her class left her preoccupied. Elliott surmises this and that there is something more. He suspects this and knows, too, that she will gauge the right moment to tell him. He touches her waist and she moves sideways for him to open the drawer for the corkscrew. She undoes her apron and then puts the bowl of pasta on the table and sits half cross-legged in her sweater and jeans while he pours the wine.

"Cabernet," she says when she's taken a sip from her glass. Elliott nods. He has observed her mental note, the quick dart of her eyes to the bottle label. He thinks once more how well he knows her—how, if she were male, he would know her entirely. In all the ways she is uncertain, catching up, she is what he was. Years ago. He has known this for the three months since they met.

He is an engineer and, to him, math is a second form of speech, sometimes the first, and he can never look at Elena without registering both that she is beautiful and that she is less than half his age, younger even than his son—younger, particularly, than his son. He knows that it is not her youth itself that draws him to her, but rather the distinctive quality of that youth—the effort she makes to show she is not in over her head—the air she maintains of being easy in New York, of being comfortable with her professors and students (no matter how brilliant or privileged they are), and of being careful to pronounce correctly every word that she knows. Invariably, he finds these things touching, for he recognizes the effort and occasional panic behind them.

She is twirling angel hair against a spoon, knotting it around a shrimp. "When are you leaving?" she asks.

"I can stay until morning."

"I mean on your trip," she says, and then she sees he is teasing.

"I'll find out tomorrow. Probably Sunday." He touches her hand. He understands that to Elena, child of short-hop moves from Arizona to New Mexico and back again (those pointless detours with her mother and whatever siblings her resident stepfathers offered), he has had an extraordinary life. Her mental note taking includes a list of all the places he's been and all the projects he's worked on. Cleopatra's Needles. The Pyramid of Cholula. The Seikan Rail Tunnel and the European Southern Observatory. The list is very long and, more than once, has prompted Elena to make carefully phrased observations (following a delay long enough for a computer search or even a trip to the library) that engineers, or at least architects, must *think* in materials. That it's very clever how the shells of the Sydney Opera House face and link each other so all of them, with just two legs apiece, have the support of four. That it was more inventive than elegant for the engineers of the Grand Coulee Dam to stop the creeping plastic clay by freezing the leading edge with brine circulating in the toe of the mass. Elliott has known not to seem amused at such comments. And besides, Elena is always right, careful as she is to exclude the context beyond what she can say with certainty.

Elena puts her wineglass down on the table and looks at him. "I've got a student who's showing all the signs of paranoid schizophrenia. I don't know if it's suggestion or acting. It's too serial to be the real thing." She pauses. "Elliott, I should have told you sooner. Hoover called."

"Hoover has this number?" Elliott feels the involuntary, upward pivot of his eyes to hers.

"Of course. It's only unlisted because of school."

"And why did Hoover call?" Elliott tries to keep the edge from his voice, tries to sound no more and no less than a father interested in his son, though it is not the easiest thing to do. At the moment, he and Hoover are not really friends. The tension between them that erupted fully when Hoover's mother finally divorced Elliott has not really dissipated, and it hardly seems that it will now that they are both enamored of the same woman.

"He tried you at your apartment. The machine was off. His grandmother is much worse. Eugenie is." Elena clears her throat as she tries the name. "He said you would want to know. And she wants to see you. It's all right with his mother. With Audra."

"The imprimatur." Elliott hears the dryness in his voice. Yet the sadness he feels is absolutely honest. He has never stopped caring for Eugenie. Old New York. Gracious, as she'd have to have been to welcome him as a son-in-law. And frequently mischievous, too.

"Hoover said he could meet you there. He thought tomorrow morning if you can make it."

"Where's there?"

"She's at home."

"At Audra's?"

"Is Audra's home? He said home. I don't know." Elena sits quietly, and Elliott sees the wariness in her eyes that has sometimes made him think he is looking back through time and at himself. Her eyes are brown with green flecks and, below them and below her perfectly elongated nose, her lips are the lips he traces in the dark and thinks of when he is at his desk drawing on a notepad, their fullness reminding him of something he read once—that it takes a hint of darker blood to bring out looks. He has not asked her if she is part Mexican or Indian, Creole, if there is anything ethnic in her white-bread Scottsdale past.

And he does not ask her now. Instead, he picks up her hand, kisses the thumbnail and then the thumb pad.

"Eugenie would want to be in the city. It must be Audra's. Your pasta is entirely perfect," he says.

"I told him you'd call."

"I will."

"And I told him I'd meet him for a drink. I hope you don't mind. When you're in Egypt."

"Should I mind?"

Elena shakes her head. She passes him the salad and he does not look at her because of the welling feeling that is desire, in part, but jealousy, too, a living thing like the snake the crazy Bronx woman forced down her daughter's throat to kill the devil she thought she possessed. Elena has told him that her affair with Hoover was a friendship more than anything, though she concedes Hoover's view may differ even now. Elliott has answered that this is not a subject they can discuss. Jealousy is new to him and he is disturbed to encounter it in response to his own son, appalled he is in a position *to* encounter it, though, in their defense, he and Elena crossed this particular line before they knew it existed. He cannot comprehend either how a relationship that was sexual in any way can be called "not really sexual," as Elena has termed it. It is an age issue, he thinks. He is not used to women young enough to treat sex lightly in the way Elena implies.

"Did I put too much vinegar in the salad dressing?" she asks, which Elliott knows is her way of asking him why he has grown so quiet.

"Not at all," he says. He stands up to pour the wine so he can kiss her neck, touch her hair which is like rough silk beneath his hand. "So why isn't my son good enough for you?" he asks and she turns to look at him, but then simply smiles when she recognizes his question is rhetorical, an apology. She untwists her legs from her chair seat.

"I'm thinking this student should be on Broadway. He's got the paranoia down pat. It's like complete sanity but with a tilt." Elena has speared a mushroom from her salad and she holds it in the air, her eyebrows tight in concentration. "Really it's like that. I had a stepfather who had a table saw and he'd flip it and lock it in place to cut an angle. It's as if this fellow's done that with his brain. If I let him get to me, though, I'm afraid I'll lose the whole class. It's not like my rich Phoenix kids in counseling. Nothing like that. Maybe I miss it. When all they make up is angst."

Elliott listens to her voice with its open vowels. From the beginning, she has intrigued him with her westernness. She's a strider. Long legs. Long skirts when she's not wearing jeans. She'd make a great model, he thinks—the long body and open face. She has the carry-to-the-back-of-the-room look that can take a whole crowd along, though there is something still awkward about her at times, something unformed. "Tell me again about paradoxical undressing," he says.

"Basic. The body tricks the mind into thinking it's burning up. It happens right before you freeze to death and if you're strong enough, you strip. Why are we talking about this?"

"We can talk about anything. Maybe you want to know if my parents named me after Elliott Ness, if that's why I named my son Hoover."

"Who's Elliott Ness? Elliott, please. I only mentioned Hoover because he called."

"A G-man, he was a G-man. They named me after Elliott Roosevelt. And Eugenie was a Hoover. Just so you know."

"Thank you." Elena pushes her chair back. "Did you want fruit with the Stilton?" She gets up and looks in the fridge.

He watches her, thinks of her, his western woman, sitting on the bed and pulling her boots on. Five seconds after he learned she was a horsewoman, he decided she looked like one. He imagined her not in New York or even Arizona but somewhere in Big Sky country with snow-capped mountains rising through the clouds and a pack of horses grazing on tufty grass beside the foothills, a chestnut nibbling at the sugar in her hand, Elena looping her arms around its neck and swinging up to ride bareback with her hair streaming out behind her.

But there is the aura of the city about her now. She has told him that she loves meeting him for a drink when he's finished work. That she likes the first taste of the whiskey and his turning all his attention to her as if the rest of his life is on hold.

Which it is. When he's with her, it is.

That has been true, in fact, from the moment they met, Elena in a contingent of people her advisor had brought to a party, and Elliott studying her all evening, watching her take things in and listening to the care with which she offered just the right rejoinder or eyed other people's glasses before accepting more wine. In the foyer, on his way out, he heard her say she was getting a cab. On an impulse he offered her a ride, and she hesitated, her pondering, dark eyes sizing him up. "I can get character references from the other room if you wait a minute," he told her, and then she'd laughed and said yes to the ride and went to thank their hosts. He drove her home, her directions full of landmarks as if she were a guidebook, and he thought she was learning the city as he had: by committing maps to memory. From his car, he watched her into the lighted entry of her building.

Two nights later, sitting on his kitchen floor, they looked through the wall of windows at the blur of diamond and sapphire lights that framed the invisible tableau of sleep and pleasure and crime: Manhattan. His city for thirty years, hers for less than one. He could sense her excitement. In the dark kitchen, she told him her fantasy of a room where the walls would not need pictures, but themselves would have carvings and thin panels of inlaid tile. In summertime she would cram the fireplace with pots of ivy and ferns and keep fresh flowers on a gilt table. She would have wall sconces to hold candles, and giant doors of mahogany with etched glass, and arched windows covered with damask curtains in a pale salmon and white to match the upholstery. And she wanted the perfect Oriental rug.

She had looked at him then and smiled. "I know," she said. "A little girl's dream of being princess. I wanted to tell you, because this is far more beautiful."

Now she has folded herself into his lap. "What's a nice girl like you doing with a man like me?" he asks, stroking her calf, and when she answers, it's as if they've been thinking of the same thing.

"If I can remember, you called to ask if I'd left my tickets in your car, though of course they were yours. You never did say how you got my number."

"A small ploy. I have my resources. But that's not an answer."

"I'm having fun?"

"Possibly. That's a start."

"I'm pretending I've stolen my mother's date?"

"You did that?"

"Not in a million years. Maybe if I'd been armed and wanted to rescue her. It's not a bad thought."

"So it's not a Freudian thing for older men?"

"Doubtful. There's nothing like that in my past."

"And that's a guaranteed predictor?"

"Maybe I want you for you. Isn't it your turn by now?"

"You like the view from my apartment."

"I meant what's a nice guy like you doing with a girl like me?"

Elliott laughed. "You really need to ask?"

"Don't tell me it's only about the sex."

"I won't tell you that. But what's your plan for this pomegranate?"

"So change the subject. OK, I'll feed it to you. With the cheese. And then will you call him?

Pretend wife. *Naggy little wife*, he wants to say. He doesn't, though, for he knows it would hurt her or hurt him, put the wrong ball into play.

The light is just graying into morning when they leave her apartment. Elliott lets his car idle, double-parked, while Elena buys coffee and bagels. A pigeon lights on the hood. When Elena comes back, her hands are full and the rope of her bag is slipping from her shoulder. She hands him his coffee, and the car smells sharply and pleasantly bitter.

"You can drop me," she says, when he has driven a little way. "There," she points, and she leans swiftly to kiss him and gathers up her notebooks, her bag, her half-eaten bagel. She grips her coffee in her hand.

"I'll call you," he says, reaching across her to push her door open. "Even if you won't be home."

"Yes. Let me know," she says. "About Eugenie. Leave a message." Then she is walking up the sidewalk away from him and he feels gloomy, feels the long, pulling arc he must make back into his own life. He waits, hoping she will turn around, but she is purposeful, walking with her long stride. He watches her pass each corner, feels the echo of her as she grows smaller. It is like looking into facing mirrors. Or, rather, it is like being in a Moorish castle where the arched doorways follow one upon another to a vanishing point that is finally only the suggestion of light.

Two hours later, he buzzes his secretary from his office and says that he is going to the apartment in Carnegie Hill. He verifies Audra's number for her. He has talked with Zurich. He has made final plans for Luxor. As he thought, he will leave on Sunday. But now there is this family business, though he does not want to see Hoover, does not want to see Audra at all, would like to see Eugenie, but not Eugenie dying, which he knows that she is.

A year ago, when they were both in Paris, he invited her to lunch at the Eiffel Tower. "I will tell my friends you escorted me to the Grand Suppositoire," she said. "Except for Sophie. For Sophie, who likes romance and who shocks easily, I will call it the tragic lamppost."

They ordered the same thing, beginning with escargot, and he answered all of Eugenie's questions. He explained about the hydraulic jacks in the base of the tower's columns and the band of girders at the first-floor level, telling her, too, about the elephant who'd walked to the first platform and the forty-five tons of paint required for the paint job and then, when the coffee arrived, she told him her cancer had come back. She was smoking a cigarette purposefully as she spoke. "They'll do a mastectomy, though who would know looking? It's all right. You can ask if they didn't do it already." Eugenie smiled and Elliott tried to laugh, but he saw the mist in her eyes as the smoke curled between them.

The doorman at Audra's apartment building lets him in and the maid he hired for her discretion, though it's been transferred now to Audra, opens the apartment door and tells him Eugenie is expecting him, that Hoover hasn't arrived yet. Elliott follows her down the hallway to a bedroom. It is a familiar walk to the place where he slept by himself in the months before Audra asked him to leave.

Eugenie is alone in the room. She is lying beneath a coverlet on a bed he and Audra bought years ago at an estate sale, a bed that Audra penciled in on her long, chosen list of their worldly goods. Eugenie is chalky pale. She is no longer any real color and this surprises him for, above all, Eugenie is vivid. Elliott expects her to move, to try to sit up against her pillows or to reach for his hand, but only her lips move.

"Excuse me," she whispers, the words coming out a breath at a time, her voice a husk of its alto, "for not . . . putting my . . . earrings on."

He leans to kiss her cheek. It is dry of scent, oddly boneless.

"Handsome." She closes her eyes and keeps them closed. "Still."

"Does the sun bother you? I'll shut the blinds," he says, but she moves her head in a slow "no" on the pillow.

"Warm. On the eyes. Audra see you . . . so handsome? My fault. Not . . . hers." The words are thin as if her vocal cords are damped. Her lips make a faint sucking noise. "Stronger, I'd shiv—er . . . like a Sister . . . Kate."

"Want to dance, Eugenie?" he says, guessing, and guessing right, he thinks. He puts his face next to hers, rocks his head in the slightest motion so their hair grazes when they touch. He has always danced with Eugenie. Eugenie has always danced. When Hoover was born, she did not rock him but waltzed him around the room, promising him a tango when he learned to walk. "Shimmy time," Elliott says, reaching to hold her hand, but he can only cover it lightly with his, feel how cold it is, and inert.

Behind him, he hears a step and the slight cough of interruption.

"Yes?" he says. He turns to the maid.

"Mr. Connolly again. He says he can't make it after all. He'll call you later."

Elliott nods. "So your grandson's standing us up," he says looking back at Eugenie, but now she's asleep.

He lowers his voice. "I'll sit with her. If you'd let me know when Mrs. Connolly's due back."

"She's here, sir. She's just waiting until you leave."

Elliott looks up. Then he nods again. "I'll let myself out." He takes his hand from Eugenie's. He leans forward and kisses her forehead, feels the faint air of her breath, though she doesn't stir.

Outside, he is glad to walk the blocks to his car. It is still chilly, early November cool, and he wants the space of the weather to help distance him from Eugenie and the pallor of her encroaching death. More than that, he wants Elena. He waits for traffic at a corner and thinks of her crossing a parking lot, her jeans white over the muscles in her thighs, her eyes checking carefully around as if she holds a periscope on the world.

He is at his desk when Hoover calls to make apologies and to relay the doctor's report on Eugenie.

"I hope she didn't sign one of those pull-the-plug things for your mother," Elliott says. When Hoover is silent, Elliott assumes that she did.

"I didn't see a nurse." He pauses. "At least her mind seems clear."

"There's a nurse. Twenty-four hours. They're giving her morphine. She's pleased. She says finally there's an addiction no one can jump her about. You're headed to Egypt."

"Yes."

"Business?"

"Business."

"If she dies while you're gone, do you want to be contacted?"

Elliott is surprised. Contacted? Through his office? Through Elena? Certainly he could give his son a number to reach him. "Yes, of course," he says. "Let me know if anything happens. I'll put you on with my secretary."

He puts the receiver down and looks at it. *Fly safe, Dad. Keep your arms flapping.* In his mind, he plays the old sign-off.

He picks up the phone again and dials Elena's apartment and gets her machine. He listens to the message, and he cuts it off before the beep and then hits the redial and listens again. He talks for the recorder: "About Eugenie, much as expected. She's very weak, still game. Talk to you later. Did I ever tell you I hate Thursdays?"

Which he does. Or he does today. Elena's last class isn't over till ten, and he would pick her up but they have agreed, in a difficult compromise, that she will always get a cab at night, that it is senseless for him to drive in rush hour from the Village for his Friday morning field checks, which are sometimes as far away as Hackensack or Yonkers. Still, it is all he can do not to call again and say he is coming, though he has his self-discipline, his hard-earned sureness and a distaste for the idea a woman could leave it compromised. He opens a folder of blueprints, takes out a notebook and a pen.

In his bedroom Elliott wakes from a nightmare that flashes in his consciousness and is gone like the headlights of a car swerving away at a corner. His eyes fix on the dresser, on the glint from a paperweight, its swirls of blown color muddied together in the shadows. He pushes the covers away, feels his own edginess and the elevation of his heartrate, the weight of the darkness. He gets up. At the window, he pulls back the shade. The city shines below him. Its distant sounds mix into white noise that is almost silence—to him, a sound like the darkest forest.

He lets the shade fall back. As a boy, he heard his mother rocking and rocking in the sleepless mountain night. He would pull himself over his window ledge, the summer moon casting silver between the trees, and see the top of her head as she arced forward on the porch below, flypapers she'd hung from the eaves barricading her from the circling bats. "Go to sleep, Ellie," she called when he bumped against the window frame.

Even now he can smell her bleached nightgown, white as bones, its scent as keen as Elena's absence. He is so far from home. Decades. Eons from the son who did not follow his father into the mines of Pennsylvania, light-years from the child ashamed of a father whose friends carried him home drunk. They brought him up the rocky path and banged on the door. They left him crying and sick in front of his wife and sons.

Elliott pulls on his robe. He has lost the language of his past, replaced it with words like berm and sewage lagoon, ice lens, *aufeis*. These are his words on a sleepless night. While his family disintegrated, they reeled through his mind and, like foot soldiers, they march through now: scarps, solifluctions, compression wave velocities, interstitial pores.

He goes into the living room and wakes up his computer. It hums in the dark. When he sees there's no e-mail, he clicks on commodities. The numbers flash onto the screen. For a while he watches them, but there is no real movement at 3 a.m. and, anyway, he does not know what movement to expect. He's no longer aware of weather patterns and harvest projections, the information that helped him sell on the bounce of the nighttime market and earn so much money during his divorce insomnia that, for the financial settlement, he simply wrote Audra a check. The risk in the market, the calculation had calmed him, had given him a numerical counterpoint to the drumming words.

He looks at the AP wire and checks his e-mail again. This time there's a message: *Families of origin class. Very intense perspectives. Went to Brewsky's. Too late to call. Glad she's still game. I can't sleep. Wish I had a comic book. Wish even more you were here.*

So they are both awake. Elliott stretches, cracks his neck against his shoulders. He pictures Elena barefoot in a T-shirt and pecking one-handed at her computer, her hair brushed out but with a tiny crimp from being tied back and a hint of snarl on one side from her pillow. He doesn't write back. He puts the computer on hibernate, feels a faint irritation that "families of origin" is now part of the string of words, that it is knotted up with transverse vertical planes, glaciolacustrine sediment, that it is part of the night.

On Friday evening a cold drizzle is falling. Elliott is late to meet Elena. He crosses the street and sees her through a window, her head bent at an angle to the window frame. The red neon of the bar sign above the window tints the rain that streaks the glass, but Elena is diffused the amber of the room's light.

"Sorry I'm late." Inside, Elliott flicks his coat to get the rain off and then puts it over an empty chair.

"Just a paragraph to go," she says holding her finger up, and he signals the waiter for drinks and waits while Elena finishes reading and closes her book. "The traffic bad?" she asks.

"I was late anyway." He reaches for her hands. "We stopped at Drummond's Y to shower. The site's a mess. It's good he's a partner or I'd fire him."

"Lucky for Drummond. But we have until Sunday night?" He hears the early note of planning in her voice, the balancing of time: her weekend work versus him.

"Until Sunday night. Or Saturday night. Or we can call it a night tonight."

"Elliott." She wrinkles her eyebrows and gives him an uncertain half-smile.

The old habit. The one he thought he had shed. "Definitely Sunday night," he says, softening his tone, angry with himself for being defensive, aware that the reason has nothing and everything to do with Elena. At his one-beer lunch, in a moment of weakness he told Drummond he was seeing an extraordinary girl.

"Hope you can keep your end up. Young tail, huh? Good for you," Drummond said, and for an instant Elliott flashed on the old days and the Connolly boys emptying a bar. He wanted to plant a jab on Drummond's bald head.

"Is this where we're eating?" Elena says.

"I thought so."

"Me, too. I ordered bruschetta to start. Am I saying that right? Here. It's coming now."

When the waiter sets the plate down, Elena cuts Elliott a piece and edges a sliding tomato back on the crust. Then, over their drinks, she tells him about her day. He asks about the student with the faux paranoia and she says he's switched to sleeping in class, and Elliott asks if it's an improvement. She says that it is. Elliott tells her more about Eugenie and about her second husband, a poet and the love of her life, who died in a boating accident off Marblehead and how Eugenie had beaten herself up over it, saying he would never have been anywhere near a yacht if it hadn't been for her money, that he was naturally poor and lyrical. As he wants her to, Elena laughs.

"Eugenie's always assumed things are her fault. Sometimes she's right," he says. "She liked me and thought that meant I was suitable for Audra."

"And you weren't?"

"I was a disaster for Audra."

Elena looks at him, but Elliott does not explain his answer, does not say that having Audra, the ice princess, was like reaching for a brass ring that was anchored in air. "She's a wonderful daughter, don't mistake me, but you know her father knowing her," Eugenie told him once. "His neatness. His punctuality. The exaggerated sense of propriety. She was always this little Prussian. Of course she's lovely and perfectly finished, but money will do that. No, I know you didn't marry her for the money. But Elliott, you did marry her for what the money made of her."

"I called my mother," Elena says.

"And how is she?"

"She's back with Joe. No big surprise."

"And Joe is . . ."

"Stepdad number three. Tom's dad, as in Tom of Tom and Lucy." Elena is speaking carefully, watching his reaction.

"The hardware store?"

"Right. You're good." She smiles and eases back in her chair, and Elliott sees the relief in her eyes and he is pleased with himself for remembering the right stepbrother—the one who loaned her the money for undergraduate school she paid off waitressing. He doesn't ask more about her mother. He knows it is up to Elena to keep up the contact, that her mother doesn't call, that when Elena calls her, her mother is still surprised she's in Manhattan.

"Maybe she thinks you mean Manhattan, Kansas," Elliott said once, and Elena looked so stricken he'd thought his joke accidentally outed the truth.

"Come to Egypt with me," he says.

Elena looks at him slyly over her drink. "Go down the Nile by felucca and sleep on the banks? Zip our sleeping bags together?"

"I was thinking more of the Winter Palace in Luxor. Or even Club Med for you, lady, though you'd like the Winter Palace. It has verandas. And it *is* palatial. Egypt built glorious hotels for the nineteenth-century tourist traffic. How do you know about feluccas?" Elliott traces her finger on the table. He is thinking of his first trip to Egypt, which was long ago—Nasser's rule—and of the tall sails gliding past palm trees as the feluccas slid quietly along the Nile.

"One of my friends. Summer. She said the facilities were a bucket hanging over the side."

"You could manage that?"

"Of course. I wish I could go. Just forget about Morena's paper and Mr. J. Crew-shirt being crazy or sleeping in my class. Egypt sounds romantic. The pyramids. All the history. A good place for people in love . . ."

"We need to order," Elliott says. He picks up his menu, and then he decides he is going to tell her something he hadn't meant to. "I got your e-mail. Elena, 3 a.m.?"

"You were awake? Really? I didn't get your message. I'll check when we get back. Or are we going to your place instead of mine?"

"No message to check. Your place is fine. Unless you want the hot tub." Elliott studies the menu, feels Elena looking at him though he doesn't look back. Then there's a heavy thump against his feet and he's aware of the clunky weight of her book bag on his legs.

"My essentials. We can go to your place," she says.

By early morning there's an icy pit of rain against the kitchen window. Elliott listens to it in the dark waiting for his coffee. Elena is still asleep. He likes thinking of her in his bed, of her mock-commandeering presence. Sometime in the night she sat between the pillows, cross-legged and eating grapes.

"You like that position," he said. "Sitting that way."

"Maybe. Maybe it's left from gymnastics." She ate another grape. "I wanted to be a gymnast, and then I grew a foot."

"Which one?"

"The foot on top of the four feet eight."

"And that's when you became a hot dog skier?"

"Approximately."

"Don't do it," Elliott said, and Elena, holding the grapes, cocked her eyebrow into a question.

"That kind of skiing? Do what?"

Elliott ate two of the grapes. He held a grape on her nose and balanced his answer in the silence. "Right. Skiing," he said finally. "You'll break something. I like you in one piece."

Elliott pours his coffee and sits at the kitchen table. He is thinking of the street fair they went to the first day they left this apartment together. They had stopped to listen to a saxophone and Elena said, "Hey, there's somebody I know. We saw each other a little, but I think he's over it. He must be over it. I should say hello. I should introduce you so he *knows* it's over."

Elliott had felt her hand slip from his. He was watching the start of a mummers' parade assemble in the street, and he tossed the core of the pear he was eating into a dumpster and heard it thud on the empty bottom. He peered inside, wondering if he'd found the only empty dumpster in all of New York City, and then he heard Elena's voice again.

"Funny, but you two have the same last name," she said, and Elliott turned around and saw his son, who was handsome in the way of his brawling uncles when they were young, but with Audra's patrician nose.

"Hoover was crazy enough to volunteer for our research project last semester," Elena started, but then Hoover put his hand on her arm and cut her off.

"Elena, he's my dad," he said. He looked at Elliott, and then, without smiling, he excused himself and moved away through the thronging mass of clowns.

"Oh my God," Elena said. "Elliott, did you tell me you have a son? Oh my God."

Later, over coffee, she had wanted to talk about it, but Elliott refused. "I don't care if the whole psychiatric panel of the AMA says we should talk about this," he said. "I'm not going to."

He hears Elena stirring now, and he finishes his coffee and starts fixing breakfast. When Hoover was born, the message arrived by telex. He was in Ankara, and he flew to New York on a plane half filled with returning Vietnam vets whose duffel bags crowded the tarmac. At the hospital, he was unshaven, hurrying down the corridor.

"Your son is beautiful. He ripped me apart," Audra said, and she started to cry and then pushed him away when he leaned down to kiss her.

"If I'd known he'd be early . . ."

"Should I have waited a week? Clenched my legs?" She was still crying, and Elliott stood awkwardly next to her in the gown he'd been given until the nurse came in carrying his son and nudged the knitted cap and his blanket and diaper aside to show off his tiny ears and tinier penis. She put him in Elliott's arms.

"He's perfect," she said, and Elliott held him. He made a kind of eye contact with the glassy blue eyes. He felt the light, tensile weight on his arm, and then a small, boxing hand grip his finger and, with it, a sense of vulnerability, a fear of loss more intense than anything he'd experienced before or since.

Except at the mummers' parade. At the mummers' parade, he'd felt the same hollow fear.

Elliott butters the toast and puts it on a tray. Elena has a child's soft blurriness in waking up. Or what Hoover's was. In the bedroom, he pushes the blankets back to make room for the tray.

"Breakfast in bed. You're a love." She yawns and works herself back against the pillows. "Cinnamon toast." She covers another yawn. "And melon. Is it a Carnegie melon? How did a miner's son get so many Carnegies in his life? You're feeding me your alma mater."

Elliott takes his suitcase off the closet shelf. "I'm going to show you how to pack an average-sized suitcase with clothes for a three-week trip anywhere in the world."

"If you're a man."

"If you're a man."

"But you're not going to stay for three weeks."

"No, I'm not, but I still want to show you.

"I already can fold your T-shirts."

"Yes you can," Elliott says, for that was also something they'd done in the night. They'd made love on the couch, the CD Elena had pulled from her book bag playing with a languorous, hitching rhythm. Slowly insistent. Quietly building. Finally blinding.

"Chausson. *Quelques Danses,*" she whispered as he rolled away.

"Some dances is right," he'd managed, and then the buzzer buzzed on the load of laundry he started because Elena didn't believe he did his own, and he got up to empty the dryer. Elena followed him and his full basket into the bedroom. When she asked, he showed her how he liked his T-shirts folded. She did one herself, and then she tipped the basket onto the bed and tossed herself on top of the heap.

"When you put your underwear on in the desert, you'll think of me," she said. "I'm still surprised you do your own laundry."

"I'm good at it," he said. He leaned over, and he kissed her naked shoulders and her neck. "You're a prime number. Let's add you to the list."

"Good at what?" she said, and he slid his hands beneath her and turned her on her back.

"I'll think of you exactly like this," he said. "I'm memorizing. And I'm memorizing how this feels going back inside. I'm memorizing you arching, and good God, Elena . . ." He could get out maybe a word per sensation. He was like Eugenie with her breaths. "Elena . . . how? How . . . can I go . . . to Egypt?"

"For a fussy boy, fussy creases to make his shirts flat," Elena says now. She takes a bite of the melon, and for the first time in a very long time, Elliott remembers the childish babble that is the interval phase of this kind of passion. He looks at his suitcase open on the floor. "Don't sleep with Hoover," he wants to say. "Not while I'm gone. Not ever." The words are choking him, sucking his breath away. He works to control the muscles in his face. There is this fissure: his life splitting between kinds of need.

Leaving Kennedy, flying out over Long Island, Elliott checks through the papers in his briefcase, and comes across the ripped out notebook page with the jotted comments for Elena's practicum questionnaire. Where, she had asked, did he feel the most comfortable and the least comfortable and, though he detests even modest attempts at analysis, she looked so earnest and preoccupied, he'd started writing. His answers are in front of him now. *I feel comfortable in my car, in my apartment, in my office, in any foreign capital. I don't like being on the water. Flying over it is all right, but a boat interferes with my antennae on the world. I also don't like the blackness of the water when you look over a railing into the depths.*

All true, Elliott thinks. He looks at the dots of light on the last spit of land. All true, especially about the water, although he does swim. In the mountains as a boy he couldn't even dog-paddle because his mother feared the uncertain depths of the mountain lakes where her brother had drowned. She kept her sons away from them, the one rule she enforced at the expense of all others. But in college, a careful, observant scholarship student, he taught himself to swim by watching swim meets and made himself a strong lap swimmer. Efficient. Precise. Eyes always open and aware.

"You are so damnably always on intake." This was Audra when Hoover was small. "When do you stop looking for what you can get from a situation and just open up? Give back? Anything but that awful watching. I think you'll come back as a walleye." She had burst into tears, which was already the pattern. It was Stage One of their lives (perhaps a form of postpartum depression, though he thought it was actually a postmarriage depression that both of them had)—Stage One which preceded hostility without tears, then affairs on both sides, a strained truce and, when Hoover was grown, the final, if slow, dissolution. But Elliott had always felt married. For all Audra's coolness and lack of humor, he had always felt married. Before Elena, the women he knew were either foreign, or they were like Audra and her friends, bored and greedy for passion, but always discreet and with built-in time limits as calculated as their lingerie. With them he felt married. Even with the German woman in Rome who shared his view that the inside of St. Peter's was a gloomy, basement gray, he felt married. But he doesn't any longer. He isn't married, and now there is Elena, the surprise of his life, and so eager to learn, so on *intake*, if one could quote Audra. Waiting with him in the rain for his airport cab, she was no longer the grape-eating sprite from his bed. She was all seriousness, careful in that way he's not encountered before in a woman. In the narrowing mist, she had the clear and steady gaze of a '30s movie heroine.

"A drink or a paper, *monsieur*?" The stewardess is in the aisle, and Elliott turns back from the dark window.

"*Le Monde*," he says. "Water. Plain, no gas."

The plane jolts through clouds and the man next to him fidgets with his seat belt. Elliott looks again into the dark night. He no longer drinks on transatlantic flights, a reluctant concession to age and jet lag, but he would like a drink if only to feel, for a moment, young and free of consequence. If Elena were here, *she* would have a drink, and he thinks suddenly, randomly, how glad he is that she is not a vegetarian, that there is not that added marker to their generational divide.

At Charles de Gaulle, he is her wake-up call on his layover, phoning from his sunny afternoon to her sleepy New York dawn. "Still raining?" he asks.

"Sleet," she answers. He imagines her in the shower, imagines her eating cereal at her counter while she finishes the chapter she is reading again, imagines her trying on the metal-framed glasses with no prescription to see if they do add gravitas, sees her slipping into the booth across from Hoover.

It is already evening when he arrives in Cairo. When his taxi drops him at the hotel, he's exhausted, dehydrated from the air of the plane's cabin. He manages a shower. He has a bottle of Evian and crawls into bed. At 3 a.m. he's entirely awake, not rested, but dumbly awake. He gnaws at a fig. For a while, he looks over his working papers, which are about soil types and rock formations along the Nile from Luxor to Aswan, about construction concepts that might transfer to the Yangtze and China's Three Gorges project. But he can't concentrate. He opens his suitcase and, when he lifts out a stack of shirts to get to his shaver, he sees a book tucked carefully inside one of his T-shirts.

At the desk, he reads the spine. *Justine*. From the *Alexandria Quartet*. He opens the flyleaf and finds Elena's writing: *I am accustoming myself to the idea of regarding every sexual act as a process in which four persons are involved. We shall have a lot to discuss about that.*

For a moment, he holds the book flat with his palm. Then he turns the page, his fingers scratching loudly in the silence, and sees the identical words—the epigraph from Freud's *Letters*. They're accompanied by Elena's brief note: *Just joking. And just quoting. See? There's nothing to worry about.*

He leans forward on the desk, his face in the teepee his hands make. Then he laughs. He pictures Elena in her NYU sweatshirt, with the too-short sleeves for her long arms and grinning her most puckish grin.

By dawn he is sleepy from reading, but he dresses and catches his plane to Luxor. At the Winter Palace, with its formal, winding entrance, the stone balusters, he finds his reservations are for the new part instead of the old. Then he learns that the dates are wrong, that the people he's meeting won't arrive until morning. How stupid! How annoying. Between the two of them, he and his secretary have messed him up.

He sends his luggage off to his room and sprawls in a chair. He stares at a chandelier, listens to British English and Arabic, smells Gauloises, and watches the clerks whispering at the desk. After some moments, a man with a mustache and a turban and white robe comes over to him.

"I am Abdul Gamal. You may call me Gamal. I will be your guide to Luxor in your now free time."

Elliott considers this and then nods assent. He will be a tourist. Along with his engineer's measurements and his notes, he will take tourist stories home.

Outside, in the sun-bleached day, Gamal shows him a map. "We will go backwards," he says. "We'll start in the west where the sun dies. The tombs. The City of the Dead. Then the market. Your meal and a purchase for your lady. Or your gentleman. And then the east. Where the sun rises you will see the great temples. This is the City of the Living."

Gamal opens the door to his jeep, and Elliott gets in. They drive in a dusty cloud until there is no road and then they walk. Gamal is speaking of the pharaohs, and Elliott knows that he has never seen so many layers or configurations of the color sand. At Tut's Sarcophagus, the goddess Selket, her body explicit in gold, reminds him of Elena. Elliott startles a bat. It is like a bird in a house, and he tells Gamal that, buried here, his mother would never have rested. Later, at the Tombs of the Nobles, a scorpion skitters over his foot.

Gamal will not join him for lunch but stands a distance away. Elliott downs bottles of mineral water. He has seen the geometry of the food stands. He has looked for papyrus paintings for Elena but has not made his choice. He would like her to be here in a ship's cabin sailing the Nile. He is thinking of the jewelry, too, if it is something she might like.

A funeral procession goes by, the women in black robes and veils, sand blowing at their hems. They are wailing, keening. It is a desolate sound. Their hands move as if they are rolling up yarn. He thinks of Eugenie and pays his bill.

"Take me to the City of the Living," he tells Gamal and they get in the jeep. They cross the Nile, and Elliott watches the feluccas. They are tall and elegant like Elena. At the Temple of Luxor, Gamal talks him through its history, and when they start up the Avenue of Rams to go the two miles to Karnak and the great Temple of Amun, Elliott thinks of what he will tell Elena, of what will please her. She will like it that Amun's wife was named Mut. And, just as it amuses her that Lord Cornbury, colonial governor of New York, was a cross-dresser, she'll want to know that a pharaoh of the Eighteenth Dynasty was a woman portrayed as a king with a beard. Thinking this, it is suddenly clear to him that he is making this thirsty day a pilgrimage for Elena. It is no longer that her presence holds him, as it has for weeks. Now her absence claims him as well.

He sits down on the base of a column, and while his engineer's eye studies the pillars carving the sky, cutting its blue, he listens to Gamal and realizes that the building of this temple, so huge and so lasting on its skimpy foundation, is a metaphor he must understand. For himself. For Elena.

"I'm impressed," he tells Gamal, but Gamal is uneasy.

"Excuse me, sir. There is someone coming now from the hotel. This is always a message. Sometimes so urgent."

Elliott sees the van. He spots a figure approaching, paper in hand.

"I will go," Gamal says.

Elliott waits, more curious than anxious. But, too, he is thinking of Elena, of Elena like Selket, scrimmed in gold. There is desire in this thought, desire and maybe jealousy. And perhaps even a kind of love.

Then Gamal returns. "A sadness," he says, bowing his head. He hands him a telex. "I am sorry, sir. Truly I am."

Elliott nods. He is prepared for the news. He is ready to learn that Eugenie has died. And it is perhaps for that reason that he must read the message twice before he can start to absorb it. It is not Eugenie who has died. A cerebral hemorrhage. A horrible fluke. Hoover is dead.

The plane lumbers and sinks from the sky. Its wheels touch the runway. His eyes closed, Elliott feels nothing but rage. Why has this plane landed safely?

When it taxis to the gate, he tests himself. He builds himself upright.

He finds Elena at the luggage carousel, and all his calculations are off. She is not even a tenth of his age, not a thousandth. His age is the age of the moon.

At the mortuary, he leaves her in the cab, and when he comes back outside he has no idea how long he's been gone. There are blank spots, time, he thinks, that he cannot recover. They drive in near silence. Once he turns to her and asks her to tell him again just why she is with him.

"Now?" she asks, looking uneasy.

He shakes his head. "Why you are with me any time."

"Well, just being with you . . ." She hesitates. "From the first, being with you. And what you are. And the same things I cared about in Hoover except that in you they're more . . . present. I mean before.

Oh God." She pulls at the rope of her bag, twisting it. "Elliott, I'm so terribly sorry."

At her apartment he makes phone calls. He talks to the coroner. He talks to Audra, who is sobbing. Elena fixes him tea, and they sit at the table. For a long time he stares at his cup. He tries sipping from it but he can't swallow. He looks past Elena at her bookshelves, at the stack of CDs.

"All these impossible things," he says. "The god-awful things like St. Patrick's. His mother having him buried from there. Should I have had his head scanned? I'm his father. Is it something I should have done?"

Elena presses her palms on the table. She starts to speak, starts again. "I know someone to talk to. Maybe you should. I do think you should."

"Were you with him?"

"I saw him."

"I mean were you with him when it happened? Were you sleeping with him when he died?"

"Elliott." She looks at him and there are tears in her eyes. "You think that?"

"He was *twenty-seven*, Elena. Why would he die?"

"You think what? What—that I screwed him to death? It was an aneurysm. He died alone, and if he didn't, I wouldn't know. We had coffee. He was very sweet. What he said was he wanted me to be happy. He was sorry about the awkwardness. He wasn't sure you could handle it."

Elliott looks toward the window. "And I've proved he was right."

There is an orange in a bowl at his elbow, and he picks it up and scores arcs around it with his knife and strips off the skin. He pulls the segments apart and eats them, though he isn't hungry. Elena is quiet in her chair.

He feels the orange's sourness on his tongue. "There were things I wanted to tell you," he says. "The Temple of Amun. The god of fertility. Of growth. The god of the wind. It's immense. Ten basilicas in size. And they built it with less foundation than a ranch house. A paltry little trench with some loose stones and a yard of sand, but it's held these pillars, these gigantic pillars for thousands of years. The hell with the grand foundation. I thought this was us. The way we came up. What we've become. Both in our own way. I wanted to show you. But this. This horror. Forgive me, Elena."

"You've lost your son."

"Yes."

"I do. I forgive you." She touches his fingers. "And what's to become of us?"

He shakes his head. Slowly. "I don't know." He looks at her, at her amazing loveliness, at the open wonder in her face. Even now, he knows that he cannot take the risk again—to love what he could lose—and that this means he must not stay with her. But it is impossible to leave. Impossible to leave her. An impossible conundrum that, oddly, he feels without bitterness.

Elena gets up from her chair and scoops the orange peels into her skirt. He watches her, her head inclined as she moves through the shadows, the afternoon light.

Watching Oksana

Once upon a time in far-off Odessa there lived a man who'd abandoned his child. He had done so unwillingly in the process of leaving his wife, but the result was the same as if he had had intent: the child did not know the father or the father the child.

For this man, known as Aleksei, the break was excruciating. In letting go of his child, he had not felt a gradual unlocking, as of hands unclasping for skaters to glide apart. He had felt a yank, a sudden splitting away that told him his daughter was wounded, cut to the green quick of her sapling growth. And yet for Aleksei there was no going back, no possible return to the anger that had been his marriage and his wife. He was left in a rage of nightmares—that his daughter, who at two had outgrown her pram, would, by her mother's carelessness, be sent hurtling down the *Potemkin* steps. That she would be lost in the labyrinth of catacombs beneath Odessa. That she would not know the excitement of a name—the Black Sea—or its floating of ancient myths: Jason and the Argonauts, the Golden Fleece. That she would grow up without Pushkin's words spiraling on the page so she must lift her eyes to breathe.

In darkness and distress, Aleksei stowed away aboard a ship, was caught, was made a soldier and sent overland until all he saw was the Khyber Pass.

And there, in 1980, the tale grows muddled, for Aleksei, as he was called only because the Soviet army held the stowaway papers that named him Aleksei Smirnov, went crazy with a war that, for him, meant killing and seeing his fellows killed and yet not being killed himself. And when he was done being crazy, done with hospitals and war, he was left with a memory that was like so many strips of tattered cloth.

"You have family?" the doctors asked him in Moscow, and when he could not answer, his discharge papers were stamped for Minsk, the home of Aleksei Andreiovitch Smirnov. A train took him there through the Russian night. Alone in his hotel, he studied the papers, and on the next morning left for Odessa.

"A holiday?" the stationmaster asked, and Aleksei nodded his head, putting down rubles.

He sat upright on the train, staring out through the window. When he smelled the sea he began to tremble, and when he arrived in Odessa, he ate smoked sturgeon, which he bought from a vendor and, looking up, saw the five domes of Uspenskiy Sobor rising into the sky. Walking unsteadily past the shops of Deribasovskaya Ulitsa, he made his way there. He lit a candle. He prayed to Our Lady of Kasperovskaya, asking for the return of his daughter's face. He prayed for his name. When, after days, neither the face nor the name appeared, he looked out at the sea. Standing at the top of Potemkinskaya Lestnitsa, he watched the big ships' cranes loading cargo in the harbor below. He looked to the steel line of the horizon. This time, with his soldier's scars, when his strength was back, he left Odessa with the official papers that had been issued to him, and as a sailor.

And so the man known as Aleksei Smirnov became a traveler along the great sea lanes of the world. With his taut, stitched-together body, neither big nor small, and with the blank spaces of memory that clustered around the bittersweet images of Odessa and a faceless, nameless child, he began a present he could make into a past. At Yalta he bought a balalaika and discovered his fingers knew how to play it. His sea bag was full of books. They had come with him on the train from Moscow, their endpapers blank, and now he wrote the name Aleksei Andreiovitch Smirnov carefully inside each cover so that, should he misplace his life again, he could start over with something to go on.

"Aleksei Andreiovitch, he is the book man," his shipmates said, but it was a light sort of teasing Aleksei knew, for he could beat them at cards, beat them in fights because of his quickness, beat them with girls because of his lambent, sea-scorched eyes and his fault lines of scars that were always alluring.

The freighters he worked on carried grain or tumbled *akvavit* the whole way around the world, making it fire. Aleksei sailed under frozen skies. He watched his laundry dry on ships' decks making certain nobody stole it. He sailed in blistering heat, in terrible storms that swung even the flat bulk of a grain carrier like a toy. He was only frightened when he stared into the huge darkness of an empty hold.

Then for the first time he came to America. Seeing a newspaper, he found he knew English. This was in Buffalo where a bumboat pulled alongside his freighter and he bought toothpaste and the *New York Times*. He was wary of America. He assumed any women he met would have AIDS; he assumed there would be efforts to entice him into spiritualism or buying a revolver. The newspaper challenged his ideas. He was fascinated by the advertisements, by black faces in pictures.

By the fifth time he had traveled through the locks of St. Lambert and Côte Ste. Catherine, heading west through the snaked route of seaway and lakes, he had lost his surprise. True, it still felt odd to be sailing between countries too alike to fight, odd to be on a freighter that needed a second set of load lines for water that was fresh. (How, he still wondered, could vast seas with giant waves not be salt?) But he had his own notion of America now, his own experience of it, and when, in December, his ship passed to the east of the aerial bridge in Duluth, Minnesota, and entered its slip on the Wisconsin side of the harbor at Superior, he had his own places to go.

An icebreaker had cleared the harbor. Aleksei, with his duffel bag on his shoulder and a cigarette warming his mouth, left the ship by himself. He was feeling oddly tired, even in the bracing cold. There was a pulling pain on the inside of his right knee, and he wondered if he had twisted his leg somehow, if in leaning back to shout to his shipmates where he was going, he had caught his foot on the ladder in the engine room. He did not think that he had. But his knee hurt and he favored it, limping as he walked up the snow-covered dock.

It was afternoon under a gray sky which dulled the lake. Aleksei had intended a brisk walk to a coffeehouse. In his duffel bag he had a book of poems, a collection of Greek lyrics in English translation, and he had wanted to read and drink coffee until it was dusk, until the lighthouse which, in summer, rolled up in the morning fog, silted light onto the darkening sky. But today he was no swift Idaios of the strong legs. The cold had settled in his knee. He was shivering with fatigue.

He stopped. He could hear the tinny sound of Christmas carols playing from speakers, see decorations mounted on streetlamps. For a moment he had no idea what to do. It was a long walk farther to where he was going and a longer walk still to return to the ship. Then a BudLite sign with a length of burned-out neon caught his eye and, shoving his duffel bag ahead of him, he opened the door of the bar which it illuminated and went inside.

The bar was not the kind of bar he was used to, not a sailors' bar with a pool table and with the smell of dust and beer dried into the wood of the floor. It was a place with silent, big-screen TVs and a horseshoe-shaped foot rail that was brassy new. Aleksei stopped in front of a barstool and then changed his mind. He braced his knee, which was actually his hip now and even his shin when it came to the pain. He worked himself backward into a booth. A chill cut from his groin down his leg, chattering an aftershock in his nerves.

He saw the waitress coming to take his order. She was broad-faced and freckle-nosed, and she was wearing blue jeans and a T-shirt. "Brandy," he told her. The pain twisted like an augur in his leg.

Two shots later, he was still focused on his leg and on the alive skin above it and below his waist. Oddly, he felt calm. He was in a bar that was strange to him, no sailors in sight, and he had a strange illness—he was sure that he did—but he was not really worried. In his experience, there was always a nurse in American bars. And, if this one time there wasn't, in America, there was still 911. Safety. Aleksei ordered another brandy.

When the girl brought it, she was watching the screen, which had switched from a ballgame to ice-skating.

She put his drink down. "She is *so* good. I've seen this five times."

Aleksei looked up at the screen. "Praha" he saw on a wall in the picture. He watched as a skater spun from a leap to her skates. He winced, felt his leg clench at the impact. "Who it is that's so good?"

"A Russian or something. She won. She's amazing."

"This Prague is now?"

The girl shook her head. "They've played it for months. Since I've worked here." She picked up his empty glass. "When I get drunk I can remember her name. Bayou? Odessa Bayou? No, maybe that's her town."

Odessa. Aleksei stared at the screen. He was stunned with excitement. The skater was young, maybe fifteen. She had bowed to the audience and she was sitting, now, between a man and woman, and holding a bouquet of flowers in her arms.

He searched her face. She was delicate in color but with dark lines under her eyes and, though her smile was radiant, the look that replaced it belonged to the lines. In repose, her face was hungry. It was, he decided, the face of an orphan.

The screen blanked and went to an ad. Aleksei drank his brandy straight down. A quarter of him was in acute, intensifying pain. He could feel his face whitening while he did not scream. His leg shrieked, and in the planet which was the rest of him, and which seemed so far away, he could feel the cracked seal on the anguish that stayed in his heart. He motioned for the waitress.

"Are you a nurse?" he said, his voice an inhaled whisper. She shook her head. "Then please. Call the number. The 911."

When he thought about it in the next weeks in his hotel room—after the ride to the emergency room in a pickup truck, after the morphine shots, and the three nights in the hospital with the antiviral drugs that kept him retching in the bathroom—Aleksei was certain he had been sick before he ever left the ship, that his leg had been nagging him across the whole of Lake Superior and that he had been a little crazy once more, this time with fever. Why else would he have quoted the "Wedding of Andromache" to the man in the cowboy hat who drove the pickup? (*And the virgins sang a loud heavenly song whose wonderful echo touched the sky.*) And why, feeling fluish, would he have taken shore leave when he knew his freighter was leaving in the morning with its load of wheat? The last run of the season. The urgency to avoid heavy ice and running aground in the St. Mary's River, though now he was the one who was run aground.

It had not been an easy thing getting a diagnosis. He'd been CAT-scanned and MRI'ed, had given blood, given urine, given blood again. When finally the doctor stood in his room, looking affirmative, Aleksei had made his job easy. There was an eruption of blistered sores that marked his backside and progressed down the inside of his leg.

"The good news," the doctor said, "is you're not positive for HIV and you don't have this because you're weakened from chemotherapy. It's right that you haven't had chemo? You don't have cancer?"

"No cancer."

"It's shingles."

"Excuse?" Aleksei was thinking fast, that this was an American deal. He got treatment; he roofed the doctor's house.

"You had chicken pox. Sometime in your life you had it, and now—nobody could say why now—some crack in the immune system and the virus woke up in the nerve root and gave you shingles. But you get it in only one nerve path. You picked a long one. Sometimes that spreads out the impact, dilutes it. You weren't that lucky."

"I do what then?"

"You leave here. Take the pain pills. Sleep a lot. In a few weeks you're well. And the drugs we gave you—that keeps you from neuropathy and chronic pain syndrome. You'll be fine."

Shingles then. That was the diagnosis and the new homonym and quirky new transit of pain in Aleksei's life. To be released from the hospital, he had signed an avalanche of papers, most of them promising the payment of apparently large but unspecified sums. Then he'd been wheeled to a taxicab, his head still in a dancy swoon. He loved the cold air, the sunlight. He rode with the window half down until the cabbie swore at him to roll it up or be out on the pavement: *You fucking better or you fucking will.*

In a room in the hotel in Superior that he knew to be the cheapest, Aleksei had sagged onto the bed and fallen asleep in his jacket and boots. It was the start of the self-monitored portion of his illness and recuperation. He had not stopped being hungry and, every day or so, he used what energy he could pry from himself to go out to buy food. The skin of his groin and leg were so tender that finally he gave in, ripped open the sash of red silk he had bought in Hong Kong for a gift—for someone, sometime—and wrapped it around himself. At odd times, he cried, which was new for him. He did not remember crying. Tears perhaps, but not racking sobs. He would lie on the stained bed cover and listen through the walls to the rhythmic banging of bodies hitting the headboard in the next room and he would cry not for those bodies or his own but from the sheer need to cry. Then he craved chocolate. For three days he ate Hershey bars and boxes of drugstore candies he pretended were truffles. When he began to itch, he scratched every bit of his leg that was not covered with sores and, once, just once, in a bath he scratched away the old layer of skin and then, drying himself, covered his leg with lotion which, for a full minute, felt glorious.

And he dreamed. He had two dreams. The one was that the captain of his ship had come to the hospital on the first night and said, "Well keep him then. It's not as if there's a real country that requires him home." The other dream was of a skater circling the ice in the darkness like a small plane teasing a ship. But this dream was a happy dream, and when he woke from it it was always with a feeling of joy. And this second dream he trusted; the first one he did not, even if his sea bag, with the name Ukrrichflot Shipping Company of Odessa stamped on its side, had appeared at the hospital and had left with him, though he had not taken it there. Somehow, in the vacuum left surrounding the morphine, contact had been made.

When the pain in his leg began to lessen, Aleksei went through the bag. Nothing was missing. He had his books, his balalaika. Everything he owned was here in his room behind the flimsy door with its loose frame and uncertain lock. The effort of taking stock, however, had exhausted him. He lay on the bed, staring at the ceiling, listening to his alarm clock tick. He had no desire to read nor any energy even to worry about money. He felt enveloped by lassitude, filled with a sadness that lacked any focus.

He drifted this way through a replay of his symptoms, which had moderated slowly as the days passed. When he had first taken his room, the television had no sound and only snow for a picture. Occasionally there were vague shadows that passed across the screen, companions of sorts. They required no attention and, as he had none to give, the situation suited him. As he began to feel better, he tried to make sense of the fleeting images. Tentatively, he would identify a man, perhaps a child, but then the snow would return and the story he'd started for himself would disappear. He played with knobs, rattled the table the television sat on. Finally he complained to the maid, and this assertiveness and the vexation which prompted it startled him. He had, he realized, presumed himself more or less dead. Now, though, there were definite signs of his life returning. He was excited, in fact, when the night desk clerk brought him a television which had sound and a black-and-white picture with only a slight double image.

"Hell of a way to spend Christmas Eve," the clerk said.

"Merry Christmas to you," Aleksei said carefully, quoting the greeting he'd heard on his trips to buy groceries.

"A fucking merry Christmas to you, too," the man answered.

Aleksei found this funny. When the man left, he laughed out loud. Then he flipped channels eagerly, but there was no skating on this TV, but churches and choirs, a stirring liturgical voice that was, even in his state of nonpractice, two weeks too early for the Christmas he knew. He listened awhile, and then he was very tired and slept a long time into the morning that was American Christmas Day.

When he awoke the day after this Christmas, he felt almost strong. His reaction was panic. His illness had drugged him into indifference, but for a man now capable of concern, his situation was clearly alarming. He hopped one-footed out of bed and got his wallet from his pants. He turned his pockets out and, dumping everything onto the bed, counted what he had. $84.60 American. There was not a coin or bill of any other currency, though he had only the vaguest memory of making an exchange. He sat back against his pillow and went through his papers, receipts. For an hour, he studied them, trying to piece things together. Finally, he had the outlines of his predicament: in another three days more rent was due on his room and by January 15 he was obligated to pay the hospital whatever it asked; he did not know where he stood legally as a documented resident of Ukraine who had overstayed his shore leave; he was stranded until spring.

Aleksei sat upright. Clearly he was headed for jail, but, in America, was he required to pay for that, too? He leaned back slowly into his pillow, back into the exhaustion that moved over him once more.

In the morning, though, he felt better again. He bathed carefully and shaved. He opened his sea bag and began to sort. A few of his books might be worth something, a few of his trinkets from the Orient. The handle of his knife was inlaid with mother of pearl, and his watch had a gold chain. There was his fur hat. There was also his balalaika.

Aleksei packed all these things, well wrapped, into his duffel bag. He needed a nap first, but when he woke up, he went straight out to find a pawnshop.

As he walked, the wind blew up puffs of white from the snowbanks along the street. The cold traveled in his leg. He wanted to run. Instead he limped. He felt the bite of the wind on his face and in his fingers, felt the fever chill that made its own bitter ice inside him.

The cold was steamed and frosted on the windows of the pawnshop. He went inside to the dank air and dim light and he was still cold. He bit his lips quiet so he could talk.

"How much?" he asked. He opened the duffel and put everything on the counter.

The pawnbroker sat on a chair, looked idly at the counter, picked at his teeth. "Not this," he said finally, moving the balalaika away from the other things. He was paunchy and had thin hair and smelled of smoke. He pushed himself up from the chair and opened the cash register. He laid two twenties on the counter, wrote on the tickets and gave Aleksei the stubs.

"For this all?"

"Take it or leave it."

Aleksei put the stubs and the money in his wallet. He wrapped the balalaika and settled it carefully back inside the bag.

Walking again, he was looking for a place to eat when he saw the BudLite sign with its dark curve on the "u." *The skaters*, he thought. *The child with the blue lined eyes.*

He went straight to a booth, stationed himself in front of a TV. On the screen, there were women in bathing suits lifting weights. He looked around the bar, hunting for the girl with the freckled nose, for the cowboy. Nowhere. Neither of them. A different waitress, much older, came to the booth and he ordered a beer and a corned beef sandwich.

"You want a pitcher?"

He shook his head. "The skaters are on?"

The waitress looked blank. Aleksei continued. "Prague. Skaters in Prague. What time?"

"These babes don't do it for you?" The waitress was tapping her pencil eraser on her pad. She stared at him. "I don't know about any skaters."

"A waitress is having spots?" He pointed to his nose.

"If you're talking about a kid, she'd be home for Christmas. You want your beer or not?"

Aleksei nodded. He put a bill and his coins on the table. The name "'69 Mets" flashed on the screen, and he lifted his foot up onto the far bench and felt next to him for the balalaika in his duffel.

The waitress brought his beer and then came back with his sandwich. "I talked to the bartender," she said, pushing her hair back, showing some interest. "With reruns, it's whatever they put on the feed. No skaters. Tonight it's the Bulls. Live."

Aleksei nodded and purposely looked away. Reruns. Feed and bulls. Livestock. He thought he understood. He was feeling very disappointed, though. Empty.

When he got back to his hotel and had wrapped his leg in the sash, he lay facedown, grasping the bed, and slept from fatigue and from loneliness. But in the dream he dreamed, he was a man in a spotlight. He was in a darkened amphitheater with a floor of prismed ice, and he played his balalaika and sang of a coachman with a leather lash and gloves, of a frozen heart that burst into flame, while, around him, a faceless skater in a shimmer of cloth skated spirals, tightly, ever more tightly.

Later, he awoke in the darkness, his mind jumbled with thoughts. He reached for a pen.

In the morning he read this: *Go to the bar where picture has sound. Can't sailors make friends? Survivors survive. Who is Harold Rydell?*

Disgusted, he crumpled the note. He had wanted directions. He had wanted answers. The name, though, nagged at him. He pulled his shirt on, zipped up his jeans. He combed his hair. In the blackened silver of the mirror and in the window light, he looked young. All this sleep. He sat down on the bed to pull his socks on.

And then he knew where the name was. He leaned back on the bed and pulled his hospital papers from the table. In the morass of signatures, there was one stamped Harold Rydell, Attorney-at-Law. Aleksei folded it and put it into his wallet. Then he took it out again and, mentally, he paced the room. What did American lawyers do? Why had one signed his papers? Did he need to find out?

At the least, he thought, he needed to talk to someone. He lay on the bed and stared at the ceiling. But who? Somebody at the coffeehouse where, in the life that never was, he read Pindar and Simonides? Or perhaps the new waitress at the BudLite bar? He didn't think so.

But a sailors' bar. Even in the off-season, there might be someone who would be all right. He clasped his hands, not in prayer but in hope. He thought that there would be.

In the late afternoon then, the sun just warming the bar stools, Aleksei Andreiovitch Smirnov, still feverish, was in a bar where he felt at ease. There were dust motes in the air, in the sunlight. There were depressions in the stools and a slant and squeak to the floor. The beer foamed from the tap and the bartender, slim in her jeans and faintly wrinkled around her eyes and her mouth, swore in loud English.

Aleksei settled himself into a booth. He had brought his balalaika with him. He was not sure why, but since the pawnbroker had rejected it, he had felt more need of it, more attachment. There were other customers, two men at the end of the bar, a couple shooting pool, a table of old men, bristly with stubbled beards, playing cards. He heard the crack of a pool ball.

This time he got his beer at the bar and took it back to the booth. He was eyeing the customers, sizing them up under cover of the newspaper he'd found lying on the street. What he didn't expect was to hear his name, but that is what happened.

"Aleksei, you too damned good to sit at the bar?"

He felt a fleshy hand on his shoulder and looked up into a big, smiling face. He stood up quickly, pushing his weight onto his good leg, and put his hand out.

"You miss the boat?" He was in a bear hug from Don Lachine, who worked the docks loading grain and was the last man to close the bars and the first man to win a sailor's money when the mood hit him and he wanted to play. He was a big Chippewa with black eyes and a ponytail, and his jeans low in the seat.

"I miss the boat." Aleksei was laughing and grinning. "Yes. Not shanghaied. Shingle leg."

"Ouch. So take the weight off." Don went to the bar and got a beer and a glass of something else. He pushed the beer across the table and fit himself into the booth. "Pepsi," he said, answering Aleksei's look. "My boy died drunk in a car. I been on the wagon."

Aleksei put his hand on the table.

"Yeah, it's rough. He was the smart one. So you got beached."

"You know Harold Rydell?" Aleksei reached for his wallet and took the paper out.

Don glanced at it and shook his head. "You look in the phone book? I'll look." He walked with his padding walk to the phone on the wall. He stood there, leaning over the phone book and then he got a pencil from the bar and wrote something down. "Here," he said, coming back. "He's on Mesaba Avenue. You got a problem with the law?"

"I don't know."

"You hit somebody?"

"No, but I am of limited means."

Don gazed down at him, sipped at his Pepsi. "If you want, I'll look over your paper."

"Yes, please." Aleksei pushed it across the table and waited.

Don squinted, studied. In a while, he pushed it back. "You owe the hospital money."

"And tomorrow for my room. I can pay American some, but money at home, worth is not much. Or how to get it. Does he put me in jail?"

"What you do is you find another lawyer. Not this one. Take a name from the phone book. They don't charge for the first time. You sure you didn't hit somebody?"

Aleksei pointed at his leg. He was feeling a lack of language to say what he felt. "I am hitting nobody. And I am sorry so much for your son." He put his hand on his heart. "I too am losing child."

Don nodded long and seriously. "We'll find you a lawyer."

On January 6, the day he knew as Christmas Eve, Aleksei was at Meryl's on the Lake, playing his balalaika and singing. He was well, almost entirely well with barely a limp, and he had his watch back, his room paid up, and he had made the first installment on his hospital bill. And he was very clean in his narrow black pants and open white shirt. He was wearing a Ukrainian belt he had bought in a store, and he had a temporary green card in his wallet which he checked very often. It allowed him to wait on tables, which he did in the day, and to perform in the bar in the evening or to play background music in the restaurant. Making money, he thought, was making him well. And he was understanding the American dream—that impossible things were often possible, that not every bureaucracy has the self-sustaining existence of a worm, that a big, quick-thinking Chippewa could save your life if he told a lawyer with a part share in a restaurant that you had performed on the balalaika professionally in the Kremlin. For Aleksei, this was all a kind of happiness, and he sang it in his songs, plucked it from his balalaika even in minor keys. He was saying Happy Christmas, though nobody knew.

And then the television sets were suddenly full of skaters. There was the girl crying, bashed on the knee, and the championship of America won by the hard-jumping blonde. Aleksei took his breaks in front of a TV set. In his hotel room, he set his alarm clock for the morning news shows and, in his hunt, turned his TV from channel to channel. On his afternoons or evenings off, he sat at a bar with Don Lachine and watched for skaters through the noise of Tonya Harding this, Tonya Harding that. Even the pool players used their sticks in Tonya Harding's name.

In his room he had seen an ad that drained his face white. The girl from Odessa had skated onto the Olympic stage: Oksana Baiul, world champion at sixteen years old. Her mother was dead. She was an orphan abandoned by a father presumed to be dead, a father who left when she was two.

Aleksei looked at his army papers, looked at himself. He had taken the age of Aleksei Smirnov—thirty-seven—and no one had ever questioned it, but he did not know his real age any more than he knew his real name; he could be older, perhaps somewhat younger. But these were all facts: in 1980 he had been in the army; Odessa was his home; he had left his child. In the smoke and mirrors that were his life, these certain memories and realities did not change. What he could not know was if another man from Odessa had done what he had, if a whole fraternity of Odessa men had abandoned young daughters one year and were lost. He could not know, that is, if this child was his.

His life, though, had gained a great clarity. Whether he was working or in his room, whether he was walking to make his weekly payment on his hospital bill or drinking a beer to Don Lachine's Pepsi, he was watching Oksana—watching for her, reading whatever he saw that mentioned her name. Like a sailor attuned to a coming storm, he was fully alert, at times so secretly thrilled he thought his fever was back.

Some of this excitement entered, unbidden, into his music. With fervor and tenderness, he sang the Pushkin texts he had set himself. He played, too, from a past of peasants and gypsies, their plaintive tunes, their dances, their dreams summoned with a clear sung note and tremolo of string. Sometimes at full break he raced horses across a steppe and held, in his balalaika, the jangling, rough drumming of their stride.

This drew a crowd. In the bar, girls gathered near the raised chair where he sat. They did not know to throw flowers, but they asked him home or to their rooms. Especially when the music stayed in his nerves, this tempted Aleksei to a serious consideration of American safe sex. And yet he stopped. The West, he had seen, had no secrets. He had read of Arkansas troopers and of the father of Steffi Graf who embarrassed his daughter into depression. If he was the real father of Oksana Baiul, desertion was enough. He would not touch her name with scandal.

"I have a bad leg," he would say, pointing to his trousers, including the article for the noun as he was learning to do. The girls would laugh, tease him a little with sly remarks, and, finally, let him alone.

This left him, as he wished, to his job and to his dogged watching of TV and reading of newspapers and magazines. He had learned the name of Oksana's coach—Galina Zmievskaya—and he said it to himself often, relishing the comfort of its familiar sounds and lingering particularly over the "skaya." He wanted to see the orphan ad again, but it seemed to have disappeared. There were no new ones. Oksana was invisible.

Aleksei asked Don Lachine if he had seen the ad. "They tell her hardships," Aleksei said. "Her mother dead and her father is disappeared long ago and supposed to be dead. She is from my city Odessa. Oksana Baiul. She is the champion skater of the world."

"I didn't see it. I'll bet you, though, Tonya Harding wants to kick her butt."

Aleksei was suddenly brave. "She is the age of my daughter in Odessa. I, too, am presumed dead and this child I am losing was very young then, like Oksana."

"You name your girl Oksana?"

"That part I don't know. My own name even is gone. Afghanistan in the war." Aleksei struck his head. "Holes. Empty spots."

Don turned to him on the bar stool and shook his hand. "Vietnam," he said. Then he was quiet and even his face went still. "You think this girl is yours?"

Aleksei shook his head. "No," he answered. "Many people in Odessa. Many, many people." Yet even as he shook his head, the idea ran through him like a freshet that she was.

WATCHING OKSANA 43

By the Wednesday she was to skate, Aleksei was almost sick again, this time from nervousness. He paced in front of the window with the BudLite sign and nearly spilled his vodka. He heard her name and sat down at the bar next to Don Lachine and stared mutely at the television and looked at an unfamiliar picture of a very young Oksana. He recognized nothing about it, nothing of the background or her clothing, and not her. He did not recognize her dead mother either, the round-faced woman in a black-and-white photo, but he could not say with any certainty that, younger, she had not been his wife. He didn't know.

But the Oksana of sixteen the television showed haunted him. She had the orphan's blue-tinted face. He could not deny this—even when her smile seemed to banish everything but joy—even when she danced, so pliantly and shockingly seductive at a discotheque. Staring at the Black Sea, at his sea and the sea of the mythical past, her sadness was transparent.

And then she skated in Olympic time, and Aleksei was all attention. He was struck by the oddness of her skates, the way they matched her legs in color, almost as if they were part of her. Her headdress was unexpected, too, a cap of black feathers that did not so much suggest the swan she portrayed as a woman who was wizened and old. And though her smile canceled the effect, made her young just as it had erased the orphan, the impression of age stayed with him as she skated. His face grew tight. There was an uncanniness in her movements, a sort of preternatural agility that toyed with awkwardness. This scared him. He held his breath. As she moved, though, curling deeper into a spiral of unquestioned grace, he began slowly to nod his head. She was performing, describing the movement of emergent beauty, showing the swan's freedom from enchantment through her own power to enchant. She was creating before his eyes.

Aleksei pressed his fingers to his mouth. He recognized the moment in his head and in his muscles. This was ballet. For all the announcers' talk of jumps and combinations, this was a body in the act of revelation. He watched transported, transfixed.

Oksana made her bow.

"She skated good. I'll buy you a beer." Don leaned over the bar. "You ever see Wonder Woman in the comic books?" He stretched one hand in front of him and one behind, his head down. "Like this. Superman, too. Phony flying. Kerrigan does it, but not this one."

"American angular and coarse chilly elements. Alexander Herzen saw this. Long ago. A Russian view. Not Ukrainian."

"If you say so."

Aleksei nodded. He was watching Oksana again, listening to her answers to questions and to the stumbling translation of Viktor Petrenko. Son-in-law of her coach, hah! He did not trust this man. Perhaps her savior, as they said on American TV. So as a fellow skater he had begged her a home. But Oksana was only a child and Aleksei did not like at all the looks between them. And why hadn't her mother made sure she learned English?

Aleksei stood up from the bar. He was angry, and he went outside and flung snowballs into the curb across the street.

He was setting tables after lunch the next day when he heard of Oksana's collision with the German girl in practice. He rushed out of the dining room to find a television, almost skewering the cashier with the forks he was carrying.

"Sorry," he said, "very sorry," but he hurried on into the restaurant bar to check the TV. He flipped the channels himself. Nothing. There was no news on the radio either and no one in either the bar or restaurant could answer his questions. He finished the tables in a state of near panic. When he finally saw the accident footage on the evening news, he was watching with a tray of drinks in his hands and had to sit down. A gashed leg and injured back. As bad as shingles. Maybe worse. How could she skate? Should she skate? Who was taking care of her? Aleksei waited on his tables and did his sets in a cloud as heavy as fog on the lake.

He did not sleep the whole night. He gave up on the bed and tried lying on the floor and then sitting in a chair with his legs up. Finally he turned the light on and read the sports pages from the papers he'd bought. He read poems, half a mystery book, then the sports pages again. He listened to head bangings and panting laughter behind the wall and a train in the night. In the frozen dawn he went out and bought coffee and rolls.

By late afternoon, the radio had made him ecstatic. Oksana had not only skated. She had *won*. Aleksei was jubilant, all but ready to do back flips through the dining room. But the evening news began without skating: a massacre of Muslim worshippers on Purim by an Israeli settler from Brooklyn, and Aleksei thought how American, that Americans killed their enemies in public.

He was playing only the late set, and so at seven he was on his stool next to Don Lachine.

"You know?" Don asked.

"I know," Aleksei said. He shook his hands in the air, beaming. "I know she won!"

"You should think about this," Don said. "That brother that showed up for Clinton? You could be famous. Maybe this girl needs a father and you are him."

"No, no," Aleksei answered. "But we're watching her skate. A girl from Odessa."

There were the other skaters first and Tonya Harding's problem with a shoelace. The bar was crowded with patrons who grew rowdier with everything that Tonya Harding did. When she began her routine, she appeared to Aleksei as if she were posing to start a war dance. Don scowled and spit on the floor. "She think she's Indian now? Miss Native America?"

When Oksana finally took the ice, Aleksei had stopped drinking beer and stopped being nervous. He looked at the bandage on her leg, looked for a sign of the back pain the announcers said she'd had injections for. She seemed all right, fine, and since she'd won, he thought she must be. He was not sure, though, about her frizzy ponytail or her costume. He didn't like the pink or the phony fur, and he didn't like the show tunes. Why American? He watched to see if she was vamping, the word a skater had hurled against her in the paper. But she was only flirting, playing, and she was dazzling on her feet. Aleksei felt himself melting, ceasing to be cross or a worried papa.

But when she had finished, the bar crowd was ugly. There were loud complaints of double-footed landings and missing triple combinations, talk of crooked eastern judges and clean Nancy Kerrigan. Of course she had skated clean, Aleksei thought. Weren't all these skaters immaculately clean?

He looked through the smoke to find the loudest voice, and then Oksana was on again in her own voice and in Viktor Petrenko's.

The loudmouth was shouting over them: "Look at that prick. For sure he's screwing her."

Aleksei was off his stool and elbowing hard past bodies. He reached for the man's collar, saw the hair in his nostrils and the hole for his earring. He threw a hard jab. Air. A hand on his shoulder had pulled him back.

"My friend likes his young skaters too much. Excuse us," Don said, and Aleksei did not think there could be so much strength in the fleshy hand but there was. He could not get loose from Don pushing and shoving him toward the door.

Outside, Don handed him his jacket. "Don't mess up my favorite bar, Aleksei," he said. His face was somber, but then he laughed. "Those skate boys couldn't even ball a hooker."

For the last night of skating—the exhibition of all the winners, all the champions—Aleksei was tired and working an extra shift. He was waiting on tables until his first set at nine, and he kept his eye on the television as he went back and forth with his orders. Most of the skaters he hadn't seen before. Now he was interested, especially in the couples—in what they did together, the terrifying moves or the astonishing ones that made the ice white heat. Aleksei was behind in his orders, rushing to catch up.

When he finished his shift in the dining room, he sat at the bar and watched. And then he fell a little bit in love. Gordeyeva and Grinkov were on the ice in their airy blue costumes, Grinkov's face with a hint of Slavic complexity, Gordeyeva with a simple and classic loveliness. Aleksei knew who they were, that she had been a child when they first were partners, that now she was his wife. They flowed in a pure line across the ice, so achingly beautiful together that they seemed in union prelapsarian, Adam and Eve without the apple.

Aleksei saw this and heard Gordeyeva speak in her very good English. But he could not keep his feelings for himself. Katya Gordeyeva, he thought, was exactly the kind of person for Oksana to admire. A role model, as Americans said.

Aleksei got up and went to change for his first set. When he came back, he moved his chair so the television was in his line of vision. He told the bartender to keep the picture on. When he began playing, the crowd was already quite large, and more people drifted in from the dining room. He started with the song of the young peddler and went on to his Pushkin arrangements and to the songs about bells that he had found were very popular—"Odnozvuchno Gremit Kolokolchik," and "Vecherniy Zvon." He saw Nancy Kerrigan fall and get up, fall once more.

When it was Oksana's turn to skate, she was a swan again, this time in white, and Aleksei was with her from the start. She skated to his balalaika, to the melodic, plangent strains that were his story of the swan. When she finished, he was startled to see his audience rising with loud applause—for him. Aleksei bowed, as Oksana did, and put his balalaika away. He sat at the bar in front of the TV and drank a glass of water. Oksana had flipped the overskirt of her costume off. She was hurrying toward the dressing room, and then she was back on the ice, wearing a ruffled skirt and colorful top over her white dress. She was skating with Viktor Petrenko in a sort of child's version of pairs, both of them smiling and relaxed. Perhaps it was all right, Aleksei thought, that he could put to rest what, were he American, he would certainly call murder in his heart. Maybe Viktor Petrenko was nothing more than a surrogate older brother, protective and kind. Really, it was as if he and Oksana were playing together. It was not the fusion of the other pairs, the two parts making a whole.

And then the show was over. All of the televisions were done with skaters, and Oksana was gone. Aleksei, bereft, hunted and read the last newspaper stories. He clipped one final picture to keep with his books. Though he tried, he could not overcome his feeling of emptiness. When he walked in the streets he felt cold. The weather was milder, but a grayness had crept inside him and it stayed there even when he took the bus to Minneapolis on his day off and bought his ticket at the Target Center for the Olympic skating tour coming in May.

When he got back to Superior, he found Don Lachine in a poker game. Aleksei sat down to wait. In two hands Don folded his cards and got up. Aleksei looked at him. "It's OK," Don said. "Without drinking I don't think so good playing cards."

They went outside. They walked down toward the lake and stood on the shore listening to the big ice floes cracking far out in the harbor. "You get your ticket yet?" Don asked.

Aleksei didn't answer.

"Me, if I had a chance to see my boy back from the spirit path I'd be in the front row." Don sighed. He moaned a little or the ice did. "Maybe she is your girl, maybe not. If it needs proving, they can do it now with DNA."

Aleksei said nothing. He knew this from Geraldo or Connie Chung—all that flipping of channels.

"You think maybe you are no good, taking pride for what you didn't do, but that is her choice, right? Or you worry about scaring her or a bad reunion, that she tells you no."

Yes, Aleksei thought—American stalking, American reunions of parents and children that want a happy ending for something impossible from the start. American dreaming which is fine for something like shingles, but not life.

The ice boomed and echoed on the lake. "The ships will come soon. The ships will come always. What have you got to lose, Aleksei, that is not already gone?"

Aleksei was quiet, touching his daydream: he saw Oksana whirling on the dark ice. He stood before her, gave her flowers as her father, took the blue lines from beneath her eyes and held her very, very close.

"It is decided. No," he said. For a second he was back in Minneapolis, clutching the purchased ticket inside his palm. He had held it, then sat on a bench staring at it and memorizing the number of his seat, imagining himself inside the arena. Then he released it. He let it flutter in the breeze to find a puddle, a rivulet that softened it and floated it away for this: to save for Oksana, to keep for Oksana what he or some other man had long ago wounded—her green sapling growth.

Mother Tongue

When her sisters asked, Janice could not say exactly when it had started. She had been caught off guard. She'd been slow to assume that the bumpy road of her mother's illness had made another odd passage, that her mother, who had never, not once in her whole life played with language, had a new short circuit in the hardwiring of her brain, that words, like the rest of her rattled new life, from now on would be unexpected.

Lippy schmippy. That was the first phrase Janice remembered from the new onslaught. Accustomed as she was to her husband's Jewish family, to the polyglot hail and rain of their language at family gatherings, the implication of her mother's new words, her new word order, had just not clicked. And anyway, it was too astonishing. But now Janice found herself telling her sisters this: their mother—their *Irish* mother—was quickly losing her English to Yiddish

They were in the sunroom of the house they'd all grown up in, their Grandpa Finnegan's house, which he'd bought when he ran his cigar business and which was filled with overstuffed furniture. Oriental rugs, faded now, had stayed on through their father's years as an insurance executive and his retirement and now their mother's widowhood. It was December and even this warmest room in the house was drafty. Chill. Janice had passed out lap robes and tea.

Alice, who was the physical therapist and the middle sister with their mother's good legs, scowled at the loose windows. "This barn," she said. "Grandpa told me once they named it the Windy City just because of this house. Even if it's in Evanston."

"We know," Janice and Sandra said together, and then none of them said anything. They sat in an unaccustomed silence and drank their tea. Janice reread the plaque on the wall above Alice's head. It was about smoking cigars. Her grandfather had written it, and her favorite part was its health advice. It warned dyspeptics (apparently, almost everyone) never to smoke in the morning, but it promised them good health if they smoked after dinner and right up to bedtime. Reading, Janice kept one ear alert for the sound of her mother, ready for the childish squeal and metallic bump that meant she'd awakened and was once more alarmed to find rails on her bed.

"You're sure?" Sandra asked finally. "You're sure it's Yiddish? I mean did Daniel tell you it's Yiddish?"

Janice nodded.

"Maybe it means she's finally warming up to him. To Daniel," Alice said, tying knots in the fringe of her lap robe, and Janice, who briefly leapt at the idea and briefly adored Alice for saying it, could sense Sandra's oldest sister, lawyerly scorn even before she spoke.

"She slipped out in her bathrobe? To take a course? She took Yiddish for Daniel? Brilliant, Alice. And when she's not only helpless but anti-Semitic. I mean she raised us all with a quota."

"Not in the Hitler sense," Alice said.

"No. In the 'not that girl for a bridesmaid sense. If you absolutely must, personal attendant.' *That* kind of sense."

"Well, it's a kind of proportion. But what? Am I opposing counsel? It's Saturday. Take the day off."

"That's her," Janice said. She was up quickly. She was across the sunroom and the living room and into the kitchen, where she could still remember her mother looking at Daniel for the first time and telling him peremptorily that a woman in the kitchen didn't mean that someone was going to cook for him and then asking if he was Jewish. Janice could still hear the words, still feel herself twisting the diamond on her engagement ring back to the palm of her hand.

She pushed the door open into her father's old den she and Daniel had converted into a bedroom. Her mother was half sitting up, and she was staring fiercely from the bed, her thin hair upright and stiff from her nap.

"*Politsai!*" she said. "*Politsai! Mazel tov!*"

It was actually Alice who suggested that Daniel's Uncle Abraham should talk to their mother. Alice had met him at a wedding with Janice and Daniel, and she was partial to him and Uncle Abraham liked her, too. "Janice, how's your sister, the hippy?" he always asked.

"Why not try it?" Alice said, her voice patched into a three-way call from Sandra's office so that Janice caught both Brahms and Prince in the background and, listening, had a split-screen image of her sisters: Alice in her dish-strewn living room on the elliptical, doing her nails with the phone under her chin; Sandra editing briefs at her desk, her suit jacket hung neatly over her chair. "At least we could learn what she's saying," Alice said.

"Why do we care now what she's saying?" Sandra asked. "When did we ever care?"

"Uncle Abraham wouldn't know *why* it's Yiddish," Janice added.

"Maybe . . . no wait . . . argh . . ." Alice's voice faded and came back and Janice decided it wasn't the connection but that the phone had physically slid away and Alice had caught it and, in the process, smeared both her nails and the receiver. "Maybe," Alice said, "maybe she's become an idiot savant and the savant part is Yiddish."

Sandra ignored her. "Janice, you'll call him?" she said. "It's a stretch, but it is an idea. Maybe there's something she's trying to tell us."

"I can," Janice said. "OK, if you really think so."

Which was why, having struggled her mother into both a bra and a dress so she'd look presentable, Janice was waiting with her in the living room, watching her rip pages out of a *Newsweek*. The doorbell rang and Janice let Uncle Abraham in from the sleety rain, pressing taxi fare from the el stop into his hand just as Daniel had told her to do.

"Janice," he said, kissing her cheek and handing over his coat and umbrella. "And Mrs. Finnegan who speaks Yiddish." He stepped over the scattered magazine pages, and Janice saw that her mother, who had lost her mind but not her backbone, towered above him.

Janice got him some coffee and a piece of banana bread. "She's better with just one person. I'll be in the kitchen," she told him.

"Three couches. In a minute. *Shlemiel*," her mother said.

At the cutting board, Janice sliced tomatoes and made egg salad and started a pot roast, only half listening to the ropy, thick words from the living room. Enough food for her mother. Enough for Jonerelle, the woman Sandra had hired to work nights when Janice went home to Daniel. There had been no real argument about any of this. The three of them—she and Sandra and Alice—had all known that Janice would take care of their mother. Sandra couldn't leave her law practice and Alice had to support herself while, for the present, Daniel and a part-time clerk could run the bookstore without Janice. And, anyway, only Janice had the patience to do it, the goodness as her sisters said, although as she voiced her one insistence and remembered the hard place, shiny like a well-polished stone, where she resented her mother as much as her sisters did and always had, Janice winced at the notion and at just how short she fell of her own ideals. "We have a home," she said. "Our life. Our apartment. Our stuff. Daniel and I can't move in with her."

"Fine," Sandra answered, getting out her notebook and putting the deal together. Sandra: 80 percent of the night worker's pay. Alice: 20 percent of the pay and three twenty-four-hour Sundays a month. Janice: everything else.

"But what about Mom's trust fund? Can't we use that to pay people?" Alice protested, and Sandra had snapped her pen closed.

"This way we're all doing our part," she said.

Janice put the egg salad into the fridge and went out to the living room. She sat on the couch. Her mother had moved to the record cabinet and was emptying albums onto the floor.

"You let her do that?" Uncle Abraham asked.

Janet shrugged. "She's still very strong."

"She called me a *grober yung*."

"Yes?"

"Young, vulgar guy. Good she thinks I'm still young. I'm waiting to hear that I'm handsome."

"Is she telling you anything? Anything we should know?" Janice asked, and her mother looked around at her, an odd smile on her face.

"*Shikseh. Zol vaksen tsibelis fun pupik!*" she said.

Janice, startled by the full sentence, looked at Uncle Abraham for a translation.

"She wants onions to grow in your navel."

Janice felt a sudden flush, a swell of tears. She got up and buttoned her mother's dress where she'd pulled it undone.

"*Zindik nit*, Mrs. Finnegan." Uncle Abraham shook his finger at her mother, and then turned to Janice. "I told her not to tempt fate," he said.

"Where's this coming from?" she asked. "I mean she could always be difficult. But in Yiddish?"

"Better then you don't know what she says. But mostly her words are mixed up. Tossed up. Landing at random. *Meshugeneh*, your mother. Why Yiddish, I don't know. But she does have the Long Island nose job."

Janice was taking a paperweight from her mother's hand and thinking, as she did, that it was past time to babyproof the house for her mother the way they'd done for Alice's boys and Sandra's daughter when they were young. Then the words registered. "What Long Island nose job?"

Uncle Abraham was looking down at a picture of a young Marlene Dietrich on one of the magazine pages. "Ah, Marlene," he said. Then he looked back up at Janice. "The nose job the doctors made. The inverted Jewish nose. No bump. The little ski slope."

"You mean Mom? You don't mean her." Janice let her mother take the paperweight back, but stayed wary, ready to catch her wrist. "You really think Mom's had a nose job?"

"My educated opinion. Uh-oh. My cab's back. Time flies. Tell Danny to visit me. We'll play cards and make money."

Janice nodded and then got Uncle Abraham his coat. "*Meh vet zich zen*, Mrs. Finnegan," he said, buttoning his buttons. "And Janice, you too, of course. See you again."

"*Shveig*," her mother said. "*Shveig, shveig.*"

Uncle Abraham nodded and opened the door. "All right, I'll stop talking," he said, and Janice watched his umbrella blowing from side to side as he went down the walk.

"Did he break the code? What did he say?" Daniel had dinner ready when Janice got home. Bread from the bread machine. A packet of cassoulet he'd defrosted in the microwave. He lit a candle, and they ate holding hands.

"I love our apartment. Everything is so ours," Janice said. She put her piece of bread down. She started crying softly. "I don't know what he told me. She's mixed up. Her Yiddish makes sense like her English. Sometimes it's clear. I've told you this, but when my dad died, I found her sitting on the floor in front of the bookcase and, when I asked what was wrong, she said, 'I won't be able to find the books. It was always your father who found the books.'"

"You think this had already started?"

Janice nodded. She let the tears streak down her face. She didn't know why she was crying. She didn't understand it any more than she knew why she'd started to laugh in the shower last week. Wildly. Uncontrollably. Yiddish! Her mother was speaking Yiddish! Daniel had stuck his head in to see if she'd gone berserk.

"She's wearing you out," Daniel said now, and Janice, with her swimmy eyes, looked at him through the lengthening candle flame.

His face seemed almost to float but it was still the slightly stern, bookish face that she loved better than anyone else's. He pressed her hand. "You've been doing this eight months. You need to talk to your sisters again."

"Seven and a half. I could be more patient," Janice said. "I could try," she added, feeling the need to qualify her statement, but she didn't tell Daniel that the school nuns, who'd inflamed her with a belief that religion must confront injustice, had not made her brave. She'd been much too timid to save the world. Helping her mother—helping her mother stay in her home was what she could do.

But in bed, curled into Daniel's back, she explained once more about her sisters. "They have more to forgive," she said and she told the stories again, of how her mother had erupted in fury when Alice confessed she was pregnant, how when Alice did what their mother insisted—got married at eighteen and had the baby and then the next one—their mother had still refused to go to the emergency room when Jeff took the boys away and Alice took a bottle of sleeping pills. And after Alice was home once more, their mother had called and told her she was a fool, that Jeff was the better parent anyway.

"How old is Brendan? It's an old story," Daniel said in a dozy voice.

"And then Sandra," Janice said. "They're too much alike. It agitates Mom when Sandra visits. They're control freaks. Both of them. They've been battling for forty-nine years."

"How come your sisters are so much older than you?"

Janice shrugged into his shoulder, thinking that she'd never asked. Not that or much of anything else. She waited a moment, her eyes tracing the light from the streetlamp that fell on the window blind. Then she touched Daniel's face. "Hey," she said softly. "Uncle Abraham thinks she got her nose fixed. On Long Island. He says it looks Jewish."

When Janice arrived at the house on Monday, Alice's son Tim was there. He had the kitchen table stacked with dictionaries and reference books. Alice got Janice a cup of coffee and flipped a book open. "Tim brought a library to figure her out. Still methodical like his dad," she said, and she reached over and gripped Tim's shoulders and cracked his back before he could move out of the way.

"She'd rather I was living on the South Side. Across from the gangbangers with her weird friends," Tim said, looking at Janice.

Alice answered him. "A little free spirit never hurt." She poured herself a cup of coffee and sat down at the table.

"Find any translations?" Janice asked, knowing she liked it that Tim had stayed his dad's son but that he still loved his mom. It was somehow OK that Alice had managed only the odd weekend when he and Brendan were small, and summer vacations that, after a week, flamed out in a chaos of ice cream and zoos.

"I think she said it was a shame for the children. '*Shandeh far di kinder*' if I heard her right," Tim said.

"And you said she told me to take a bath," Alice said.

"Right."

"But any revelations?" Janice asked.

"No."

"Did she recognize you?"

"Maybe. Probably not. She knows Mom. She tried to close her hand in a drawer."

Alice nodded in confirmation. "All I need for working on clients. Which reminds me. Am I leaving for work? Tim, are you? Do they give you translation days off?"

"You can borrow this stuff." Tim stood up. "Acquire another language, Aunt Janice, while she's watching Barney."

Janice laughed, though she was embarrassed that the books had been Tim's idea when she and Daniel were the ones with the bookstore. She gave Tim a quick hug and then found gas money for Alice when she came back into the kitchen.

"Thanks. Sorry," Alice said. "I meant to switch cards. This one's maxed out."

Janice walked her to the door and waited. Tim's car was already rounding the corner, and Janice watched Alice wave as she got into her own car. When she was gone, Janice stood at the window a moment and then, gathering herself, she went back through the kitchen to her mother's room and opened the door a crack. She looked in. Her mother was awake, looking at the galaxy Daniel had glued to the ceiling. "Ready to get up?" Janice asked, wondering if Alice, with Tim's help, had managed to get the bed changed.

"*Veist oy* . . ." her mother said, her voice trailing off, and Janice knew what she was saying this time.

"With this one, everything's 'it seems,' " Uncle Abraham had told her. "No more life that is. Everything just seems."

"You mean it seems as if the stars are right in your room?" Janice asked. She tugged her mother's slippers on and slid the bed rail down, lodging her hip, thin as it was, against the bed to support herself as she lifted her mother upright. When her mother was sitting, Janice waited a moment before helping her to the floor, doing everything in slow motion so that her mother didn't grow light-headed, buckle, her greater size knocking Janice over and collapsing them both to the rug.

But when her mother was standing, she pushed Janice firmly aside and headed for the closet. "*Klaider.* Do it fast," her mother said, and she started pulling her blouses and pants, her suits and dresses off the hangers, tossing them aside as she worked her way to the back of the closet.

Janice watched her. *Klaider*? She didn't know the word, but she could guess. At the store, Daniel had shown her a German story—"*Kleider machen Leute*"—and translated the title as "Clothes Make the Man." So clothes, she thought. *Klaider*: the Yiddish word for clothing.

Janice started picking up garments and rehanging them in her mother's wake. Her mother was talking to herself, and clothes in wool and polyester flew at Janice in a perfume-scented whirlwind.

The odor, stale as it was, brought Janice up short. Perfume. *Perfume.* She'd already forgotten her mother had always worn perfume.

"What are you doing?" Janice asked finally, though she didn't expect an answer she'd understand and she didn't get one. Her mother neared the back of the closet, and her voice grew more guttural, excited. Then she was backing up, turning around and plowing across the littered floor, a cotton tunic and skirt clutched in her arms. Janice had never seen them before.

"Do it fast," her mother said once more. "*Mach es shnell! Klaider.*"

This time, Janice took her words as instruction. "You want to wear these?" she said. She unbuttoned her mother's nightgown to pull it off, automatically averting her eyes from the body that had always stayed secret, though now she knew it by heart. All its wrinkles and lonely strands of hair. Its arthritic bumps and scarred and surgery-dinged breasts. Its acid breath and diaper smell. The skirt was short for her mother but, otherwise, the clothes she'd found fit her. The waist buttoned and the tunic, softened with age, molded itself naturally around her shoulders.

"Very nice," Janice said, but her mother was on the move again. She was at the dresser, pulling drawers askew and hurling out underwear and sweaters until she'd found a long black scarf. She wrapped it around her head and neck and then looked in the mirror and Janice looked too. Her mother's eyes were bright, and she was smiling her inscrutable, closed-mouth smile. She looked pleased, Janice thought. And she looked very much like a peasant Janice had seen once in a picture book about Crete.

"*Mameh,*" her mother said.

"Mama?" Janice asked. "You mean mama?" she said. She waited, but the word didn't come again.

"I suppose it was funny. Of course it was funny. If I looked up the right words, she told them to drop dead, and I swear one of them understood her. It was horrible, but, yes, it was funny." Janice was seasoning the chili and Daniel was setting the table. She was telling him about the day and the visit from the Sodality women from the parish. Not that her mother had attended Sodality even when she was well, but Sandra had arranged for the women to come. She hadn't warned Janice and, when the doorbell rang, she and her mother had been in the kitchen, her mother drooling oatmeal and still dressed in the black scarf and tunic and skirt. Janice had let the women in, and her mother had followed after her into the living room, a sticky mess of oatmeal on her face. Looking back at her naked, bruised legs and bare feet beneath the skirt, Janice, who'd never in her life felt sorry for her mother, suddenly did. Then, her mother had walked forward, making her hostile command—*Folg mich a gang un gai in drerd!* Her steps had been punctuated with an insistent rumble of farts.

"They beat a fast retreat," Janice said. "But hey, I nearly forgot—" She reached for her purse and took a letter out—pale blue, almost pale lavender—and handed it to Daniel. "What could this possibly mean? What's Piser Original Feingold?

Daniel shook his head. "A funeral home? *Yahrzeit*'s the anniversary of somebody's death."

"I looked that up with the 'drop dead.' But why do they want my mother to light a *yahrzeit* candle in memory of Susannah Weiss Kornbluh? Who's that? Who's Susannah Weiss Kornbluh?"

"If you don't know, I should?"

"Maybe I'm going a little crazy."

"Maybe call Sandra."

"I will," Janice said. "I was going to."

Instead, she got Charlie, her brother-in-law. Sandra had gone to bed with a cold.

"Probably Daniel's right. Probably it's a funeral home. But I haven't met the Susannah person," he told her.

"Apparently, she's dead," Janice answered, and she was thinking of how basically tidy Sandra's life was: pretty girl turned into attractive woman. Big, good-guy husband. College-aged daughter who'd never stopped being sweet. The exactly right job. Swimming and ski vacations. Yet in spite of all that, Janice still sensed there was a gap. At times, she wondered if Sandra, who'd gone to law school because their father insisted she should, wouldn't be happier on expeditions to the South Pole or driving dogs in the Iditarod.

"How about this?" Charlie said. "Your mother's forgetting English and speaking Yiddish, and the first language is the last to go. She's got a Jewish nose job. She's getting reminders to light candles from a Jewish funeral home. She's anti-Semitic. Maybe your mother's Jewish, Janice."

"That would make her anti-Semitic? She's Irish, Charlie. Irish Catholic. Like Dad was. Ruth Keneally Finnegan."

"If you think so."

"You don't?" Janice felt a jangly sense of anticipation waiting for Charlie to answer. She tried another question. "Charlie, do you and Sandra know something?"

He answered her this time. "Maybe Sandra does. You could try calling her office tomorrow."

It was past two the next day before Janice had time. After a manic morning of newspaper shredding and pan banging, her mother was finally asleep in a chair. "*Ek velt. Ek velt,*" she'd kept saying and Janice had followed after her with a dictionary and a phrase book until she understood her mother was proclaiming the end of the world.

"What's up?" Sandra said sniffling, when the receptionist put Janice through.

"Not Mom. Fortunately. She's asleep for the moment. But Sandra, there was this notice in her mail. It's a reminder about the death of a Susannah Kornbluh. A Susannah Weiss Kornbluh."

"Grandma Anna we never knew."

"Grandma *Keneally*?"

"I've got a client waiting—" Sandra sneezed. "The Anna's short for Susannah. I went to Mom's safe deposit box last week. I was going to tell you. Grandma Anna was a Weiss. She married a Kornbluh after she divorced Grandpa Keneally. Got that? And the W. Mom always

62 WATCHING OKSANA

said was just a middle initial? On her marriage license, she's Ruth Weiss Keneally."

Janet was quiet, watching the phone cord she'd twisted unwind. Then she started twisting it again. "They met when Dad was working in New York. I wonder if it was on Long Island. Or if it has to be."

"I've no idea. I'm in San Francisco tomorrow. My paralegal's got the info. I'll tell him to call Alice so Tim can surf for more. If we care about this. If it matters to anybody."

"It matters to me. I mean I'm fine with it, but—"

"Sweet, I have to go. Talk to you. Love you."

"OK. Love you too. Take care of your cold." Janice kept the phone in her hand. Her mind was racing as she looked around at her mother snoring in the chair. She leaned against the doorway, and then slipped the phone back in place. "Not *ek velt*," she said looking at her mother, "but pretty amazing."

A week later, Sandra called and suggested they have a party for their mother on her birthday, which was the Sunday before Christmas.

"She won't know it's a party," Janice said. She was thinking about her dad lying on the rug in front of the radio and holding her high, high in the air while he teased her mother across the room and said she'd been an easy girl to court. That it only took twenty-five cents and the bus ride to Jones Beach. Her mother had shushed him. But Long Island, Janice thought. Wasn't Jones Beach on Long Island?

"She was always good about birthdays," Sandra was saying. "Her strong suit really. Why not do it? Ginny'll be home from school. We'll make it a family party. Charlie can cook."

"You mean three pizzas and Chinese?"

"Right." Sandra laughed. "Wait, and I'll call Alice and patch her in."

"No—" Janice started, but she was already on hold. In a minute, Sandra was back.

"Who was the guy who answered the phone?" she asked, and Janice assumed she was talking to Alice.

"A guy. A friend. A Caleb."

"A guy you liked enough not to kick him out after the pancake breakfast?"

"Watch your tongue, big sister. If we're having a party, we should have matzo balls. Janice, does Daniel know where to get matzo balls?"

"I think you make them," Janice said.

"We should learn that stuff. We should really get into it," Alice said. "I should have guessed this before. Really, I should have guessed it a long time ago. She fed me chicken soup when I got my first period. You think I look Jewish? The prettiest girl in my class was Jewish."

"You look like Mom. She fed me chicken soup after my *honeymoon*," Sandra said.

"Her video's almost over. I have to go . . ." Janice leaned back to look into the living room. "Another minute."

"If you can think of something to tell Brendan," Alice continued. "Tim's OK—he thinks he should join MENSA—but Brendan's not having fun with this. I mean this is my son the Palestine supporter. He keeps saying, 'It goes through the mothers, right? And now I'm a Jew named Brendan?'"

"I'll try to think of something," Janice said, and she got off the phone. When she turned around after rewinding the tape, she saw that her mother had fallen asleep in her chair. Janice sat down on the couch across from her. Though she'd managed to get the tunic and skirt into the wash, her mother was still insistent on the scarf, and it was wound around her head, the fringe sticking out on top. At first, Janice had worried that it would catch on something, strangle her Isadora Duncan–style (though without the flair), but it had ceased seeming like a hazard. Instead, the scarf was her mother's signature now just as her perfume had been earlier, and it meant that Janice had stopped worrying that she should try to color her mother's hair so she looked more like herself—more like the person who, though she'd never been quite what could be called stylish, had always been very well groomed. It was hard even to conjure a picture of that mother any longer. She'd been replaced by a stranger. There'd been this alien abduction.

Lately, Janice had started taking the photo albums out trying to find that earlier mother, trying to think who she was (a decent hostess; a mother who had left each daughter with at least one memory of her kindness, in Janice's case the time when the dog had spattered her Sunday dress with mud and her mother had laughed instead of scolding her; a woman who never cried at home, but always cried at the movies). Since the Yiddish had appeared, Janice had particularly noted the gappiness in the albums. There were photos of her mother when she was a baby, but she wasn't with her own mother in any of them. Then the record leapfrogged abruptly to her mother's teenage years where she stood next to her father or vamped for the camera with friends. When Janice's own father entered the picture, the Finnegan family history began to unfold: a heavy dose of Sandra, a dabble of shots of Alice and Janice. In due time, the grandchildren appeared, though Janice had noticed they were often miscaptioned for each other as they grew older—Ginny, with her abundance of long curls, as likely as not mistaken for Tim. Janice thought there were the two stories visible on the album pages: the mysterious distortions and absences in her mother's past; the more recent distortions and absences in her mother's mind. And there was a link now between them, the old language that inhabited them both.

Janice looked out to the kitchen counter and the laundry bag filled with ironing she'd lugged with her. She was wondering if she could set up the ironing board so its metallic screech wouldn't wake her mother. While she was considering it, the phone rang. Her mother stirred, but Janice caught the phone before the second ring, and her mother's eyes stayed closed, her head tilting farther against the chair wing and a buzzy little snore starting in her throat.

It was Tim. "I found something," he said. He sounded excited and he immediately launched into an explanation of Internet sources or of documents that could be acquired through the Internet, Janice wasn't sure which. He'd been hunting in censuses and the Social Security Death Index and inquiring about cemetery records and death certificates and divorce records

"And you said you found something?" she asked, uncertain just where he was going with all this.

"Have you ever heard of a Henry Keneally?" he asked. "Does Syosset ring a bell? It's in New York. On Long Island, as a matter of fact."

"No," Janice said, which covered both questions. She listened while Tim rattled off his finds: her mother with an older brother no one had heard of who died when she was nine, their parents granted a divorce the very next year. Tim had discovered the whole family in Syosset in 1930 when the children were one and four. He'd also found a record of Anna marrying Theodore Kornbluh just months after her divorce, and an entry for her daughter and ex-husband in a Chicago parish directory in 1941.

"Did you quit your job? My God, Timmy, you're fast. Have you ever thought of being a detective?" Janice was astonished, and Tim was appropriately modest, but he added that Sandra's paralegal had hired a genealogist who'd done most of the digging.

"Very interesting. It's a lot to process. Uh-oh, she's waking up," Janice said and she told Tim good-bye and went over to her mother, who had the frightened look in her eyes she sometimes had now when she'd just awakened. Janice knelt on the carpet and touched her hand. "I didn't know you had a brother," she said.

Her mother turned her head rhythmically from side to side. "*Hot ir kinder?*" she asked, which was something she asked a lot now.

"No, Mom. No kids for me," Janice answered. "Nobody but you."

"Maybe it's time. Maybe we should have a child," Janice said to Daniel. It was Saturday night, and she'd brought sandwiches and beer to the shop to help him with the holiday orders.

"All this stuff is hitting the family button?" Daniel sliced a book carton open with his mat knife. "Exactly where are things information-wise? Information Weiss."

"Nothing new." Janice put the sandwiches onto plates. She'd already told him that Tim had located the right Keneallys on Long Island, and she said now that there'd been what looked like a relevant Kornbluh, but it hadn't been a fit since her Grandma Keneally didn't have children with her second husband. "The only thing that seems sure is that Mom stayed with her dad when her parents were divorced," she said. "Basically, she stopped being Jewish when she was ten."

"Until now."

"Until now." Janice picked up some books and then set them aside and started organizing order forms alphabetically by customer. When she'd first heard the Jewish names and Sandra's revelations, she'd thought there was maybe a bigger mystery, maybe some ongoing hidden need for secrecy. Maybe even something about the Holocaust. When her thoughts were really melodramatic, she'd imagined her mother had survived a death camp, that she'd done it by her wits and body and then been ashamed forever. (For this scenario, she'd canceled out the Irish grandfather she didn't remember and had it covered that her mother had never had an accent. She'd thought, why not? Why not a rich family and maybe an English governess and connections after the war?) Now, however, since Tim had kept her mother firmly in America, she leaned toward more pedestrian explanations: a child who felt abandoned by her mother. An infidelity, and a father who made his daughter ashamed of the woman who'd betrayed him after their son's death. A father (Janice's grandfather!) who skewed her mother's worldview. Thinking of it, Janice wondered just what her own father had known, how much he was part of the secret.

She opened the cash drawer to look for a bottle opener, and then handed Daniel a beer. "Sandra keeps saying it's all speculation, and there's no guarantee it won't stay that way. And I think I'm OK with that. That I don't need to know all the details, though I am curious what she was doing back in New York when she met my dad. But I know it might be better—cleaner—just being a puzzle. And, anyway, could it ever, deep down, not be a mystery when a person actually gives up her identity?

"Although maybe you're right. About it hitting the family button. I mean at least you and I know who we are. Or sort of. I've been thinking about this. Would you have married me? Would you have fallen in love with me if you'd thought I was Jewish? Or somewhat Jewish?"

"You're asking a Jew that?"

"I'm asking you. You weren't that unhappy not taking a Jewish girl home to your parents. It's true. You liked the rebellion. And if it was hard for your mom to be generous to me, she still was. Is. Would that have been different if we'd known?"

Daniel opened another carton and sat back on his feet. He took his glasses off and wiped them on his sleeve and, when he looked up at Janice, he had a kind of tiredness in his face that made her think just how wearing all these months had been for him, too. He put his glasses back on. "How could anything change the fact that I love you?" he said.

Janice felt the same warmth in her face that had burst on the scene the very first day she'd met him, the touch of recognition that made her forget the skinny, mousy person she felt that she was. She reached for his fingers. "You're a wonderful man," she said. "I'm the luckiest woman on the planet."

"You think I'm wonderful because I'm a Jew who doesn't care if you're Jewish?"

"Of course not," she said, chagrined at the question. "I just meant that you're wonderful. Full of wonders."

Later, when they'd walked home over the scruffy remains of snow that were hardened on the sidewalk from the last storm and climbed the stairs to their own apartment, Janice was still feeling a little distressed. She'd not meant what she'd asked. Or she'd not asked what she'd meant. Both really, though of course the wonderful part was right. There was hardly a way she could overstate it. Daniel amazed her. Sometimes when he was sleeping, she lay awake just to have the sense of being with him. He was so much more than she'd ever hoped for. He was smart and kind, and he loved her and, slight as he could look in his clothes, it was deceptive. Without them, he was a beautifully made man. She'd been surprised at herself, but the fact was it had always thrilled her.

In the kitchen, Janice unpacked the last of their store picnic and checked the refrigerator to see what to get when she went shopping in the morning. She set the sour cream that was turning pink on the counter and sniffed a half jar of peaches to see if they'd begun to ferment. She could hear Daniel watering the plants—his turn at the Saturday night ritual. He was whistling and Janice could trace his progress from the sound, and decipher his mood from the tune. An opera chorus, she thought. Something lively. Maybe Rossini. If her question had bothered him, he was over it. She was the one who was still smarting, feeling uncertain about things.

Janice tasted the peaches and put them back in the fridge, remembering Alice's warning when Janice had first started taking care of their mother. "You've got a great guy," she'd said. "I know there's this filial responsibility thing, but you don't want it wrecking your life. Honest to God, do you think she's worth it?"

Janice had been taken aback. Quickly, she'd assured Alice she was OK and that Daniel was supportive, that he entirely understood it was something she felt she had to do. And maybe because she wasn't used to getting advice from Alice (or regarding it highly on the rare occasions when she did), she didn't let Alice say anything more. There'd been a look on Alice's face, though. Janice still remembered it. She'd had the strong sense that her sister had been about to tell her she was letting a fear of happiness destroy her future.

Janice went out to the living room. She waited while Daniel checked the ivy plant for signs of spider mites. When he put his arm around her, she whispered she was sorry for asking such a dumb question, and he laughed, which was what she'd wanted. "I can't remember the question," he said. "You might as well have been talking to your mother."

"New question then." Janice tilted her head, her chin lodged in the warm spot between his neck and his collarbone. "Alice told me once—and true I was seventeen and she was working off a bong hit—that I'm so scared not to be perfectly decent . . . she said I'll never catch a clue about living. Was she right?"

Daniel held her back and looked at her. He smiled. "Think about it. Is she ever right?"

"I don't know. Maybe. Maybe about that. Maybe."

The question stayed with her the whole weekend. It was on her mind in the aisle at the grocery. She thought about it on Saturday and Sunday while she was waiting on customers at the store. By the time she'd navigated through a bright Monday morning of Yiddish outbursts, the idea of herself as someone afraid to make a mistake or to come up short of expectations had begun to haunt her. Just what was she doing? And what was it, exactly, about her and her mother? She got it about her mother and Alice, her mother and Sandra, but what about her?

She sat down on the floor in the living room and watched her mother ripping up the new stack of magazines she'd brought for her. In some ways, her mother hardly seemed even human to her anymore. She was more like an animal a person might watch scampering about in a zoo. Janice didn't know how long it had seemed that way. She hadn't charted the changes. But she knew there were things about her mother that had been unsettling long before her memory had started seeping away. In fact, Sandra had told her once that it was too bad that, being the youngest, she hadn't known their mother when she'd had an actual charm, which suggested that the start of her illness lay far in the past. Janice really didn't know. What she did know was that she'd always been her father's daughter more than her mother's and that she'd liked the company of the school nuns much better than her own mother's. They'd valued her. They'd praised her, and her mother rarely had.

Janice looked at her mother's flattened hair and thought she could have done a better job of brushing it. "Maybe I'm doing all this in hopes you'll really love me, or say that you do," she ventured, but her voice didn't even raise any Yiddish in reply. She wished that it had, for she'd come to crave it, that odd and comforting rhythm of sounds.

Her mother was trampling the strips of magazine into a solid mass, and Janice watched her, thinking once again that in all the months of observing her, she'd had a crash course in memory. The way she'd put it to Daniel was that, without memory, life lacked connective tissue. There was no way not to be confused, no way not to be thwarted in every single moment. Yet her mother had lived a life of blotting out memories even before they'd been stolen from her. Janice couldn't help wondering why.

She felt a sudden wave of love. "We're all still here, too. You've got more than that troubled past." She tried her own Yiddish. *Mameh*, she started, but she stopped. "What?" she said, and she dodged quickly so that the magazine her mother had thrown sailed past her head.

The afternoon of the party, Janice was putting on the antique opal earrings that had been her mother's last gift to her. She was sure they'd been an afterthought since her mother had pulled them from her jewelry box and handed them to her unceremoniously on her twenty-fifth birthday. She cherished them anyway. Screwing a back on, she allowed herself a rare fantasy: her own daughter's birthday. Twenty-one, she thought, and she'd hand her a glitter-wrapped box with the earrings inside and say it was a gift from both her mother and her grandmother.

She was checking the first earring in the mirror, and telling Daniel she didn't really mind spending her free afternoon at her mother's party, when the phone rang. It was Alice, and she was hysterical. Janice couldn't understand her. She was still clutching an earring in her hand, and she gave the phone to Daniel and waited while he listened.

"Yes?" she said, the earring digging into her palm when he put the phone down.

"Not good," he said. He hesitated, looking at her. "She's not dead, your mother, but she took a swing at Alice and crashed into the sink when Alice ducked. She hit her head. The paramedics are taking her to the hospital. She's out cold."

Janice had already turned and run to the coat tree. She grabbed her purse and jacket, and heard the jangle of Daniel's keys as he followed her out the door. In the car, she was rigid in the seat as they drove. When she realized she was still clutching the earring, she pulled the mirror down and put it on. Then she held her purse against her face and kept it there even when Daniel rested his hand on her knee.

They were the first ones to arrive at the emergency room. Alice came in a minute later in her fur-trimmed boots, her mascara leaking into blotchy marks on her cheeks. "What did they say?" she asked. "I think she cracked her skull. I mean she really hit hard." She started sobbing. She buried her head in Daniel's shoulder, and then switched to Janice's.

"They haven't told us anything," Daniel said.

"Did you reach Sandra?" Janice asked. She felt scared, but she realized she was feeling oddly calm, too, as if a long day's journey was suddenly growing short, and the landing lights had come up in the night sky.

Alice hiccoughed her answer. "They're at O'Hare getting Ginny. Sandra never answers when it's me, but Tim's calling Charlie's cell. Why did I duck? I should've just taken the punch."

"Oh . . ." Alice reached quickly into her purse. "I found this." She handed Janice a thin booklet with a blue-and-yellow cover. It was faded. Old. "Mom dumped her jewelry box out, and the lining came loose. This was underneath. Is it Yiddish?"

Daniel opened the cover and looked inside. He nodded, and then he showed Janice the date. 1939.

"She was ten," Janice said. Carefully, she turned the brittle pages, aware they were more proof that her mother really had grown up with Yiddish. "Poems," she said. "And an inscription. To Ruth from Mother. '*Tsu Ruth fun Mameh.*' "

"I'd like it," Alice said. "You know . . . if. And there's a letter."

Janice nodded. She was still paging through the book trying to see where it came from. Prague? Berlin? The Bronx? There was nothing that said, nothing written and no printed place of publication. She handed the book back to Alice and took the folded sheet of onionskin Alice was holding between her fingers like a forgotten cigarette.

"We're having the party here?" Brendan asked, making his way through the miscellaneous strangers waiting on their own emergencies, and Alice started crying again, and the resident came out to talk to them. Severe trauma to head and neck, he said. Mrs. Finnegan on a respirator. They'd be able to see her soon.

Janice was trying to absorb it all. Were they really moving past the medical part of things? How could it be happening this quickly? How could it be that the Yiddish words she'd grown so accustomed to could evaporate as rapidly as they'd come?

She unfolded the sheet of onionskin. It was clearly a letter to her mother and it was very short: *The neighbor is writing for me. She said you were here looking for your mother. Don't. They moved out of Syosset, and your mother can't bear to have her heart broken again. I thought Keneally took you to Chicago. Good luck to you from your Aunt Lottie.*

Janice sat quietly. She was shocked, but she realized there was as much information in this letter as Sandra had learned, or as Tim had found. More really. Her mother had gone to New York looking for her mother and had received this dismissal that had twisted its way through her life until it had wounded them all.

The nurse came for them and Janice folded the letter and put it away in her own purse. For the moment it was hers, though she knew she would read it later with her sisters.

She went into the room and quickly stifled a cry. Her mother had tubes running everywhere and machinery clicking and a swathe of gauze on one side of her head. Her eyes were closed and, except for the programmed rise and fall of her chest, she was perfectly still. "Sandra needs to be here," Janice said.

"She is. They're here now." Daniel was at her elbow, and Sandra and Charlie were coming in, snow dotting their good wool coats.

Ginny was with them, and Janice gave her a long hug. Ginny stood for a moment looking at her grandmother and her rig of equipment before pulling a chair close to the bed and beginning to stroke the hand that was bandaged over needles.

"Happy birthday, Grandma. We brought you a cake and we'll eat it for you," she said, and Janice remembered that, before the worst of her illness, her mother, had mellowed as a grandmother. She'd been a better grandmother than a mother. "I wanted to hear you talk Yiddish," Ginny said.

Charlie was munching on chips. "Anybody have some cards? We wouldn't have to worry about Ruth kibitzing. That's Yiddish, isn't it?"

Sandra shushed him. "We need a priest. I brought the living will."

"You're pulling the plug on her birthday?" Charlie asked, and Sandra gave him a quick, sharp look and stuffed his bag of chips into his pocket.

"What we actually need is a rabbi," Brendan said. "I don't care anymore if she's Jewish. If she speaks Yiddish, we should get her a rabbi."

"Oh my god Uncle Abraham," Alice exclaimed. "I invited him to the party. He'll be on the front porch in the snow with nobody there."

Daniel shook his head. "He'll be here. Your mother never leaves the house. The neighbors will tell him about the ambulance. I'll see about a priest. If there's a chaplain," he said, and he squeezed Janice's hand.

Tim moved his chair next to Ginny's. "We should sing 'Happy Birthday,' " he said. He and Ginny fumbled for a note, and spottily, hesitantly, all the rest of them joined in. It was the familiar, strange music—Charles Ives-ish with the Finnegan tin ears.

When they were done, Sandra started to cry. "I don't want her to die. I want her to be peaceful. I want her to have peace, but not to be dead." She looked up at the window. "All this snow. When you were born, Alice, and she brought you home, it snowed and I thought babies came from snow—"

"Daniel's come back with the priest," Janice said quickly, keenly aware she was upset with Sandra. She was angry at her for being the firstborn and for having her memories and this grief—easy for her— and for not ever having learned what she might have. "Alice, Daniel was right. Here's Uncle Abraham."

He was peering in at the door. Janice beckoned to him, and he shook his head shyly and stayed outside. She motioned to Brendan to come with her.

"Brendan wanted a rabbi," she said in the hall. "Is there a prayer you could say?"

"This Alice's boy? One of hers? Janice, your mother's not dead?"

"Not yet."

"Maybe a prayer. Not Kaddish afterward. Nobody to say Kaddish since Danny won't. But there are others, too, that will break a rule. We can maybe do this in Yiddish."

Uncle Abraham bowed his head. Janice listened to him, to his rising voice and prayer. She heard the priest saying his own prayers as he moved around the tubes to anoint her mother. In the room, in the hallway, there was a presence of words. As the twilight thinned at the windows, the words twined around each other, and Janice realized that of all the prayers she had said in the last months, she had never said one for her mother.

"Your servant Ruth," the priest intoned, and Janice thought what a beautiful name it was, though she had not thought so before— a name that had once belonged to a child.

Uncle Abraham said it too. "Ruth," he spoke in his cantor's voice.

Janice stepped into the doorway. She looked at the bed. She looked at her mother, who was hardly more than a white face and gauze and white sheet, all her family gathered around her. Sandra and Alice were weeping.

She is leaving, Janice thought. My mother is leaving. I am released.

She leaned forward and clutched at the sheet. Daniel was next to her, but she couldn't look at him until she found the word that she wanted.

"Mother," she started. She closed her eyes for a second and then it came to her with the surprise of a gift and with a clear certainty. She felt Daniel's arm around her shoulders and the word finding its way through her body.

"*Sholem*," she whispered, tears stinging her eyes. She let go of the sheet and reached for Daniel's hand. She whispered again. "*Shalom*, Ruth, Mother. *Sholem*."

The Fields of Flanders

It was for tea that her mother had asked her and Victoria, dabbing powder on her cheeks where her tears had left them swollen, still had plenty of time. She pulled her cap down over her hair and tried mugging in the glass.

There. She looked all right. Maybe her eyes were glittery—maybe they had that dark, swimming edge her father said made them like Waterford ("though I hate to see you cry, love," he always added, "even if it looks that good on you"). But it was her mother she was going to see and, in an hour, if the water spigot stayed shut, she would look just fine.

Victoria pressed her hands against her cheekbones and then brushed them across her eyelids and turned around. She surveyed the room. Even during her crying jag she had kept working. Even when she was screaming into a pillow so the upstairs neighbors wouldn't hear, she had kept on straightening and arranging. She'd found the silk flowers she and Chase had bought in France and put them in an outsized glass in front of the window where they looked just right, with the white scrim of curtain behind them that caught the sunlight when the sun shone, and invented it when it didn't, which was now.

Victoria put her coat on and took her car keys out of her purse. She had gotten everything right. The room was perfect for later when she'd come back bringing the chops she'd planned for dinner and the salad greens and wine. She would come in determined. She would be in her brightest mood with her cheeks just glowing from the chill, with the feel in her of London, of being in London, of driving and shopping in its streets. She would sink into Chase's lap, laughing with all her packages, and hold the lettuces over his head while he undid her coat and kissed her all over, and she would tell him between kisses, all her mother's new stories, with even the accent secondhand—Victoria's version of Clarissa's version of the German manicurist, the French waiter—and they would extricate themselves from the chair in stages and fix dinner, Chase chopping vegetables expertly on the marble counter, and get a little drunk on the wine and then make love with the silk flowers devased, finally, and planted all over them.

The doorknob rattled when she grasped it, and Victoria glanced back over her shoulder—one last look before she headed for her car. The room was perfection. For all that it was, it was still a place that defeated her in the ultimate sense of things. It broke always in two. Today a zigzag line split it apart. At other times there was a blocky kind of separation like the difference between red and black on a checkerboard.

Chase said it was her artist's eye that made her see things that way—that other people wouldn't, that he, in fact, did not. But it was not her artist's eye. Victoria knew that it wasn't. There was something emotional, not visual, at center that had made her this crazy and sad, that showed her a room divided between them—Chase's books (he might as well have brought his Bunsen burners home), Chase's young and round-faced daughters gazing from their portrait with their distant, matching smiles, Victoria's china cat, painted and fired at her grandmother's knee.

She sniffed once more into her car keys and then charged away down the outside stairs.

The shopping was first. At the greengrocer's and in the queue at the butcher's she was preoccupied, staring at the ceiling and then her feet.

"How much again, miss?"

Victoria nodded and then, waking up, looked at the meat on the scale. "Fine. It's good." Mentally she'd been off in France, riding with Chase, holding the door handle as he drove stubbornly, intently, on the right side.

"Is it all right? I mean do you mind?" she'd asked. "The right side?" and Chase had laughed at her, squeezing her thigh.

"You getting out, *Vick-y*?" He said it to tease her, making the name loud and broad like some gangsterism, like something from Chicago where her father had lived.

"Victoria," she said, and she'd relaxed against the seat, explaining herself to herself: wasn't it the first time that she'd traveled anywhere with a man who wasn't her father, though who was to notice this latest of the many firsts that ran back to the beginning time when, shaking with pleasure and fear, she'd slept with Chase, refusing to know, to admit to herself that he was some woman's husband?

"Your meat, miss."

Victoria paid and went out to her car.

In the off-licence, she bought wine and tried to shrug off the last Belfast headline to the clerk, who was from Londonderry. Then she was ready to head for her parents' house. Not home (it had never been that to her, purchased as it was when she was sixteen and off at school). It was only her parents' house.

A car shot out from across a side street and Victoria braked for it and then accelerated up the streets of Mayfair. She was running a bit late after all. She backed into a parking space, squealing her tires, and then scooped her packages into her arms and ran up the steps of 116, the house her cousin called the Fuchsia Door, as though it were a pub.

"Sorry I'm late. I'm here," she announced, going into the hallway. She put her packages on the table and hung her coat on the rack.

"In here, Vick. In the kitchen. The sun's nearly out. We can have our tea in the window."

"Whoa, Oliver. Not my chops." Victoria scratched at the orange cat of the house who was on his hind legs at the table, one delicate paw probing the butcher's wrap. She picked the chops up and went out to the kitchen.

"Christine made scones. Your timing's right. They're just now cool enough." Her mother was sliding things onto a plate, and Victoria kissed her and put her package of chops in the fridge.

"Don't let me forget that."

"You like these—the Calvin Klein's? Gertrude got them in New York. I can walk in them or breathe. Not both."

"I thought you wanted a bikini."

"You believed me? Thank God she didn't." Her mother moved the teapot onto the table and sat down so her blue jeans disappeared beneath the cloth and she was all one shirt of many colors and a broad-featured face that had grown more beautiful, clearer as the years went by.

Victoria sat down, too. She had that from her mother, didn't she—her lack of fear of getting older? She had that and her long legs and her gray eyes.

"Darling, how's school? And Chase? Is his paper done?" Her mother was pouring the tea and Victoria felt herself stiffen. At the questions—at Clarissa's self-conscious attempt to be a sort of mother-in-law. It was the only thing Victoria had ever seen her be clumsy at.

She waited a moment. "The first draft. He's put it away for now."

"And your painting? Is the light in the flat good enough? You know your father can always find you a studio."

"He told me. You told me." Victoria took a sip of her tea and picked up a scone. This was *not* a subject she had more to say about.

"Well I did think we were going to have sunshine." Clarissa stirred her tea, her free hand on her neck. She was looking out the window and she, too, seemed for the moment to have nothing to say.

Victoria picked at a raisin in her scone. The silence was something she recognized. So maybe she had planned on Clarissa's stories, forgotten the awkwardness, but it came back to her strongly now. This was the same quiet that had fallen between them more and more. Since Chase, actually.

Victoria moved her chair back from the table. And didn't Chase have an explanation for this as well—two of them, in fact—the first one plain enough, that it was awkward for a mother and daughter sorting out the business of being women together? Victoria had listened and told him that, instead of doing chemistry, he should write for the women's magazines.

It was his other reason, though, that tore her up. She had clapped her hands over her ears and screwed her eyes shut to make him stop talking. And he had stopped, though not before saying more than she'd wanted to hear: "Do take it all on yourself, Vick. Figure every time you're in bed with me it's the same as some shopgirl having it off with your father. Making Clarissa the deceived wife all over again."

"Would you like more tea?"

"Yes—lovely." Victoria pushed her cup across the table. Why couldn't the phone ring? Or even the doorbell. But there—she had something to say.

"I do like that. Isn't it from your *Othello* costume?"

Her mother glanced down at her shirt, which was really a tunic, riotously painted in stripes. "I think so. Maybe it is. You remember that?"

"Of course." Victoria laughed. "Why wouldn't I? No right man for the part and my mother with the low voice playing Othello. Of course I remember! But now that I think of it, why did you wear that shirt?"

"I don't know if I know. Well maybe to distract the audience. Or maybe to worry them over the shirt so they wouldn't trouble over what was in it."

They were both laughing and Victoria spilled tea on her napkin.

That was home—home and the West Midlands and all the plays and all the evenings she'd spent upside down in a folding chair in search of other children with their heads down amongst the grown-ups' legs and shoes while people got murdered or were set swooning on stage. Clarissa had been the star always—almost always—accomplished enough to have acted for real, people said, though she gave it up for good when they moved to London. "Why play at it," she'd said, "when the center of it—the real thing in all the world—is right here?"

"Funny you should mention that—*Othello*. Those plays. Funny, I guess, I should wear this. It's what I meant to talk to you about. In a way. Oh, the bloody phone."

Good. Her deliverance, Victoria thought. But there was this lovely memory, too: the scent of her mother in her stage makeup, Clarissa in her dressing gown in front of her mirror, painting her cheeks a fiery red or dark brown.

Victoria got up and stood at the window, looking out at the garden. She pressed her hand against the glass. She was thinking of her father still—her father and his girlfriends forever. Always they stuck in her mind. Even when she'd told Chase, she had felt it was something he could already see in her, something he could find like the strawberry mark on her buttocks.

"Why does he have to? She's so extraordinary. And why does she stand for it? Why does she?" she'd said, and Chase looked back at her with even eyes.

"Well she *is* extraordinary. Maybe he wants a respite from that—something thoughtless now and again. But she's loyal, your mum. She'd stick with the *Titanic* if she'd stock in the company. I don't know, Vick. Was she trained by nuns?"

Her mother was ringing off now, and Victoria moved away from the window.

"Love from your father. He's got some dinner thing."

Victoria picked up her spoon. "You were going to tell me something," she said, running it around the rim of the saucer.

"Yes." Clarissa sat down. "You're right I was." She looked at Victoria with an odd expression that turned slowly into a smile. "*Othello*, Victoria. Do you remember when we got the London actors coming through on their tours?"

"I guess so. Did they wear purple shirts? I remember that."

"Maybe. Some of them. Some of the time. Purple shirts, Vick?" Clarissa looked at her over her tea cup. "Darling, it was when we did *Othello*. No, maybe it was *Murder at the Vicarage* we were doing when Claude came."

"Who's Claude?"

"*Murder at the Vicarage* or at least something he had to show me the blocking for on stage. He told me he decided when our hands crossed. You know—the textures together. He's a great one for textures."

"Decided what? Who's Claude?"

Her mother still had the smile on her face.

"This morning I woke up knowing I'd tell you. A lover. My lover, Victoria. For twelve years."

Victoria stared.

Her mother looked down at her cup. "You were young when it started. Very young. And I was discreet, which gets to be a habit. There now, I've told you." Clarissa put her cup down, turned it in the saucer. "I'd catch the train to London after you left for school. Or we'd have a day or two of holiday when we could manage it. Oh, Victoria, the loveliest times."

"A lover?" There was something extraordinary happening inside of Victoria, something skidding around in her the way Chase said particles did inside of a cyclotron.

"Yes, a lover. The most amazing lover. Maybe you saw him, Vick. He said he knew when our hands crossed, but I'd made up my mind before he ever got onstage. He was so lithe, but brawny, really, in the shoulders. And with that wonderful voice, the seduction built right in."

"Clarissa!" Victoria put her hands on her mouth. She was laughing. She could not keep herself from laughing. Maybe she had seen him. She felt sure that she had. "But where did you go?"

"Everywhere. Hotel rooms, rented rooms, dressing rooms, beaches. Of course beaches! Wherever there was a dry rock or a bit of sand. Did you know, darling, when you can't wait any longer or if you're a bit short on funds, you can buy a round trip to Richmond and spend it the whole way, going and back, locked into, demolishing your own little compartment?"

Clarissa stood up and moved from the table. "And all the marvelous lost rooms at Hampton Court.

"And Sissinghurst Castle—especially Sissinghurst Castle in the late autumn when the tourists won't try the cold and rain. And endless gardens everywhere with an infinite privacy of hedge—"

Clarissa leaned back against the sink with her hands behind her. Her face was flushed, her eyes far off, and Victoria, who felt split nearly in two from the grin on her face, remembered exactly the smell of stage paint.

"Victoria," her mother said. "Vick, if this country had a single poppy growing for every place that Claude and I made love, the whole of England would look exactly like Flanders."

She couldn't help it. Really she couldn't. Victoria was shrieking. She jumped up from the table and hugged Clarissa. She hugged her again. "But I never knew!"

"Of course you didn't."

"And Daddy—does he know?"

"No. And he never will." Clarissa turned to the sink. She leaned over and scrubbed at the tin from the scones.

"But can I meet him? Claude?"

Clarissa started the water running. "Not likely, I think. Unless, of course, you're going to Australia."

"He's there?"

"He left a year ago—something with films. And then he stayed."

"Is it all over then?"

"It was over before."

"Is that sad? I mean are you sorry?"

"Maybe not. No. It was time."

"Clarissa, you amaze me! Really you do." Victoria clapped her hands against her head. "I can't believe this."

"It's all right that I told you?"

"Yes, of course it's all right!" Victoria thought she was still spinning, still whirling around in the cyclotron. She could feel her watch where she'd banged it into her head; she looked at her wrist.

"It's so late. Oh I do have to go. Is that awful? Chase will be home."

"Already? You don't want more tea?"

"Well it's lovely—"

"But you do have to go." Clarissa had cocked her head, her shirt collar stretching open across her clavicle. "Then take some scones with you, darling."

Victoria hugged her mother again, felt the quick dampness of her hand on her cheek.

"Don't forget your meat." Clarissa nodded toward the fridge, and Victoria collected her chops. She took the scones Clarissa put in a sack.

"And I'll rinse these cups," Clarissa said. "Just quick, and I'll walk out with you."

In the hallway, Victoria pulled her coat on and gathered her packages. "Lovely tea. Lovely, Mummy." She was grinning again, into Clarissa's smile, and didn't she feel a startling, an absolute happiness as she went outside? She nearly flew down the steps.

For a black moment, then, she stopped on the last one, a wave of uncertainty sweeping over her. She looked back for her mother who had come halfway outside and was leaning against the door frame—tall, self-possessed, poised as always. Yet there were the tiny lines by her mouth, the small marks of tension Victoria had always recognized when her mother was concentrating or thinking out a role. Victoria hesitated.

But Clarissa had shifted her shoulder against the door frame and she waved now. She smiled and the lines were gone. "Love to Chase," she called.

Victoria waved back. Of course it was true! How could she even think of doubting it? Of course this Claude, this lover, was real!

She clutched her packages against her coat and crossed the pavement. She opened her car door and, pushing the wine, the scones and chops in their wrappers across the seat, she got in. It was just dusk. The street was jumbled with traffic. Lights were blinking on in the houses. Streetlamps spilled light. People on corners were lighted through silk—phosphorescent with light. Each lamp, its soft-edged glow like a luminous flower, shimmered around her.

Victoria's heart raced. Something wide and billowing was opening inside her. She eased the brake free, nudging the car into the lane and then speeding up. She'd tell Chase about Claude. Yes definitely she'd tell him. Somewhere between the chopped vegetables and emptied vase—and if she remembered—she certainly would.

Moving

When Alix Shalli first became symptomatic, her husband, Jefferson, was not alarmed. "I know what's going on in your head," he told her. "These are sensations. If you embrace them, if you tell yourself they're not dangerous, and they're not, you'll be fine."

Alix was huddled on the couch with the needlepoint pillows and their son Jacob's stuffed bear. She mumbled something unintelligible into the cushions, then rolled halfway over and looked at Jefferson with an expression he identified clinically as fatigue but which appeared far more hostile. "If you knew what was going on in my head," she said, "we'd have gotten divorced years ago."

That was in May, the loveliest day of May, and by a Saturday in November Alix was well except for the odd, quickly aborted setback, and Jefferson was unpacking boxes in his new apartment, dusting off his Little League trophy from fifth grade and putting it next to the textbooks that had already bowed the shelves. He was standing at the snowy window and beating his chest in liberation: no walks or driveway to clear.

It had been his call to leave. He had not been dumped, scuttled by a wife eager to find herself. Instead, sensing Alix's restiveness, her desire for more empowerment (the unspoken statement that grew brighter in her eyes as she and her self-chosen therapist conquered her disease), knowing her relief yet resentment that he had been right (she was not doomed to a panic-driven life, phobic at markets and school plays), for one last time he had made eager love to her cool love and then pulled out the suitcases.

His call. All the way. Every step. He had seen her through her illness and then beaten her to the punch and for that he was pleased. At forty-two he'd avoided the cliché. He'd deferred to her wish to find herself before she had even asked.

And he? He would buy a sports car. He would take a vacation fly-fishing in Alaska and date twenty-nine-year-old women from health clubs and an occasional hospital resident for conversation. He'd call his brother-in-law a right-wing nutcase and eat carbohydrates that were in no way complex. He'd get a divorce where he wrote the ticket and let Jacob sleep in bed with him when Joseph teased him to tears and let Joseph tease Jacob until he'd taught himself by himself it was wrong.

Jefferson pitched the empty box on the pile by the door and sprawled across the gigantic new mattress the sheets wouldn't fit. It was a bed bought with well-laid plans for his future but, at the moment, all he could think about was his sons. He wanted them squirming across him and trying to reach for the soft dice he juggled from hand to hand just out of their grasp. He wanted to smell their hair, damp and dark with sweat. He wanted Jacob's earnestness: "Dad, give me a book. I need to read on the toilet." He wanted Joseph's voice mimicking cartoons.

Twelve blocks away. It was as far as the sun.

Jefferson punched a pillow against the wall and got up. He pulled his jacket on and went out to a pay phone and left a message for his lawyer—*his* lawyer, right?—that he'd see him on Monday. Then he drove to Target and Toys "R" Us. He bought a new battery for his pager and one of every game and one of every toy his sons had at home, plus two rooms' worth of Vikings and Twins posters he knew he couldn't put up on his rented walls. With his Bronco crammed full and with food from Leeann Chin balanced on his lap, he drove back to his apartment, the Minneapolis skyline leading him in the rearview mirror. Trip after trip and tracking wet snow, he carried bags up two flights of stairs. Then he ate at the sink reading real estate ads. By the time he threw out his fortune cookie and his pager went off, he'd circled three condos he thought he could buy.

In May, a year from the day when he'd heard the word "divorce" aimed from the couch, Jefferson Shalli was settled in a condo with rooms for both boys and a piano to play jazz on and the right to see his sons for four weeks a year, every weekend, and an as yet to be determined midweek day that was dependent on his patient load. He had stopped driving past his former house late at night. He was taking flying lessons. Although there had been dates, many women on the passenger side of his XKE, for the moment flying seemed more possible, safer at least than the under-thirties at his health club. It was Tuesday, and at 6:01 he had landed a Cessna after a slow roll so right that his flight instructor owed him a beer. Now he was in his kitchen drinking a vodka martini and pressing the collar of his one clean white shirt, wondering if Alix would be where he was going, if Jacob had stuck an invitation to the boys' school fund-raiser on her refrigerator, too. Jefferson ironed the front of his shirt and the cuffs, and dressed with particular care. It had been months since he'd seen his wife—ex-wife now—without the buffer of lawyers or sons.

    She was there in the reception room, looking young in green as she always did, with the lean body that meant the taut quadriceps in blue jeans, the slim inner thighs, though tonight she was wearing a dress. They nodded at each other across the room, sipping wine, but for dinner the seating was a problem. They were together, name tag by name tag, hers with the new hyphenation. They stood awkwardly. Around them, people noticed the mistake, and Joseph's teacher from last year started to redden.

"It's my fault. I'm so sorry. I thought you were still a together couple."

Alix smiled then, slipping into her seat. "Together people. All right. Even if we're not together anymore. But it's fine." She looked at Jefferson expectantly, and he sat down.

"I like your dress," he said, though he was thinking about her hair. That it was different, longer maybe, with more sheen.

"Thank you, Dr. Shalli. I like the shirt your sons got for your birthday." She smiled, and he smiled, and he felt the old wordless understanding, which was an odd fit with the place where he was, the day that she'd met him for lunch and told him she was selling the house and buying a condo.

He had been entirely furious. "Uproot the boys?" he'd said and she'd looked at him without speaking. "Alix, where is it they're supposed to play?"

"You mean where do they play catch with their father? Who's got the condo? You're the one that went first, Jeff."

And he'd signed then, signed again and again. The realtors' forms. The banks' forms. A ream of paper from accountants and lawyers until now the woman next to him had quit her editing job, had joint custody of his sons, a hyphenated name, a part ownership in a bookstore he had never set foot in, though his check closed the deal, and a condo with a crew to shovel the walks, and not one foot of grass.

"Can't you give them some space?" he'd asked, and Alix had looked at him evenly.

"It's not happening, Jeff. I won't be one of those wives who asks her ex-husband to mow the lawn and fix the snow blower and then sleeps with him out of gratitude. You left. You're history, my friend."

She was speaking now with the apparently single man on her right and Jefferson shook off the memory, hearing her voice. She was in her deft, small-talk mode, the one with an edge. "No, he doesn't shrink you. He's not Freudian. Not Jungian. More Pavlovian. Even Skinnerian. We raised our boys in a box. They're out now. They're eight and ten."

"Alix," he said, and the man laughed, uncomfortable perhaps, but recognizing the joke and clearly admiring the teller. Jefferson looked at him. Good upper body. Not ugly. He'd expected any time to hear Alix was seeing someone, but not this man, not anyone with a face.

"So who's babysitting?" he asked. She didn't hear him, or pretended she didn't. He edged his belt against the table, trying to work his finger inside his pager case to set off the beep.

"I'll be good," she said quietly, leaning toward him, and he cut into his chicken.

Outside in the warm night, when he saw the man from the table had disappeared, he walked her to her car. "How's the store?" he asked.

"A lot of work still, but I love it. I really do."

"And you're feeling all right?"

"Fine."

"Your medication's OK?"

"Jefferson—"

He reached over and opened her car door. "You know, don't you, I'd never have left if you hadn't been well."

"And you wouldn't have left if you didn't know it was what I would want. Do I know that? Do I even know I was well?" She tossed her purse on the far seat and got in behind the steering wheel.

"I'm not sorry we waited."

"What?"

"The thing I said when Joseph was born. He was beautiful and I meant then how crazy we were to hold back from that. Me, I mean. You were ready. But they're perfect. They're absolutely perfect right now."

"They like your car. Very smart of Jaguar to build a midlife vehicle that fits kids in the back."

"Right." Jefferson backed up, absorbing the blow.

"Thank you for not smoking," he said, watching her drive away, realizing for the first time that there had been no cigarettes, no European mouth spray, that she'd quit. He yelled after the car: "THANK YOU FOR GUARDING MY CHILDREN'S LUNGS."

By August, with school approaching, Joseph wanted a backboard. "I don't have a hook shot," he said, desperation moving into his voice. He walked down the hallway. "Does Joseph Shalli make the lineup without a hook shot? No, Joseph Shalli sits on the bench."

Jefferson made promises about gyms. He led neighborhood searches to find a hoop that, for safety reasons, gang matters, had not been replaced with a tennis court. "We'll work it out," he said, rejecting the offer from Jacob to throw balls back out to the alley that Joseph hooked successfully through his bedroom window.

"So what do we do, Dad?" Joseph said.

Jefferson had the answer only when the words were out of his mouth. "We'll buy a house."

On a Saturday in November, they moved in. Jefferson had sold his condo to the resident he'd meant to ask out until he'd discovered she was married and pregnant. With the house, he'd gone larger than he intended. He owned an updated kitchen for a real cook, four bedrooms, a study in the attic, two-and-a-half baths, and a basement with a workshop and a serious poolroom. The driveway was blacktopped under the snow, and the basketball hoop was already in place. To counter the huge emptiness of the dining room, he'd bought a table that seated ten.

"It's cool, Dad," Joseph said, and Jefferson unpacked the new snow blower and cleared off the driveway and they shot baskets with a black Hoyas basketball until their feet were soaked and Jacob's fingers were freezing.

"It's a house, guys. Real wood," Jefferson said, taking them inside, holding Jacob's fingers in his hands until they were warm and drying feet with a dish towel that was all he could find. The kitchen was sunny, the winter light reflecting blue off the tiles and patterning the ceiling with arcs like the lead of the windows.

"Let's have a party," Jacob said.

"For Christmas," Jefferson answered. "We'll have one for sure."

On the next Thursday evening, loaded with decorations from the Christmas section of Macy's, Jefferson ran into a sprite on his way past cosmetics. She was all glitter and costume, and clearly in a paid and playful mood. "Mistletoe," she said. She held it over his head and left lipstick on his cheek and the corner of his mouth and a scent of Dune that stayed in his beard. He drove home pulling glitter from his hair and put white lights around the porch and toppled off the ladder, and broke his left arm.

Alix's message, relayed later through Joseph, was direct: "Right choice of arm. Good you weren't hooked on the surgery rotation."

She was right, but the day before the party—a planned Sunday cocktail hour of old friends, the new neighbors, the boys' friends (he'd vetoed Jacob's plan to invite his Cub pack and demonstrate how all fourteen could fit on the bed)—he was paged to talk a patient out of shooting his wife, and he wished he had picked maybe urology. When he finally saw the man lodged in a hospital ward, he drove home preoccupied, the man's litany of complaints running through his head—all of them familiar, all of them suddenly weightless in the face of an onslaught of questions. Why do people get married? Why do they make families to unmake them? For that matter, why had he done it himself? For an instant, frightened, he could not remember at all.

It was snowing, the soft, floating snow of an all-night snow, and the flakes sparkled and burst on the streetlamps. Jefferson pulled into his driveway. His nurse had called Alix to pick up the boys and he expected the house to be dark, but there were lamps on in the living room, a bright glow from the kitchen. He walked up the sidewalk, the pinpoint-white Christmas lights tracing the rectangle of the porch, the oak gargoyle on the front door spitting its pursed wind into the snow. He stopped with his hand on the doorknob. They were all wrapping gifts beside the Christmas tree—Joseph and Jacob and Alix. He could hear them laughing, see them so easily, the blinds not yet closed against the evening.

Even in the snow, he felt the clearness of the cold, felt the clearness in his mind. How much time, how much money and outright loneliness it had taken to come to this—back to a home with an inside and out. He opened the door. The paper crinkled quiet. Quiet faces turned in his direction.

Two pianos. Two kitchen tables. For a burning moment, Jefferson considered the possibilities.

Eleven Days to China

Think I wanted to give my firstborn to the Chinese and before they've even got their act together? Not me. You can guess again.

I mean he did go. That much is true. A flight to Tokyo and then Beijing, but no way that took place because his mother said go on, kid, save the world. It was more me saying don't go, you son of a bitch, which makes me the bitch but OK. Didn't we need him at home cleaning up the mess his father left with his brother a zoned-out pothead and his sister having low self-esteem? Haven't I worked two full-time jobs?

There are things I would be happy to do for any son of mine—like let his friends sleep off their high school drunks on my living room floor or, when they didn't have their licenses yet, take the whole bunch out to the desert so they could shoot off their pop guns at the lizards and watch them splatter. But Travis meeting an ambassador and going to the Forbidden City and being paraded around on some bus at my taxpayer expense? If he wanted that, he could've told me to forbid him Phoenix.

You raise your kids. Maybe you get them to Mass sometimes and even switch and get born again once in a revival tent, and when you throw a ketchup bottle at their no-good, whoring father, you clean up before they see it and maybe you say a prayer being thankful the bottle's plastic that time because your aim's right on and what good is somebody's mother doing permanent time for killing his dad? Forbidding a city, though. I could've managed that.

Travis Donald Sanagamon, U.S.-China Friendship Volunteer. Peace Corps. They found a fancy name: China D. This, to me, is like *Rocky III* or *Naked Gun 2½* or whatever number it was before O.J. meant that name was finished. Not that I ever thought O.J. did it. There are women who tell me with my experience of men (you can read that Donny) I should be Denise Brown's number one supporter, but I could never see that O.J. had the time. Forget the forensics. You know how long it takes to scrub a carpet clean of just one spurt of ketchup?

I am not agreeing with violence against women. But women can egg a man on or throw the first punch. I know women that fight back for real.

When it hit me Travis was leaving, he had eleven days to go. The dishwasher timer was broken, and I was at the sink washing glasses and looking at my cactus garden. I had the air-conditioning on, but with my hands in the water I felt warm anyway. It was like when Travis was little and I was pregnant with Josh, and Travis would stick to my legs like a hot little bug and I'd push my bangs back with a damp wrist trying to keep the soap from my eyes. I remembered him on my legs. I could feel it like it was right now, and it was then this thing came out of me like the whistle of a train, like the whole damned train. This wail. *They're sending him to China. To CHINA.*

I mean Travis is my ace in the hole. No slight to Josh or Jenny and I love them every bit the same, but he is the one truly perfect thing to come out of the whole crazy turmoil of Donny and me. Donny knows it, too. At school, Ms. Gomez or Mr. Harris or Dr. Evers would compliment us to death and then, before we went on to Josh and Jenny's teachers, Donny, who in the looks department is like Travis's graying twin, would say, "One of us must have fooled around. How can this kid be ours?"

But *China*. I am from a big family, five kids, and even with three of us in Arizona, it's hard to stay close. Dottie lives in San Diego, and every year she arranges the family reunion here, and Leon comes in from San Francisco and, no, in spite of what Donny blabs around, Leon's not gay. My friend Maureen's husband left her for a guy and her brother came out to her the same day and Maureen's totaled in Margaritaville, but I still wouldn't care if Leon's gay.

However, Leon isn't.

I left the dishes in the drainer and went down the hall to Travis's room. He was packing already. He'd been packing for two weeks, checking things off on a list and weighing books and Wite-Out and markers and his camping stuff on the bathroom scale. I sat on his bed. "We got Mexicans right here you can teach English to," I said.

"Hispanics," he answered. "Chicanos. Chicanas."

"Well they're right here."

"Mom," he said without looking at me, and when I picked up a shirt to fold it, he pointed toward the door and I kicked the shirt under his bed on my way out.

"You think the Chinese need you more than Josh and Jenny do? What if your Uncle Glancy gets pneumonia again? What if it's worse and you aren't here?" I was talking to a shut door and the volume went up on Sting, who is the one performer I recognize that Travis plays. I knew already he was gone. With him not even answering about Glancy, I knew it.

The fact is Travis worships Glancy. Glancy's my baby brother, and back when he was nineteen he was in an accident with his Harley, and he would've made the Paralympics this time, but he was in the hospital again during tryouts. He's got a woman living with him here in town. Her and her two little girls that every time I see them I wish I'd had another girl for Jenny to have a sister, except after she was born I decided no more kids with that bastard. No pushing down and Donny walking in loaded, hitting on the nurses. I was jealous for one reason only: if they had wanted to, those nurses were entirely free to clobber Donald S. Sangamon since they weren't in the middle of having a baby.

Glancy's got spastic legs and you wouldn't believe how strong they look from all that surprise clenching. But he can't move them even a bit on his own and even if Glancy gets along fine, I'd lock my boys up before I'd let them on a bike. Hear that, Mr. China Ambassador? You give Travis a motorcycle, and I'm writing to *60 Minutes* before you can spit.

I was hoping Travis would come out to the kitchen after I talked to him. Maybe get a Coke or pick up a dish towel to help even if he didn't say anything. Maybe get out the chocolate chips and start making cookies, which I taught him to and he is better at than Jenny. But his door stayed shut, *loud* shut on all that music and packing, and here I'd never even thought about it before that one of my kids would leave Phoenix. Let alone the state.

My dad was the one that decided to come here. He was in Tucson during the war, and his mother had bad lungs and he wanted her to come out after he and Mom and Leon got settled, but she stayed in Kentucky. My dad always said it was still a smart move in case one of us kids got asthma, but we never did. Once he went to California for six months, but his job fell through and he came back and took the house off the market. He owned half a gas station when he died. My mother lived off his share that his partner bought, though he cheated her good. She lived on that with her Social Security until she strangled to death on a piece of meat in a diner where they didn't know the Heimlich move.

I miss my dad the most. One summer he taught me how to scrape a boat and paint it and what's the good of that in the desert, but we had a great time. We listened to old Linda Ronstadt music she sang with the Stone Poneys—Linda's a Tucson girl—and when he died the whole family went in a pickup caravan out to the desert. Sunset. The sky boiled orange from the copper mines. Mom said to shake his ashes where he could see the rain falling down the mountains in sleeves, and so we did. Even now, sometimes a screen door bangs shut and, before I remember, I wait to hear him coming in with the grease spots on his shirt and the *Standard* embroidered on his pocket. I tell Jenny, don't you get down on yourself. Your grandpa was as sweet on you as anybody could be.

Josh is my bigger worry, and I do not understand how Travis could walk out on that. Josh is a sweet boy, not planning for himself like Travis does, but just blundering into things that hurt him. His eyes are bad for a boy and we got him glasses when he was nine and that helped except for the names he got called. I even took boxing with him after Donny left and I thought that helped, and so did my sister Angie who had the idea, but she is married to a Mexican and lives in Nogales and she is half in another country in all ways. She named my niece Ling-Ling, and Donny says to me, "Wait till she gets to kindergarten. Ling-Ling Ortega. Your sister the ding-a-ling named her baby after herself."

I was mad he said that, but then I laughed because I knew it was funny. It's not like there were never any good times with Donny and me. I mean we got together, right? What a dumb kid I was. Donny had this line he practiced on every girl he saw and I was in the 1 percent that bit. It wasn't even a line. It was poetry, or he said it was—poetry from the spirit of his grandfather who was part Navajo—and it was high speaking about things that are mystical and like aliens. I thought wow. Now I know it was poetry the way three sheets to the wind is poetry, but he said I was pretty and that I'd remember his hands on me the same way I remembered using my body to swim or hit a ball. Like you don't forget how to ride a bike. And this is the part that was best with Donny and me. The way he touched me before I knew it wasn't just me he was doing it to. Also, when he took the time, he was good with the kids the way a charmer is.

I am thinking this is what hurt Josh more than anything else. When Donny left, Josh had so much rage. Finally, I had to close his door just to keep the feather lint in from when he pounded his pillows. They don't tell you in counseling that when your family breaks up, one kid lives in the library and one puts fingernail polish on her eyebrows and the other one turns your house into an allergy zone. How do you get there from when Travis was a baby doing crawling races with Donny, and I thought this is easy, this is how it's supposed to be?

When I went to see Donny about Travis leaving he was at his trailer building a barbecue pit, though why this is necessary for a trailer I have no idea and, anyway, what's wrong with a Weber? I pulled up in my Camaro, which being my father's daughter I have kept mint in spite of two boys. I waited, and I thought Donny would come over to the car window, but he had his trowel and he kept spreading mortar on the bricks and smacking them together though he knew I was there.

I got out of the car and showed him where the mortar had squeezed over the bricks. He had overalls on, which must be the idea of some woman I never met, and a painter's cap that looked basically ridiculous. He told me I could mind my own business and what did I want?

"You could talk to your son," I said. He was using his plumb line and his T-square, and he was sighting past my legs entirely on purpose.

"You are talking which of my sons?" he said, which could be fighting words if I let them because we both know when Josh needs talking to is when you can't, but I do know my sons are the only ones Donny has in spite of any implications. I let it slide.

"Your big-shot, saving-the-Chinese son," I answered.

"About what?" Donny said. He was pouring in the water for more mortar, and I didn't tell him it was too much.

"About how the job market is now and what will it be in two years and Glancy has been sick and Josh could use the example and what about Jenny. To say nothing of me working two jobs, which of course you wouldn't know."

"You don't want him to leave."

"I didn't say that. Well if you put it that way."

"He can go where he wants. He can get a Ling-Ling. The real kind."

"You can shut your nasty mouth," I said, and then good-looking Dennis Mateo came out of the trailer and I was entirely surprised. In court, Donny said we were drinking tequila once with Dennis Mateo and I started kissing him. Kissing Dennis. I don't remember that, which I'm alive enough I would, but I know Donny was lying anyway and this is why. I've got a friend at work whose husband died, and she's with this married guy who's a long-distance trucker. I don't think they messed around before, but she's one of those women that needs a man, and this guy's it. I don't think it's right. I never believed in people fooling with somebody that's married. I always saw it from the other side. Maybe Donny didn't make me jealous, but he made me humiliated. So I don't think I kissed Dennis Mateo, though if I was kissing somebody married, Dennis would be all right.

"Josie," Dennis said, heading for his car, and I told him hi back and maybe it stopped me from beaning Donny right then with the trowel instead of driving off. I knew there was no talking to Donny, although if you ask me, he didn't want Travis going either. He's just too mean-stubborn to say it.

I'm not defending myself, but this is relevant fact. I am careful about my kids. Growing up, I knew my mother was a little shaky. She'd lose it sometimes and just whale on us. My grandma was mute from a stroke she had with her last kid, and Mom lived scared, kind of nervous it would happen to her and she wouldn't be able to tell anybody what she wanted. When Glancy got paralyzed, she was just frantic. "Will he talk all right? Will he be able to talk to us?" she kept asking and we told her, "Mom, cool it. It's just his legs." I have thought sometimes what she went through with that meat stuck in her throat.

But this has made me draw the line at physical violence with my own kids. The week after Travis left, when Josh didn't come home I would not have hit him even if he'd walked in the house instead of them calling from the emergency room to say he was freaked out loony on bad dope. I got Jenny up to go with me. She was mortified somebody'd see her without her makeup on. I yelled at her. "Forget it, Jenny. Hurry up. It's not an improvement." Which is basically true, but I shouldn't have told her that.

The truth is I was mad at myself for saying it and mad at myself for being the kind of mother that would have her kid half-dead on pot—all right, angel dust—so he can't think straight and maybe that's why I ended up back at Donny's, which is where he was, no Dennis Mateo this time, and too drunk even to get his sorry ass to the hospital. Donny's a lousy carpenter and a worse bricklayer. He had more leftover bricks than bricks in his grill and that made me mad, too, and that's half why, when he came reeling and stinking out on his steps with me yelling in the yard, that I grabbed a brick and sailed it at him. He was too drunk even to see it. I swear he passed out and then got knocked out besides, though the doctor will not admit to that since I threw two more bricks before Jenny tackled me when I thought she had blubbered to sleep in the back seat.

This is how I am in this predicament. The psychologist says I feel betrayed by Travis and that is why it happened. That Travis escaped me and my mother love, and that getting dumped by your own child after their father leaves can make a person snap.

I don't know if that is so. I know I am here. In the night I am locked up, and in the daytime I am walking the streets of Phoenix picking up trash with the chain gang. I have raw skin. I have a hip I did not know would be arthritic starting to be so from walking funny. I have met women you would not believe. The worst part is the newspaper. Angie brought it. There is Travis in his college picture and the article about him in China. And there smack next to him is his mother with chains and the garbage. It does not say I am his mother, but people will know. The *National Enquirer* will make this discovery and there will be headlines at the grocery store: "Chain Gang Mom Has Good Seed." "Peace Corps Son of Maricopa Mom."

There is something I have done so very wrong in all of this. Something worse than maiming Donny or leaving Josh and Jenny alone. It's about Travis who'll be coming home now, though he's way too good for us. It's about Travis, but words and more just fail me when I try saying what it is.

Treasures

"Can I get it? It's only sixty cents," the child said.

"Get what?" The man, his face dark with a prickle of short beard, settled the pipe he had been fingering onto its rack on the display table and looked over his shoulder. "What is it you want?"

"The chicken. I just said. It's pottery. It's got a hole in the bottom and a nest with an egg in it. The paint isn't chipped." The child's fingers were working as she went through her list. She was a small child, just eight, and she had large gray eyes that were a shade lighter than the coat she was wearing and brown hair that had a look of careless array about it as if it had been combed before she slept but not after.

"If it's what you want," the man said. He dug in the pocket of his jacket and took out his coins and gave them to her.

"Nothing better than this today?" He turned back to the woman who was sitting behind the table and rested his eyes at the base of her neck. She was not a young woman but she was a woman who had always attracted him with her mocking laugh and her clothes that were not so much low cut as too small for the full bursting size of her. "Is this it?"

"What? You think I would keep something for you under the table?" The woman laughed. Then she leaned forward like a conspirator. "There is something. The child needs a snowsuit, a blue or red one like the others have. Look on the new rack for a change. Believe me, forgive me, you should."

The man took a bill out of his wallet and laid it on the table. "She's all right," he said and, with an elaborate slowness, a kind of insolent care, he picked up the pipe again and, bowl first, fit it into his breast pocket.

He moved up the aisle. It was early morning and only a few other people were bent over the displays and browsing among the flea market tables. Some of the vendors were still setting up, and the back door to the building kept opening and shutting as they hauled in their wares, rays from the just risen sun streaking off and on across the aisles as though they were wired to a light switch. Where grandfather clocks and porcelain stoves had been dragged into place, melting snow stained the floorboards wet and, in spite of the exotic nature of some of the exhibits—snake oil, sabers, elephant teeth—there was a general character to the room of cluttered domesticity. Women dusted armoires and polished mirrors. They fussed armloads of quilts and calico aprons into puffy stacks. Men, baby-faced from the cold, pushed their fingers through their hair to shake it free of the snow that had collected in their trips back and forth across the parking lot.

"Let's go," the man said, touching the child on the shoulder. He had made his inventory earlier, walking swiftly down the aisles, his eyes shifting in diagonal sweeps across the rows of goods, missing nothing. He reached into the child's pocket and drew her stocking cap out and pulled it over her hair. "It's snowing, remember?"

"Well it's early for snow," the child said matter-of-factly. She was carrying her chicken wrapped in newspaper and, using its head, she stuffed her pocket lining, which had pulled out with the cap, back inside her coat. "Did you buy anything?"

The man didn't answer. He pushed the door open and the child, ducking under his arm, tried the world with her tongue first, catching snowflakes. She went on ahead of him, receding on the periphery of his vision like an edge of snow.

"Papa, do you suppose the chicken's good?" The child was balanced on one foot on the sidewalk beyond the parking lot and she waited for him with snowflakes on her eyelashes.

"You're the buyer. Whatever you think."

"I think it's good."

"Then it is good." He pushed the collar of his jacket up and nudged her forward along the sidewalk. They were not far from home. They would stop at the corner and cut across the field beyond the dairy store and in three steps more they would be at the back porch of their house. They had come this way often, in two years a score of walking trips to the flea market. The first time was when her mother had left and he had taken the child from her bed and buttoned her coat on over her nightgown while she blinked herself awake. When they went out of the house and he realized she was walking stocking-footed in the snow, he'd carried her all the way.

"You didn't buy anything?" The girl was squashing the field weeds into the snow.

"Here," he said. He took the pipe out of his pocket. "Give it to your chicken."

Inside the house, he stood at the window, watching steadily as the snow floated winter down.

By New Year's, he had begun to wait, edgy as he was every year, for the start of the farm auctions. The number and quality of flea markets close to home and farther away grew uncertain as the winter progressed, and when his urge to buy, his gambler's sense that his luck was running took over in him, he and the child piled blankets in the pickup truck, and then started on their set tour of salvage stores and the city rag companies. He bargained harder in the winter. He would name his price and never waver from it, looking steely-eyed at his adversary until, when it was a man, he nodded or walked away or, when it was a woman, she turned her eyes and muttered yes or no. In February he purchased a carved turquoise screen in exactly this manner, staring away a male clerk and then drawing a wary yes from a woman behind the counter. In March he paid almost nothing for a pair of oak doors with beveled glass windows. He was surprised at these successes. He bargained harder in the winter but he did not expect as much.

It was the auctions that excited him. When they started finally in the spring, the barnyards smelling of thawed manure, he and the child went out on weekends canvassing the county and to the north. They slept in the pickup at night, and they ate noon meals while they leaned against empty hay wagons, their plates filled from Tupperware boxes of potato salad and buns and from black canning kettles of barbecue. They wandered through side yards and buildings, the child's hands stuck in her pockets and he, with one ear tuned always to the nervous slide of the auctioneer's voice—*you give five give five—five do I hear three?*—looking for old cultivators and for markings on the underside of tables and for the right color and style of antique glassware.

He knew when to plant himself beside the auctioneer's stand and, with a flick of his index finger make his purchase, or instead yield to the amateurs, the dangerous high bidders.

"Can I have a puppy?" the child would ask, pulling at his sleeve. "It's got real fur on the tail." Or "I found a jar of buttons," she would tell him, and he would reach in his pocket for coins and give them to her, his eyes never moving from the auctioneer's face.

By autumn he had made one real find—a salt-glazed plate with an undulating yellow ribbon painted on it—and a handful of smaller acquisitions—first edition books and bullet molds—and had picked up a truckload of cardboard boxes filled with the detritus of country living. From the boxes, he sorted out what he could use for trade or sale and then left the rest for the child who filled her room with strings of beads and old dolls whose cracked skulls and chipped lips she hid with a skillful cover of bonnets and high-collared dresses she made from feed sacks.

At Christmas a box came from the child's mother as it did on Easter and on her birthdays. It was wrapped in shiny foil and it reflected the light of the tree and the distorted silhouettes of cornhusk dolls and glass bells.

"I like it under the tree," the child said and when he told her to open the box on Christmas Day, she looked at the new dress inside and tapped on the pocket radio and then laid the foil back on top of the box. "See. When the paper moves, the dolls dance," she said.

It was their fourth Christmas alone and they had their own traditions. They ate chicken and canned artichokes and listened to Christmas carols. When the tablecloth was folded away and the tree lights turned off, the child would wait expectantly and he would nod, the key to the back room in his hand, and they would go down the outside hall and unlock the door on the whole world of his treasures.

The child walked on tiptoe. The room was cold and he took a shawl from a clothes tree by the door and handed it to her. Years before he had found display cases—ponderous walnut and glass discards that were strewn with a department store's pneumatic tubes across a dump—and they divided the space of the room now the way shrubs make a labyrinth. The child walked lightly beside them, her breath hanging blue in the air above her nose. Each Christmas, with infinite care and growing absorption, she chose a gift.

He watched her now. She rubbed the back of her hand along a stoneware crock. She peered through the glass at rows of necklaces and enameled pins and counted the feathers in a hat and squinted her eyes at the tiny, perfect bird that was sewn beneath its crown. She picked up flatirons in both hands, balancing them for weight. She ran her finger down the edge of an ax head and sprawled out half the length of a Cleopatra couch, staring at a mounted owl through the bowl of a green stemware glass and then tilting a prism back and forth in her hand so the room was filled with rainbows.

"Can we light the lamps?" she said. She slid her wrist along the rough underside of the horse tackle in the corner and lifted a brass kettle and then a coal hod and, as the room flickered golden, she twirled a weather vane, sending the cock due north, and opened and fastened a leather trunk and a painted trunk, hitched an entire train of railroad cars together, and posed in front of a mirror with a salmon-hued dress, trimmed in peacock feathers, tucked daintily under her chin.

For an hour she was lost in the bookshelves, turning through yellowed catalogues and pushing ripples of gold-leafed pages into her cheek. He had lit a fire in the stove, and as the room grew warmer, she took the shawl off. She folded it carefully and laid it on a cane-bottomed chair and spread her fingers out to cover the fan that decorated the chair's back. She wiggled her fingers, waited and wiggled them again as if she expected the fan to accordion open and shut in imitation. Then, clasping her hands behind her back, she resumed her walk along the aisles.

The afternoon was finished. The windowpanes had turned a mottled black and gray, a mix of outer darkness and frost that had gone thin as the room heated up. The child dawdled at a phonograph. She lifted its arm, her head inclined, and to the man's eyes she was centered perfectly in the frame of a window, her flushed skin and the purple horn of the phonograph set in its coldness. In a moment, she went on, abandoning the phonograph without settling a record on it to limp in place. She slid between two counters, her elbow bumping a rope of prayer bells and sending it jangling and clinking in the air.

He stirred at the sound, shifting his boots on the fender. Without looking at him, the child seemed to know he was ready for her to make her choice. Her eyes swept in one, long, idiosyncratic course around the room. Past stained glass windows and parking lots of pressed-tin cars, past milk cans and blown-glass paperweights, past coffee mills, chocolate pots, ancient surgeon's rolls of instruments and old photographs in cherry frames, past a Tiffany lamp and stacks of sheet music. Then, after lingering briefly on a hand-carved violin, they settled finally and unequivocally on a butter churn.

"I want this," she said, crossing the room and squeezing her fingers closed on the top of the dasher. "I'll learn to make butter."

By the following Christmas she had.

By the next Christmas she had turned the armload of frayed silk dresses that was her most recent gift into a shining, star-centered rug. She had begun to grow faster as well. The mark on the doorjamb by the stairs climbed six inches from New Year's to New Year's, and he did not know which surprised him more, that the child's face had lost its roundness or that she used these things he had bought as being preserved but past use.

He had been much readier for a change that didn't come. He had thought that as she grew she would leave him in a sense, saying no to their weekend diet of salvage and rag stores, trading their excursions to the north for a friend's slumber party. He had been waiting for the change, he realized. He was restless, full of old cravings and desires. For the first time in a long time he looked hard at the ample woman in the flea market, but the child never wavered. She learned to start the pickup, coaxing the heater to half power on frozen mornings, and the woman, when he looked at her, seemed older and like someone too much used.

In another year, the child barely seemed a child. At fifteen, two years later, she had the look about her of a full-grown woman and had taught herself skills that were rare but wholly adult. She could make soap, using lye and stamped molds. She could split wood and bake bread. She could take a gun apart and put it back together again and make lace and play the harpsichord. For a while she took on a kind of Gibson girl, pinched-waist coquettishness and he wondered if the change he had looked for earlier had suddenly arrived. He went as far as calling a dealer to the house to make an appraisal of what he had collected, thinking that maybe it was time to sell things off, to make his own change. Yet he was uncertain. When the girl returned from school, a velvet bowler in her hand, and stood, with no trace of the coquette, silently in the door to the back room, her eyes fixed not on the man with the magnifying glass and notebook but on him, he made up his mind.

"I'm not selling. It's just for the insurance," he said.

They went on as before, their lives together divided between forays for collecting things and the growing assault of the room in the back on the ones in front. The girl learned to weave and to make hard cider. Her loom stood in front of the bay window in the living room and her apple press by the door to the kitchen. She discovered a cache of feathers stuffed in sacks in a barn loft, and the comforters in the bedroom got feather beds to match. She fixed a music box that was broken and it unwound while they ate, plucking out songs. There were china eggcups on the breakfast table, finger bowls at dinner.

She had become a bargainer, too, with a skill that matched his own. More than that, she had an uncanny sense of value. Even with a stranger, she seemed always to know who understood his merchandise and had priced it fairly and who had missed a find or was hawking something counterfeit.

"Did you ever wonder," he asked her, "if some of what we buy is stolen?" She shook her head and laced her fingers behind her cap, leaning into them, and yawned.

"No." She looked past him as he drove. "You can always tell how things are used."

And so their lives, their home filled up with treasures. When he began to smoke a pipe, the pipe rack with its briars and meerschaums was carried from the bottom shelf of a display case in the back room to a table near his bed. The girl lined her own room with cameos and miniatures, satin pillows and hand mirrors set in abalone shells.

When she was twenty, he thought the change had come at last. She was tall, well formed, clear eyed, and bright skinned, her hair a shiny coil at her neck and crimped above her eyebrows. She looked utterly ripe, and he waited for an indication that some natural trade-off in the scheme of things was infusing her with that psychic and sexual energy that was dying in him. But he could find no sign at all that her eye was moving somewhere else. She learned to carve and mended the sheered-off claw-feet of a piano. She drove the truck, spelling him on long distances. She read *Godey's Lady's Book* and dipped chocolates, setting them to cool on long strips of parchment.

"Invite your friends," he said. "You still have friends from school?"

The girl was stirring soup. She ladled it to her mouth and blew on it and tasted it. "Hand me the bowls?" She frowned at him, shaking her head, her cheeks, from her own heat and the heat of the stove, the color of apples.

In the spring she teased him to the auctions, and in the fall, she hung velvet curtains at the windows, their hems spilling out across the floor. A set of Dickens turned up on the bookcase by the mantel, and he spent one winter looking at the spines and another keeping the row straight. Then Thackeray took over, and Balzac.

When she was twenty-five, he no longer waited. He had taken to wearing a slightly tattered, velvet smoking jacket in bed, and she had started pinning her hair up and dressing in gowns with lace bodices and long, flounced skirts that touched the top button of her shoes. She had always arched her neck in a certain way when he spoke to her, but its swanlike curve was rare now, replaced by something slower and more angular in her movement. She kept her sewing basket filled with yarns and embroidery threads and carried a parasol in the sun. When he looked at her he saw a faint yellow to her skin, a thin, antique patina.

He stared at her across the room, at her profile and the fall of her dress, etched plainly against the darkened doorway. He stroked his own skin.

He would grow old at her side, he thought. He would grow old, older and older still, until one day, he grew as old as she was.

II

AMERICAN SNAPSHOT

American Snapshot, 1993

There was a boy in the other fourth grade, in the class that was not designated the opportunity room. The boy was black and alone, and I do not remember his name. This was in the fifth year of five years in Ohio. I remember him, though he is the only one I remember from the fourth-grade class that was not the opportunity room. He wore a white shirt, his eyes luminous in the dark hallway which snaked around the stairwell.

In New York there is a woman who dances. If you see the page in a given *New Yorker* where dead Sammy Davis Jr. leaps in his khakis in a cinnamon-colored ad for the Gap, if you pass the page where a pale and beautiful black family discovers a greenhouse, the young father falling out of the composition like a stranger, if you then wander back through the good woolens and Ralph Lauren athletes and forward again, you will find her: Twyla Tharp announced as demonstrating process without benefit of costume at seven thirty on the day before and the day after Dave Winfield, at home in Minnesota, hit a baseball safely in the Big Leagues for the 3000th time. Neither *The New Yorker* nor the third edition of the *American Heritage Dictionary of the American Language* mentions Ms. Tharp's race. She is not black.

In New York and, yes, profiled in that same *New Yorker*, there is a director who replaced Joseph Papp's successor at the Public Theater. He is intellectual, gifted, African American. He is from Frankfort, Kentucky, as far from Ashland, Kentucky, as Ashland is from the school near Chillicothe, Ohio, where the boy I remember was not in the opportunity room. Of the Catholic school's three black children in Ashland my six months there, one was in my fifth-grade classroom which was neither opportunity or not-opportunity. I remember his name. François. I remember the soft Caribbean accents of his English: *Our Father who art in Heaven.* I remember him.

But in *The New Yorker*, George C. Wolfe, gay and the director of *Angels in America*, considers his race, his past: What was in the shops of Frankfort? "What was so precious that a little six-year-old boy couldn't touch, couldn't walk inside of?" In St. Paul, my neighbor upstairs, who is not black, is gay, angelic-looking, and racked with coughs. Is this a connection? When I play the piano (poorly now, as if my hands are covered with dust), I worry that the sound disturbs him. I skip "Ase's Death," going straight from "Morgenstimmung" to "Anitra's Tanz."

Perhaps this piano belongs in New York. It is historic in the way of the first hit that might lead to 3,000. In New York a pianist—young, gifted—was the first African American to win a major piano competition, and this piano is the first that he played. His sister would have played it, too. For a month they were angels in my parents' house, both of them in white nightgowns for kisses goodnight. Menah and Awadagin. Menah and Awadagin Pratt. At my mother's funeral, Menah played the piano and Awadagin the violin, their father having announced they would, driving up in the early morning, and, for the instant, piercing the shock of my father's grief as, numbly on schedule, he hauled garbage cans out to the curb. This is Ted: "Mark, the children will play."

For Awadagin, still gangly, it was pre-dreadlock days, while for Menah—a decade before the funeral of Arthur Ashe (intellectual, gifted, black, and not gay but dead of AIDS)—there was still hope for

Wimbledon Center Court. Would we have predicted Wimbledon more than *The New Yorker* announcement of the city debut: "Awadajin Pratt in recital at Alice Tully Hall"? It is as text, actually, that I mention *The New Yorker* once more, because we midlanders with our weekly magazines and our own printing of the *Times* are wired in, an inevitable part of the hot center, the radiating diversity: New York's gunshots and sleek fantasies land here.

From my home, it is fifteen blocks (eleven on the crow's-flight hypotenuse) to Dave Winfield's childhood home and to St. Paul's Oxford Playground where he played his early ball. It is not necessarily a safe walk. The police crime grids and a day's log of sirens suggest this. In the 1930s and 1940s, those Depression and war years that preceded Winfield's birth on October 3, 1951 (a birthdate precisely two years, seven months and two weeks before the Supreme Court decision in *Brown v. Board of Education* that was announced on perhaps the last day of my life I saw the boy who was not in the fourth-grade class that was the opportunity room), the blocks of his neighborhood were the prestige address for a striving black family. Enter the child who eighteen years later was the one black face on the all-city baseball squad. Enter the child who grew up in the neighborhood's years of blight, though perhaps he did not notice this, living just doors from the neighborhood sandlot in a modest house ten blocks from where a teenage boy, named for two presidents, was shot to death twelve days before the 3000th blow. Is this a connection? Possibly. Possibly not. There is a loose circle of time and place, but still light-years of distance: a death for a boy who could not strike even a single hit toward 3000. A death, that is, at zero.

What if I had a party? I mean no disrespect. Not a wake. Not about the dead boy. What if I had a party for these people in my life I do not know? What if the cheap fares were on and each person outside of walking distance could fly in and some of the zillion questions that go unanswered in a lifetime—those questions we could wish for a god, however computerlike or in need of patience and all eternity, to answer—would be answered for us, for me?

When I work on the guest list, the party wrestles me like an octopus, changes. The roster is past ten, not sit-down anymore. There're names that are for sure—Twyla and George C. from New York. And Awadagin. And Menah from Vanderbilt, though perhaps she's moved on, and maybe she and Awadagin have forgotten I exist. Which is all right. They are important to me, loved, but we are, nonetheless, nearly strangers. I think they would laugh, talk in low voices, the brother-and-sister game, and Menah would twist her jewelry: a gold medallion at her throat, bracelets on her arm.

The hardest reach is the boy from the not-opportunity room who would be a man long since, though possibly a dead one. (Why do I think this?) I could try a search. Pick up the phone. Write for school records. Write for census records. Did his father farm? Find a copy of the school yearbook that has his name. Maybe he lives in the forever darkness, but does he remember what I remember—the buckeyes on the autumn grass, the pear tree on the far edge of the school grounds close to the scandal we children all knew (the plain but passionate woman who lived on the school road and gave up her twins and a pretty husband to live with a stranger—*une affaire de coeur*), the basement bathrooms with the concrete troughs and the stench that flashed stronger when the water pumped through for the hourly flush, and on the playground the layout of a lost house in the grayed two-by-fours we strode, testing our balance at recess?

I have questions for this man. What has he done his whole life? Who is he? Does he love the name Sojourner Truth the way that I do? And if the thing could be arranged, would he want African Perfection, the neighborhood drill team, outside the window *right now*, all flashy uniforms and sharp moves, dancing in the street light?

François, too. Our fathers worked together, and perhaps somewhere there's a paper trail to check for a lead. But François must come.

I'd want Johnnie Mae New. I mean, shouldn't this party have a life? She was here the college summers I worked in St. Paul, and maybe she still is. Then, if she got mad, got hurt, it didn't show. Instead she did her job and she laughed. She made jokes with the nurse's aides about the doctors' finger cots in the hospital supply room—mini-rubbers, sheaths by the dozens—"What do they do with *these*?"—though it's really serious now, isn't it? Her uniform got its edge from her black skin. You knew the whiteness of a hospital dress when you saw Johnnie Mae New.

I would like Nelson Mandela as well, and also, though less so, de Klerk, F. W.—his dimming counterpart on the started journey from a forked path. They are forging a government while the large question here is what to do with the one we've got, this big tent of peoples. Would they want to know all this? see this?—that the genie grown out of the bottle stays polymorphous, slippery as hell?

I am quiet at the thought of Nelson Mandela and Dave Winfield together in a room of my home. What could hold the presence? The careful, suit-and-tie dignity that is both burden and command: respect me. Fear me if you must, but always respect me. Maybe somebody's mother said it—that dignity is a mask for rage. Maybe it's me who's that mother.

Twyla and Dave are an easier pair. Besides New York (Dave, the ex-Yankee) they have this in common: both are about the body and about legs, about what the mind chooses to do with a physical self uncommonly graced. She is a wild card, the random choice here with her white skin and her bookend appearances bracketing the 3000th hit. I do not know why it feels she belongs. I do know I would ask about her name—that is, if the two of them are not talking of process together, if she and Dave Winfield are not standing in front of the dining room window where the streetlight on Laurel, caught in the slip between two buildings, glows in a night that never quite darkens the city. In the daytime white squirrels circle its base, rocket through leaves. But it is night and the movement of this man and woman, who are angled toward each other to accommodate the difference in their heights (which is also about legs), is largely implicit, a geographical history that resides in nerve-drilled memories and in the memories of people who've watched them. What are they saying?

My body was the opportunity.

For me it was always the art.

Invite Harry. I would want Harry here, our first neighbor from across the hall. "Harry, I like your sweater. You knew, didn't you, you'd look that good in the hallway?" Laughter. Happy, book-reading Harry, aching for his family to sell their house in Hyde Park and move with him up to Dayton Avenue, Harry with the gold-black skin in the hot wool colors.

This is a true thing. As a people, a white people, we did not always know that more than the eyes of a black man are uncommon. We had not studied skin so well—the olive and blue hues and sheen—the august power of pigment. But this also is true: a balding black man with a golden tint to his skin looks better in a carved oak hallway than a balding man who is pink.

I have had Alice Oliver in my dining room. When the ad went into the paper for the NordicTrack that wanted a room I wouldn't give it, she came as a surrogate, a trim black woman from Marshall Avenue, writing her check for a Spanish friend whose husband wanted the ride. They had beaten out a hundred callers, I think it was more, and Alice Oliver, who arrived as a gracious encyclopedia with entries on mansions and on the Laura Ashley–primped gingerbread on Summit Avenue, and on the houses built a century ago for the mistresses of prosperous men, went right ahead and slid her lady's feet onto the skis and nearly flew out the window.

I would want Alice back and Evelyn Fairbanks, not precisely her contemporary, I think, but close enough, the person who knew the uptown side of Dave Winfield's neighborhood before he got there (the middle ground between Oatmeal Hill and Deep Rondo and gone now because of the freeway), and who wrote it all down wonderfully, a life, for a child, that was without race. Except for this: "I knew blacks were better than whites. I also knew whites *thought* they were better than blacks."

There are possibles: Garrison Keillor, who once lived up the block, and Trish Hampl, who lives down the street, though she might be in Prague, and the ghost of F. Scott Fitzgerald, who was born in the brownstone I see from my window. But I don't think that they're coming. I don't think it's a fit.

I would like a glittering affair—crystal gleaming, a new chandelier, African prints. We would start in the living room, though it's small for this crowd, and it might be sad with the cough upstairs, but it's good he's still coughing. Thank God he's still coughing.

I see George C., taking a cream puff, wince at the sound, and that's one of my questions. Does it matter for him if the one crusade piggybacks on the other, gay rights, civil rights? To be born into a manner of being, to be born into a manner of desiring—does he find the first case the broader class and demanding of precedence? Or is this all about want, about need?

The list isn't finished. There's the mother of Cleveland Washington, dead boy, shot boy. Of course she's invited. Do we ask her to tell her story, to say what it's like to bury a child?

And, definitely, definitely the Triangle Market folks who gave us Christmas when we'd just moved in and had not known that the stores from one end of St. Paul to the other end of Minneapolis would close early on Christmas Eve. "I got steaks. You want steaks? I got a turkey."

Their baby girl was in a basket, behind the counter, next to her father, and this year there's a boy baby instead, even tinier and with a name like Awadajin, though I know that's not it. The father, twenty-something, brings his family into my hall, cradling the baby in an arm, holding his daughter by her hand, and I do not ask him or his wife if it frightens them as much as it frightens me: a child in the city right next to a cash register.

There are physical players besides Twyla and Dave: here is Menah on tennis, Awadagin on performance, and the grocer on meat:

For me it's about extension.
For me it's the back and the arm weight.
The butcher know it's all in the wrist.

I take a picture of everyone together—the tripod set up for the $15 Holga from China, the camera with imperative settings: single portrait, nuclear family, committee, the Alps. Even so, choices. But I can place people by heart: taller in the center, shoulders interleaved, a second arc of people sitting in front with the baby on a lap, the little girl—beribboned and flounced—leaning against a chair.

Click. Freeze again. *Click.*

There is the instant smile after each snap and then, the photographs done, bodies loosening, the chairs back in place, the return to sound, and one afterthought: a single picture of Nelson Mandela holding the baby. For posterity. And this done, drinks and more food.

They are making a fuss over the baby. Nelson Mandela unhands him. The women pass him around and, when he wants to cry, his mother takes him again, rocking him on her shoulder, eating, carefully, one slice of kiwi.

Awadagin plays Franck, then a lullaby, and maybe this is matchmaking. Perhaps Awadagin Pratt, son of a mother who comes from Pittsburgh and a father born in Sierra Leone, will play in South Africa.

Drinks all around. A toast to Dave Winfield, man of the hitched killer swing, longer than even his very long body—a belated tribute to Dave Winfield for batting in all kinds of weather and for being safe three thousand times.

Plus a toast to the end of apartheid.

The women hum. Johnnie Mae sways. The little girl circles, dizzy with tiredness, and pulls at a hem.

The baby is sleeping. He is lying, not in a basket, but in an infant seat propped on the table, his quilt breathing its jigsaw color above the lace cloth. Dreams come, flutter his eyes.

And when he falls, it is not so much that the table is jarred or that his sister, trying to see, has pulled at the cloth. It is just that there's been a collapse. The seat has malfunctioned, toppled him, lurched him to his father's one-motioned catch. He hiccoughs awake. His sister, startled, buries her face in her mother's leg.

Legs to choose from. Everyone's legs. They arrive in a wave.

You caught him, man.

Oooh, rock-a-bye, baby!

"You all right. Shhh now." The mother talks to her leg, reaches the baby into her arms, counts him safe in each part. "It's your brother about broke hisself. You all right. You look out for your baby."

A voice almost calm. The baby unharmed.

But the South African worry crease is back on the face of Nelson Mandela. Fright has come like a spirit, and arrived with a voice. Low at first and then rising, it is the keening of the shot boy's mother: "That boy baby. Don't you watch him out of your sight."

"Sister, Sister." All of them touch her, New Yorkers and not.

And I am crying, crazy, the lone white face here, with F. W. a no-show and Twyla gone after the twilight, and they look at me, these dark, stern faces, look at me as though I haven't the right, but I keep crying anyway.

I hope it's OK.

III

LAURA

Birdman

If this were a true story, I would want the straight facts about the Birdman of Alcatraz. For certain I'd need the exact dates, precisely when it was he spun away the thin-strand filaments of his sanity and life, no longer incarcerated in California but in Missouri at a prison called the medical center. Was it for the criminally insane? At home we called it the institution, nothing more.

My father worked there. My parents' friends were the neighbors on our gravel road of tract houses and my father's coworkers and the people my mother knew from church or spoke French with. There was one friend with a new baby. At four, I was in thrall. I liked the baby well enough—on my father's side particularly, I am from a long line of people who like babies inordinately—but when this friend came to visit my mother, what kept me eye-hungry and in a state of alert was the leisurely nursing, the long hours of the afternoon when the friend from Provence talked and sewed and then idly, with the tuning-up squawks and fretting of the baby, opened her dress in the sun of our front window and showed her soft, functional breasts and intricate nipples. I stared, watching the coaxed juncture of mother's breast and baby's mouth, keeping the tugging circle of the baby's head at the edge of my vision so I would be neither misunderstood nor understood.

"How sweet," the friend said in her husky English. Her hair grazed the inverted question mark of one white breast. "It's so dear Laura stays near the baby."

My mother smiled at me, and I felt almost safe: dishonest yet affirmed in my goodness, the trio shaping up already—ego, superego, id.

If I have not invented this, twisted the dates, substituted the famous name for a nonentity's, it was Robert Stroud my mother and her friend were laughing about as they talked. He had said something hilarious for its idiocy and I, making my way farther into the cardinal sins, spoke up in pride and a child's anger at unfairness: "Don't laugh. It's not his fault if he's crazy."

I remember the power of bringing their silence. The two of them stopped laughing, looked at me, cleared their throats. This really did happen, though afterward I could not listen to my mother's version of events without a flicker of shame.

"We felt this big," she would say. "You were so young and so sensitive to people's feelings. And you really loved babies."

And I do love babies. This—unquestionably—is true.

But about the Birdman. Perhaps it was years before he would find his way to Missouri and old age. Whatever, whatever. At some point in my childhood, he became ensconced in my personal mythology, not as the man who caused the laughter in my mother and her bare-breasted friend, but as a sort of criminal version of St. Francis of Assisi, a man in leg irons but with arms outstretched for incoming birds. In a way, this was a parochial matter. My brother and I, with fewer moves than the army brats but plenty of changes of address, took a definite pride in the stars of the prison system. Federal stars, that is, past and present: big-time criminals who had crossed state lines or done something huge like a kidnapping. Baby Face Nelson. Machine Gun Kelly. Roy Gardner: the twentieth-century Jesse James. Al Capone. We cared about the prisons, too. Our personal ones were borderline—places like Terre Haute and Chillicothe—but we knew our father had trained at Leavenworth, lockup for the hardest kind of man, its name like leather and dust and tough-riding cowboys. We knew we were proud of a serious thing.

We didn't feel mere team loyalty. And we were not simply awed by crimes or personalities. There were side issues, too. Mine about the Birdman were these: did he want to escape carried by birds like the princess in "The Wild Swans"? Did he twitter, flutter? And scarier, scary, did he think a bird flying loose in a cellblock meant a death in the big house?

By the summer I was ten, such matters were a well-established part of my imaginative life. But my real life, or at least my walking around and talking life, had a new set of particulars. We had moved once more, this time to a prison in Kentucky and my father, because of a promotion, was entitled to dependents' housing in the looping cul-de-sac of houses adjacent to the prison grounds. Following the hierarchy, our house was at the top of the loop, and following the federal nomenclature, where we lived was the reservation. Our house had a large screened-in porch and a wooded hill that rose behind it. I had my own room for the first time, a corner room with a blue rayon bedspread, which looked nearly like watered silk, and two double windows which my mother fitted out with ruffled organdy curtains that crisscrossed in the French style. I loved the curtains like a true obsessive. I continually adjusted the tiebacks to make them exactly even and to get the drape of the fabric right. This was in the daytime when there were real possibilities that friends would arrive. Maybe the three sisters with identical hair (short bangs and one loose brown wave chopped off straight before it could turn under like a pageboy), girls who were unhappy, uprooted Yankees, transferred with their father from Connecticut. Maybe the warden's daughter who was confidently thirteen and feature-perfect pretty and who lived apart (as the associate warden's daughter did) in a grand house with a spacious lawn and front view of the prison.

At night my windows posed a different sort of challenge in exactitude. I had entered a period of deep, prepubescent modesty triggered by the catechism classes from the other institutional force in my life. At ten, I was seriously Catholic. The nuns I knew had taught about Saint Maria Goretti, dead at eleven from resisting the lust of a farmworker who was afterward repentant for making her a martyr by—what? Stabbing her? Hacking her to death? Her chasteness, as the nuns presented it, was both an ideal and the minimum requirement. I felt this deeply, so deeply that I still have the holy card with her picture. *Printed in Italy.* Painted, she is very serious, a young beauty in three-quarters profile with a yellow full moon for a halo and her arms crossed forbiddingly on her robed chest. She is holding flowers, white lilies, a general motif of the card, and because her image was indelible and because the view out my side windows was of the prison yard and because that summer the escape siren wailed nearly every night and I heard the pounding-on-earth of feet running away, I worried over my window shades, pulling them securely past the glass of the window, pulling them flat against the sash like a talisman so that no one, no one at all could see inside.

But in the drenching daylight I walked to the warden's house, my hair moist and curly and still an undecided blond from the early summer sun. I was short that summer, square at the waist but with my mother's slim legs, my kneecaps already brown. I climbed the steps to the warden's house, the prison at my back, and rang the bell for his daughter, who was almost my friend. We did the family's morning dishes together, taking turns scrubbing the Revere Ware with SOS pads until there were gritty bits of steel wool in our fingers and our palms smelled of soap and bacon fat. Sometimes we talked in her parents' room. More often I walked back toward home and read about starlets in the movie magazines of the ponytailed girl whose house was out of the loop, an afterthought cottage in the lee of the hill. On the days they didn't have headaches, I played jacks with the Connecticut girls on the sidewalk by a willow tree, the red guard tower on the prison fence looming over us.

Waiting for them one afternoon, I met the prison's birdman. He was not the real one from Leavenworth and Alcatraz and Missouri, but his job was to cut lawns, to tend the grounds. When he found a robin's egg he gave it to me since it would never hatch, and from then on he was the birdman. He was around forty, more than six feet tall, and his hair was dark and beginning to thin. He was serving time for beating his wife unconscious and bloody, the one felony on an otherwise clean record, but that was something I learned later—and the hard way, as my father would say. For the moment, this trustee with sweat on his neck was the first person to lift a robin's egg from the grass and place it in my hand. The wonderful, smooth blue.

"Keep it," he said. "Blow the yolk out and you can keep it forever."

The Connecticut girls arrived then, and the conversation was over. They eyed the birdman suspiciously. They were frosty, especially the oldest. Darla? Darlene? But I did not talk to this birdman so much as I listened. When he was cutting off suckers from a lilac bush, he pointed to a cowbird and told me it laid its eggs in the nests of other birds. Another day, as he was weeding salvia and I walked by, he told me I'd just missed a hummingbird, that it could hover like a helicopter because it kept its body straight and beat its wings so fast it supported itself on a current of air. He told me, too, that every bird has a distinctive contour to its wing that governs its flight—stubby for the dodgers, long and slender with a giant span for the great albatross which glides for hours over the sea without one beat of its wing.

I was intrigued. If I was wary, if every prison child I knew was wary as we'd been taught to be—each of us with our own experiences of traveling with our fathers and a man who was genial yet manacled—I could not help thinking that this man, this person who had been within the space of a bird's egg of touching me, was a man of potential stardom.

For a week or so, this mattered a lot. I would look through my curtains as the birdman mowed the lawns and wonder if he had it in him to do what Robert Stroud had done.

"He used a razor blade to cut long strips of wood from a soapbox," my brother told me from his bunk bed when I asked. "That's how he made his first birdcage. In secret in his cell. And before that, he trained sparrows to play dead with their feet in the air."

There was the matter, too, of the book—*Stroud's Digest of the Diseases of Birds*—written from research done on canaries in a Leavenworth cell. It could require a great deal, I realized, making fame strike twice in the same place, and I thought about it a lot.

Then I lost interest. My new friends and I had entered the intoxicating world of secret clubs. More than that, there were clubhouses. The girls met in a freshly painted, white chicken house, chickenless behind the warden's garden; the boys, usually long gone on their bicycles or running the grass thin in football games inside the cul-de-sac, held meetings in the loft of the warden's unused barn. Their club seemed especially secret, hidden behind those broad, closed doors, but we were no slouches. We had a password. We had a sign which, by Fate, made us peculiarly sisters: all of us—and it was by heredity we knew—could splay our hands with a V between the middle fingers and the fingers themselves pressed into tight pairs. We had the perfect handshake: our hands, locked at the crotch of the V.

Finding an initiation rite was more problematic—we suspected the boys were doing something with rabbits—but Tanya, the warden's daughter and our president, was thinking. In a hot July week, the phone call came at last. The official ceremony was scheduled for two o'clock sharp.

I caught up with the Connecticut girls on the way down the loop. "We're not doing it if it hurts," the youngest one told me. "Or if there's any kind of blood." She giggled, nervous, her hair flapping where it would have bounced if the whole pageboy had been there. "What about you?"

"I don't know," I said.

The door was closed when we reached the chicken house. "I'll do the knock," the oldest sister said, and then we all gave the password, altered for the day of the week and with our own numbers added on. I was 1010, one ten for my age and the other for my birthday day of the month. In the whole club, I was the only one with a golden birthday that year.

I pictured candles burning. Maybe incense that smelled like church. Probably costumes or some kind of robes. But inside it was like other days. Everybody was in shorts, the same as always, and we did the sign and handshake and sat on the usual boxes, and all of us said Tanya's outfit (this one with polka dot piping at the armholes and on the cuffs) was really cute. She had the start of a bust, and the girl with the ponytail actually had one, but the rest of us in our cotton tops, cut off at the midriff, might have been ironed flat.

Tanya got the meeting under way. We stood for the oath of secrecy and our treasurer reported we had a balance of ninety cents from dues and that her mother was giving us calico for curtains and to make a skirt for the orange crates the Connecticut girls had donated so we could have a vanity table if we got a chair and mirror. It was like a regular meeting, but then Tanya stepped into the middle of the room and put her hand out in the sign.

"And now everybody has to go through initiation." She looked at the associate warden's daughter, who was our vice president. "Carol and I already did it, so she'll help. But everybody else has to go outside until we call you."

This was excitement. Finally. We filed out the door. When it closed behind the last person, the littlest Connecticut girl started to cry. She was holding herself through her shorts, and her sisters scolded her and the older one took her hand and hurried her up the path to the warden's house. The rest of us stood expectantly. No jokes. No gossip. Just waiting. I could still smell the chicken smell from inside and from the dirt under our feet.

I wasn't first. The ponytail was. They called her name. She said the password and her number and went inside and she was there for three or four minutes, at least that long, and she came back out almost smiling in a sardonic, thin-lipped way that didn't really say anything except whatever had happened probably hadn't hurt.

"What did they do?" we asked, but she didn't answer.

The middle Connecticut girl was next. She looked up the path for her sisters. She hesitated. I thought she might run away, go home, but then she cleared her throat around the password and went inside.

We felt the minutes plod by. Finally she came back. She didn't look at us, but I looked at her arms for welts, marks—for any sign she was different. She was flushed, maybe, but nothing else showed.

And then they said Laura, though my club name was Medusa, and it was my turn. I opened the door. I had made up my mind I wouldn't be scared. I walked into the chicken smell, which was like the mold on a swimming towel left in a hamper and like a scratchy dryness I felt in my nose.

Tanya and Carol were standing in front of the far wall. They were next to the sagging-hinge cabinet we'd dragged down from the warden's garage and set on the boards nailed over the cistern. For a moment, I was sure I knew what was happening. The cabinet looked different, moved, and maybe a board was exposed, pried up. They would dangle me by the ankles into the pinging darkness of the cistern where the damp concrete and black water stood waiting. I stopped in the middle of the room. How did you kick off the bottom, scissoring to the surface, when the bottom was fathoms away?

"Scared?" Tanya asked. She looked at Carol with a smirk on her face.

"I'm not," I said.

"Come here then. Close your eyes."

I walked forward, cheating an eye at the floor through my eyelashes. I wondered if I could swim in the dark. If I could forget about spiders and snakes and if my legs would hold out as long as I needed them to tread water. Then I heard the bucking wood sound of the swollen drawer in the cabinet being pulled open.

"All right. You can look."

I opened my eyes. Carol was giggling with her hand over her mouth. Tanya had a picture in her hand. It was a drawing, or a watercolor I decided, remembering the landscape my mother's friend from Provence had signed and given to her as a farewell gift when we left

Missouri. There were soft, smudgy blues and pinks in the fabric that was the picture's foreground, and the fabric itself was chiffon and draped so the reclining girl beneath it, her hair so evenly black, was covered except for one braceleted ankle and the arc of one breast and the brown ring of nipple which shifted the color of fabric pulled thinly across it.

I looked at Tanya. "So what?" I said, though a narrow spiral was moving inside me.

"Next," Tanya said.

I turned, ready to go back outside, but Tanya pulled tight on my arm. "Next picture, dummy," she said to me. She motioned for Carol to take another one from the drawer. This one was of a blonde with green eyes and with more jewelry than clothes. She was in watercolor, too, with a flood of afternoon window light touching her body.

There were more pictures, at least six, and I looked at them all, sparks and showers jumping inside me.

"And this one," Tanya said finally. She made me take it, hold it, the picture of the girl in the ice blue gown with her legs spread open to the side and a mirror placed so her smooth, quiet vulva was isolated in the reflecting circle.

"Oh," I said.

And that was all. "You're initiated," Tanya pronounced, taking the picture and closing the drawer. "Go back outside."

The next week a storm blew the willow tree down and knocked the shingles next to our chimney loose. I went up on the roof with my father. He was dressed in his Saturday afternoon sweatshirt to put the shingles back in place, and I was helping—holding the hammer while he positioned a shingle, holding a shingle while he hammered away. I sat with my legs over the peak of the roof. I looked at the hill behind us, which seemed very close, and at the ground by my windows which didn't. I was thinking of the nun who'd given me the picture of Maria Goretti, how she'd said if a rapist came toward you on the roof of a high building, the only right choice was to jump.

"Would we die if we fell off this roof?" I asked my father.

"Maybe not." He was talking through the nails in his mouth. He took a big swing with the hammer and I pulled my hand away and he laughed. He took the nails from his mouth. "You'd crack a few ribs."

I nodded. I looked down over the black roof and down the loop to where the willow tree had been. It was gone except for a small stump. It was all cleaned up, but it wasn't the birdman who'd done it. Two men I'd never seen before had loaded the branches into a pickup truck and taken them away.

I straightened the stack of shingles. "Do inmates get their jobs changed?" I asked. "Like at school. Do their jobs rotate like chores?"

"If you mean where's your bird friend, he's reassigned." My father looked at me over the hammer, and my mouth opened and closed. I hadn't known that he'd known.

"We can talk about this, Laura," he said, eyeing me evenly. "There's a reason you're not to make friends with the trustees, not even to talk. They're criminals. Maybe they're not all bad, but at some point they've done something so out of control they've wound up here. If they're trustees, it means we trust them like we'd trust an attack dog we let off a chain inside a fence. There's still a risk."

"I didn't really talk to him," I said.

"Keep away from them," my father said, and it was the end of the conversation, the end of it the way it always had been when my father spoke in that voice, the way it had been in the ever so long ago with my patent leather shoes kicking against the driver's seat, the driver with a holstered gun and the man at his side with slicked-back hair and a red splotch on his neck, the man who smiled at me and smelled of tobacco and wore handcuffs while my father wrote notes on a legal pad and the yellow summer air blew over us and it was a long way to my aunt's home and somebody's courthouse and I wasn't to ask my father again how much farther, and then, driving home, I slept on his lap.

I nodded slowly. I handed him a shingle without speaking, the earliest feelings still squirming together: security, resistance. So the birdman was gone. So the person I thought had read my face after I left the chicken house—the one person who saw my skin turn crimson with knowledge at the willow tree, the one person who surely had sensed the nature of my sudden flight—was out of my life.

I thought that. And I thought, too, that no matter what the nun had said, my father wouldn't want me to jump.

Then it was August. In the daytime I read more, though there was still the power game of the clubhouse and its hidden pictures, at times lure, at times threat that the secret would out. At night the sirens had stopped, but still I tightened my window shades and, though I could fall asleep readily, in the deep night I awoke terrified, frightened about infinity, that it had no end.

"I have so many windows," I told my mother when she came into my room in the darkness. "They let the night in."

The summer was almost over, rushing away like the whoosh of air that flattens a balloon. Our clubhouse was quiet and life was about tablets and book satchels, about first-day-of-school clothes laid out on beds for private showings. For me, fall meant another new school and I was headed there without friends since none of the other reservation girls went to the Catholic school. We didn't even start on the same day. For the school nuns, Labor Day was the beginning of a two-day retreat, and so when the prison mail van stopped at the bottom of the loop and the wearers of the new dresses with eyelet on the collar or the boy-shined brown penny loafers squeezed onto the wooden benches in back, my brother and I weren't there. He was off on his bike with his BB gun, and I had figured out an errand to do. My blue sweater was missing. I thought it might be in the clubhouse, and I needed it back.

My mother was at the piano practicing vocal scales when I left. She was at the break point, up at the top of her range, and I don't think she even heard me when I closed the door to the screened porch. I walked down the center of the loop through the patchy football grass. I wanted my own first day of school when things started to happen, but

I was still in my shorts and in my sandals with the straps curled on the ends and the red dye scuffed down to the sandy-colored leather.

I decided on the longer way, the walk down the road in front of the reservation instead of the shortcut across the lawn that faced the prison. I could see the guard in the corner guardhouse that jutted up over a tree, but there was no one else anywhere. I bent down and pulled a fuzzy weed from the ditch, slipping it from its casing. I bit into the green tip. A tractor was buzzing and droning across the field, but even at the intersection with the county road that passed the prison and climbed the hill there were no cars in sight. I walked on up the road and turned on the familiar path that ran beside the warden's garage and led back to the clubhouse. Leaves shaded the path. There was the faint but growing chicken smell and then, as I passed the garbage can where Tanya's brother emptied the trash, a stronger odor layered over it—a harsh vinegar smell like the smell from bananas my mother sometimes put on the refrigerator and forgot. I went on to the chicken house and unlatched the door, lifting up on the metal hasp and pulling it forward. I nudged the door open to go in, and it creaked shut after me.

Inside it was musty, like a shut-up sickroom. I pushed the window open, but the stick to prop it open was gone so I lowered it back into place over the sound of a truck, maybe the garbage truck, and recentered the curtains. The Connecticut girls had reclaimed their orange crates, but I looked under the other boxes and around the cabinet for my sweater. Nothing. There were lower doors in the cabinet and I opened them and eyed the cobwebby, empty shelves, felt into their corners.

And then the drawer.

It had swollen tighter as the summer passed, but now it almost leapt open when I pulled it. It came out entirely and I went sprawling and so did the pictures. On my knees I picked them up, startled to be holding what I had seen only in passing since the afternoon of our initiation. I looked at the stack of gauzy faces, at the arching bodies. Then, like spotting an ace in a hand, I found the picture of Maria

Goretti in my mind, her face so serious and sternly beautiful I had never even noticed the color of her hair.

I was studying the air, the wall, when I heard a raspy cigarette cough outside. The door opened and in walked the birdman.

I inhaled. The birdman back? Inside? Inside our clubhouse?

I hugged the pictures, crossing them with my arms the way Maria Goretti held her lilies.

He was surprised, too. He pinched the cigarette out of his mouth and flattened it with his heel on the cement floor.

"My school didn't start yet," I said quickly. The birdman was looking hard at the pictures, at the back of the pictures as if he'd seen them before. He didn't seem friendly, and I was sure all at once that he knew it was my fault he'd been transferred. I turned away from him a little, edging against the cabinet. "This is our clubhouse," I said. "I thought I left my sweater. But it's not here, so I should go."

"You got a chicken house clubhouse," he said, and I hoped he was going to leave, but instead he took a Snickers out of his uniform pocket and undid the wrapper and crumpled it onto the floor. He took a bite. In two swallows the entire candy bar was gone, and I thought of my mother who made us chew our food thoroughly, proper mastication she called it.

He was looking at me again, and the sunlight shimmering into the window through the leaves made a sort of quiver to his arm that gave the edge of his sleeve a tremor like a wing's. "What have you got there?" he asked. He stepped toward me and I smelled the vinegar-banana smell that had been in the garbage.

"Nothing," I answered, a hole I thought was appendicitis opening in my stomach. "Yesterday I saw a tanager."

"Show me your pictures."

"They aren't mine. They fell out of the drawer. They belong to somebody else. Tanya. The warden's daughter."

"Let me see." He had moved another step toward me with his hand out and I took a step away from him along the wall.

"I can't. It's part of the initiation I can't. I did see a tanager." I could hear myself talking, but I was watching the way he had planted his feet and the strange way a shudder traveled the length of his body. "Did you ever know the Birdman?" I said. "The one from Alcatraz?"

He looked at me with a sudden sharpness in his eyes. He was all eyes except for the khaki. "What do you know about any birdman?"

"I knew him in Missouri. The real one."

"Stroud?"

"He told me about bird diseases."

"Canary diseases?"

"Yes. I drove with him to St. Joseph. My father took us. We went past warehouses and he told me he made his first birdcage out of a soap box."

"St. Joseph?"

"For court. He fed the pigeons on the courthouse steps." I nodded my head for emphasis, and I thought I had him diverted, but I was running out of material. I didn't want to mention the Birdman's razor blade.

"You lie good for a kid. Your father know how good you can lie? He know about your dirty pictures? You got a club here for girls that like girls?"

"We're all friends," I said uncertainly, and all at once, I felt as frightened of the birdman as I did of the infinity in my room.

I was hunting for my breath. Why did I have these pictures? I could run fast. Could I run away? And why was the birdman here? There was no escape siren to say he was missing, though if he had come in the prison garbage truck . . .

I swallowed hard and darted a look to see if my sandals were buckled tight. He had moved away from me. He was punching his fist against the wall in an even rhythm, steady but not hard. Maybe I was going to be kidnapped, maybe murdered and left in a ditch. Maybe the birdman meant to rape me, though what was that? What was it you jumped off buildings for? I had a picture in my mind of my mother's

Missouri friend and her husband groping each other on their stairway, which was the image I'd put with my mother's description of how babies were made, though I'd learned since from Tanya that sex happened in beds and where did you find a rooftop with a bed? Where, for that matter, had Maria Goretti's field hand intended to rape her?

"Little girl, you can give me those pictures or you can take your medicine on the floor and I can Jesus Christ spend my whole life in this hell. Why are you *here*?" The birdman hit the wall, louder and louder, and I thought I had my chance.

"Run!" he yelled, surprising me so that I froze like a block.

But then my feet kicked in, my sandals were flying, and I was through the door, pictures scattering up the path, past the garbage truck that I knew later the warden, from his bedroom window, had spotted just sitting there parked, the warden who was home for an early lunch with his wife on the first day of school and had called the guards who were on the way so I would have been saved, I would have been, but I was running, running, and this much is true—I saw a crow land in the newly cut field. Feet first. Its wings up, up like parachute: a fine black silk easing the awkward, inevitable fall.

Journeys in the Hidden World

It had been snowing when Laura's children came home from school. After David said she'd gone past three minutes on the egg timer for her "Minute Waltz," Mollie stopped practicing and knelt on the window seat, her face against the pane. Laura, who'd come in from the kitchen, kissed the back of her head and watched the snow drift humpbacked over the trees. In the fading light, the lilac bush looked like pussy willows. The branches were gray, and the fat parts that were dried-up buds had swollen into glassy sacs the shape of lemon drops.

"Did I hear your father?" she asked. She saw Mollie's face in the window reflection, and she thought again that Mollie's chin and eyes were more like hers than David's were, though all three of them had dark eyebrows beneath lighter hair, and their noses were nearly the same, something they'd discovered quite early and still confirmed, when they thought of it, front and profile in the hall mirror.

"I didn't hear him. I didn't see any cars."

"I hope he didn't get stuck. David, did you put the lid on tight when you took out the garbage? Maybe that's him now."

Laura went to the window. The car lights she was looking at went on past the driveway, and for a second she leaned against the window frame. Then she moved back from the window and switched on a lamp. "Mollie, set the table. You've finished practicing?"

"Yes."

"And, David, what about your homework?"

"I don't have any," he said. He was on the rug with the cat going up and down on his chest. He rolled over and the cat fell off and sat up purring to get its ears scratched.

"He never does. I had homework in third grade. Even in second."

"Set the table, Mollie."

Laura thought they were all waiting now. They didn't say it to each other, but all of them were listening and all of them kept glancing out the window into the snow and the falling darkness.

"Hibbards are home," Mollie said. "Their lights went on." She put the silverware down at the last place and went back to the window seat. Laura saw that the lilac branches were lost in the shadows, though she could still see dim house shapes all along the street, the bright rectangles of windows and lights dimming as curtains were closed. Then everything blinked. The refrigerator stopped. It made a coughing start and went quiet again and the whole room, the whole house and street were dark.

"I didn't turn the toaster on," David said.

Laura laughed. "It's not the fuse." She waited, listening. "It must be the snow. It's wet snow, so it's heavy. Maybe there's a break in the lines. Maybe there's a problem at the power station."

"So how long does this last? How do I do my homework when it's so dark in here?"

"You told her you didn't have any."

"Well if I did."

"Light the candles, Mollie. You can light all of them if you want. We can still eat." Laura was down on her hands and knees crossing newspaper with kindling in the fireplace.

"Are you going to cook on that?"

"The chili's already done. But we should eat before it gets cold."

"Chilly chili?"

"Yes, David. Even if it's always hot."

"We could pretend this is *Little House on the Prairie* and we live without any electricity at all and that we're waiting for Pa, who's lost somewhere in a snowstorm," Mollie said. "You could be Ma."

"Mom is fine. And I'd prefer, Mollie, to think your father will be home any minute and that the lights will come back on. Put the hot pad down for the chili."

"I bet it was like this outside when Vladimir got lost on his way to get married." The candlelight flickered on the table and Mollie's fingers, and Laura watched her turn the spoon in her bowl.

"That dumb story?" David said.

"It's Alexander Pushkin. It's not dumb. He's a very famous writer. Or he was. Mom, is he dead?" Mollie looked up at Laura.

"Very. For a long time."

"Did he live in the Bahamas?"

"Only when your father told you the story. He was Russian like Vladimir."

Mollie blew on her chili and took a bite. "I like the part where Vladimir's in a panic and his droshky keeps tipping over and he gets snow way down inside his collar and he's so cold he can't feel his face."

David looked up at Laura. "It's cold in here. Is the furnace electric?"

"The starter is. When we're finished eating, we'll sit by the fire."

"I still think it's gross the bride married the wrong man and that Vladimir died. And how come the peasant's son found his way in the storm when Vladimir couldn't?"

"Ask your father when he gets home." Laura had left the table and was poking at the fire.

"Remember I get to tell him first," David said.

"Tell him what?" Mollie said.

"About the cow the guys at the meat locker were strangling and it got loose and came to school and threw up all its guts."

"You are so gross. You think I'd want to tell him that?"

"They were all chasing it."

"We could make animals on the ceiling from the firelight," Mollie said to Laura, but David, following her into the living room, protested.

"All you can make is a crocodile. That's boring. This is boring. Mom, tell us a story."

Laura had left the fireplace and was standing at the window, but she came back again and stared at the fire. "Yes, I suppose I could. Let me think," she said. She tied David's shoe and, when she sat down, Mollie leaned against her back.

"How many different kinds of coins do you have, Mollie?" she said after a minute.

"I don't know. Lots."

"How many countries have you been in, David?"

"Was it ten?"

"Close."

"It was twelve."

"And that's just the number of countries the people in my story have been to—all on one trip. There're four people—a man and a woman, a girl and a boy."

"It's a story about us."

"They took a trip on a shoestring."

"We took a 747."

"They did, too."

Laura leaned forward and pushed a log back with the poker. "Eventually anyway. But they started on a DC-9 and went from there to trains. They took ferries and cable cars and ponies and vaporettos and a double-decker bus that shook so hard their giggles broke . . ."

"That was in Rome. It *is* us."

"The thing is these people seemed restless. It was as if they were looking for something."

"We found a lot of stuff. Remember the snails on the beach? Where was that?"

"The North Atlantic."

"But there weren't as many snails as there were bees when we climbed Tornado at camp. There must have been ten million. Really. *Bees!* And six girls were probably allergic and Jenny Kidder's even got medicine she has to take if she gets stung plus she has to get to a doctor in fifteen minutes but her mother made her leave it at home so she wouldn't break the bottle. We had to keep going to the next clearing and that's when I got the blister on my foot."

"I bet the people were looking for a TV. How come we didn't stay longer in the room with the TV?"

"Actually these people were always in a hurry. They flew to Reykjavik, to Luxembourg City—all right, Luxembird, David—and they went to sleep in this dark skinny hotel room with carved beds and when they'd slept twelve hours to get over their jet lag, they got up and ate a sausage and caught a train to Germany."

"You can skip Germany. I didn't like that part."

"I was going to—except for the Moselle. Except for Karl Marx's house since it looked so impressive. So clean.

"And as a matter of fact, these people rushed off again. They went to France and the woman had her birthday with strawberries and croissants for breakfast and in the evening they ate dinner in an old-stone-walled restaurant with the sun slanting in golden and warm at the windows, and the tables set with green glassware and giant vases of flowers."

"They should have stayed there."

"They went on. They did Switzerland in the blink of an eye—Basel, Lucerne, a walk down a mountain for another birthday dinner—for the boy this time—a cake with ice cream and whipped cream and more strawberries—enormous ones—and two-inch barrels of chocolate."

"David, remember that cake!"

"They went farther, deep into the Alps, searching to the end of the train routes until they ended up in—*voilà*—some little subdivision of a ski resort. They stayed in a brand-new house in a room with two feather beds for four people. There were bare white walls. The feather beds were white and there were white crosses in the cemetery and pictures of soldiers who'd died in the wars. They left and went to Vienna and in the night were awakened roughly on the train by men in uniforms. The passport control."

"It wasn't the Gestapo?"

"It wasn't. There is no Gestapo now, Mollie. Vienna frightened them, though."

"But the English bookstores, the coin shop . . ."

"Yes. And the Rembrandts and Brueghel. They went on anyway. They went to Venice, to the wonderful light, to the pink buildings swimming up out of the Grand Canal and a beautiful, brown grandmama of a hotel owner who smiled and cried *ciao!* every time they came in the door. It rained and they went to San Marco's and the children played tag in the Doge's Palace and were scolded by a grandpapa guard. '*No, no, bambinos.*'

"But even that didn't keep them. They rode on to Ferrara. They shared the fruit they'd bought with an Italian who talked to the children by folding paper hats. They raced through the treasures of Florence and then remembered Rome for a beautiful umbrella they saw in a shop window on the Via Veneto and for the papist takeover of the Pantheon and for an enormous orange moon over the railway station.

" '*La luna!*' the woman pointed to the ticket seller, and he nodded back, perfectly calm, perfectly placid, as if there were always such a moon—always such a tourist to announce it.

"Still they hurried. They took a rushing train ride up the white beaches of the Mediterranean coast and stopped at Nice for an afternoon, an evening. There were fishermen on the shore casting lines for squid far out to sea.

"Then Antibes. The covered market, the villa where Picasso lived for a moment after the war. They walked among the rooms—among the sculptures and chunky plates, the rising walls. They listened for Picasso as people wait for God in church. And then, in Avignon, a man ate fire.

"It was after that that something changed. They kept up their frantic pace—it was not that that was altered. Slowly, though, imperceptibly, the impression they were running toward something was replaced by the idea they were running away instead. In Barcelona, puzzling out trains, they passed a sign so often—*A Tarragona*—that at night they dreamed of it like a prophecy. Then two weeks later in a tent in Ireland, they read that a lorry on the coast road in Spain had careened in flames into a campground, igniting sunbathers and campers with a chain reaction of explosions from their own cookstoves."

"A lorry's a truck?"

"Yes. A truck. In Tarragona. On the coast of Spain just one of the disasters that they skirted now with the random charge of their travel—the bomb at Versailles which they missed by a day, the fire in the British Rail sleeping car in the south of England when they were heading north, the arrest of terrorists in London at a cultural center they'd toured the day before. They were in a minefield, somehow, its perimeter drawn by their trip the way cities are linked by routes sketched on a map."

"Mom, I don't get it. I don't understand. Anyway, this is getting scary."

"Is it? I suppose it is."

"Did all that stuff really happen? I don't remember it. What about Scotland and Wales?"

"I remember the roosters and burros and cows in the field next to us when we woke up in Ireland. And the old man with his bucket of milk."

"I remember when it stormed."

"And we could hear the waves crashing all night and the wind shook the tent so hard it was like sleeping in a great big bowl of Rice Krispies."

"Mom, what were they looking for? What were those people in such a hurry about?"

"I don't know. Maybe they wanted to get their money's worth on their rail passes. Maybe they weren't sure themselves. Maybe they didn't know if they'd found what they were looking for, so they should go again. Maybe they need another shoestring."

"At least the kids would be old enough. How come you took us when we were so little?"

"You were as old as you'd ever been."

They were all stretched out now, their toes reaching toward the fire. They fell quiet and, in a while, David's breathing grew huskier.

The cat jumped them then. It landed square in the pack of them with its tail up, and they were laughing and tussling when they heard the banging at the door.

"What? It wouldn't be Dad at the front door—" Mollie was sitting upright and David held on to the cat. Laura stood up. The nameless banging came again, and she moved to the door in the darkness. She hesitated.

"Yes?" Her voice had slipped into her throat.

"Open the door! I'm *freezing* out here." The sound was broken apart, yet it slammed back together as it came through the wood, and Laura was unlocking the door. She pushed it open.

"Oh Zack, you're a snowman. Where were you?" She was holding him, helping him with his coat, with his gloves. They were iced like his whiskers. She kissed the ice from his whiskers onto her face.

"There's a fire," she said, and the children had him then. They were hanging on him and puffing on his face and hands while Laura dragged a log across the hearth and hoisted it into the sparking flames.

"Where's the car? I'll get you some chili. What happened?"

"There's isn't a damned light in the whole town. The car's dead. The alternator went. Are my boots frozen on?"

David was tugging at his boots, and Mollie was working at the laces, and Laura, handing Zack a bowl, thought the laces were like the lilac twigs. "They're wrapped in ice," she said, and she watched David pull one boot off and then the other, though Mollie kept on at the laces.

"*There,*" Mollie said. She laid the shoestrings on the rug near the fire. "We're in business, Mom. Not one but two."

"What's she talking about, Laura?"

"Shoestrings. Is the chili warm enough? Are you warmer yet? We were telling stories. Travel stories. About traveling on a shoestring."

They were all on the rug in front of the fire watching ten toes defrost. The four of them were sprawled for a long time in a shadowy tangle, the fire snapping and hissing. It burned down to embers and they were all warm-faced and dozy when the fridge hummed and the lights came back on.

Floating

1 952. There is more than enough room for Jamie and Laura on the waiting room bench, so Laura squinches closer to Jamie to show their mother there is room for her, too. Lucy Palmer shakes her head and stays standing, their green suitcases wedged against her knees. Jamie elbows Laura away from him and the skin on the back of her legs tugs on the polished wood. She catches herself on the bench arm.

"Sit still," Lucy Palmer tells them. The station clock is a big circle on the wall behind her. Laura watches it skip two minutes at once, and then stares at the run next to the dark seam in her mother's stockings and the tiny bulge of blue vein just above her ankle. Her mother has sit-down wrinkles on her suit skirt and a smeary soiled spot below the waist where Jamie's Hershey bar melted, and a little tear in her hat veil right above one corner of her glasses. Otherwise she looks very nice.

"Did they forget it's today?" Jamie says, slouching on the bench but in a knee-cocked sort of way, ready to bolt, to race a stranger to the platform door if a train whistles. Lucy Palmer shakes her head again and keeps her eyes on the station entrance. Laura sees the blue vein pulse. In Nashville, her mother, flagging porters, rushed them through the station. They made their connection panting with a minute to spare, climbing carefully up each tall step of the Pullman car as if it were the first step of an escalator. Behind the train the summer moon was rising in the sky where the engine curved into the distance and stars. Now, though, it is full daylight and they're in Savannah and Uncle Peter isn't here.

1994. On the eve of her forty-ninth birthday, paging through a photo album—leather, solid, and thick—Laura Cray has stopped at a series of black-and-white snapshots with wavy edges and with her mother's handwriting beneath the images: *Savannah, Summer '52.* In the picture that strikes her most, there is a palm tree, a stucco house in shadow. Her young and languid aunt is seated at a table in the yard, holding baby Chloe, and Laura and her mother and brother are lined up with her uncle, and at the picture's edge, there is the maid, trying to disappear and almost succeeding, her dark face suspended on a white uniform that bleeds away against the stucco. Laura does not remember who took the picture. She does remember that days earlier—a week? two weeks?—her uncle was late, that on their arrival he was not there to meet them.

This is what interests her now. She touches the stiff black corners on the picture that hold it to the page, touches the faces, but she does not remember why he was late and why it was important beyond the lateness and why it is just this picture she finds compelling. As she traces the outline of the bodies, the phone rings, and she closes the album and puts it away on the shelf beside the fireplace.

1952. Laura is in the ocean, floating, the sunrays pooling in the water that closes almost over her and rims the green sheen of her swimsuit where it stretches oval across her belly. She sucks herself down into the water. A sliver of the suit remains, then grows into a wide clown-tie on the water as she bounces back up. She did not know that salt and waves can carry you so high, but they do. She smooths her stomach, feels the wet slick of the green, pushes her finger on her navel through the fabric.

She is lazy in the water—barely sculling with her hands and holding her feet up high to count her toes, and then letting them splash back. She will tell her friends she has been in the ocean. The *Atlantic* Ocean. Back home in Ohio she will tell Mary Sue Clintock about tides and salt and the white beach and the boulevards of sand that look poured out by the Morton salt girl. Sitting on the rug in the front room of the Clintocks' house they'll deal out the "Flinch" cards, and she'll tell as much as she can before Mary Sue breaks in and asks, "Well *was* it a trial separation?" Laura has practiced not answering. Why would her parents need a trial? And if her parents had wanted a separation, hadn't they already had one during the war?

Jamie paddles up next to her and grabs her hair and dunks her. Water rushes up her nose. For a scared second, Laura flails in the blurry water. Then she's upright, standing on something sharp. She pulls her foot up to look at it. There's no blood and, as she lets go of the foot and watches Jamie dive into a wave, she feels very serious, knowing she's not going to tell.

1994. When Laura picks up the phone, there is circuitry in her mind. Or fiber optics. Or whatever the scheme is that links the receiver to the places that might be calling: local places like Minneapolis or St. Paul, distant places like Bangkok, Monterey, Houston or Chicago or Middlebury, though if it's Monterey, for tonight all bets are off.

Laura lifts the cord away and says hello. A woman's voice answers hers and in a minute things are sorted out, that Laura is not her daughter (her children are both away at school), that she can be at the gallery in ten minutes to join people for dinner, that Zack won't be with her because he's in Bangkok tonight and for a week of nights on business, unforeseen, and that it really is her cousin Chloe after all these years and the recent correspondence, and that the man who met Chloe's morning flight from Monterey—San Francisco actually—was very helpful.

Laura reaches for her coat and straightens the couch pillows. She turns off the lamps on the end tables and turns on the rose Tiffany lamp next to the piano. She picks a piece of lint off the rug on her way out to the car and the bitter January night.

1952. Laura has her sheet tucked in neatly around the comforter on the floor in the sewing room. Her pillow is against the wall, but she wants a cover even though it's hot, even though the air is heavy in the room and the tree leaves, which are shadowed on the wall, are still. She pulls at the bottom of the sheet and makes a triangle that tucks her feet together and angles across her waist. Jamie is on another comforter in front of the closet. She hears him rolling around on the floor, punching at his pillow, knocking against the closet door.

"You awake?" Laura whispers.

Down the hall, a light goes on in Chloe's room, and Laura sits up. She feels a drip of sweat trickle down her back. The light goes off and Laura's sure it's her uncle who walks back down the hall. She can hear far-off voices in the living room, and she wishes her mother would come in to get in the daybed for the night.

"So go to sleep," Jamie says.

"Uncle Peter got Chloe up."

"She's weird for a baby."

"She's not."

"You're weird."

"In Georgia you'd think they'd have a refrigerator full of cold pillows."

"Their blood's different. They're used to it hot. Or they sleep in the altogether."

"You're lying."

"You're a dope."

Laura pulls her pillow over her ears and knots herself up in a ball. Sometimes Jamie makes her cry, but she won't let him do it while they're visiting. And Chloe isn't weird. It's like she's off limits. At home they get to hold their baby cousins, but here Essence the maid has Chloe all day long, and at night she's Uncle Peter's. She's a staring baby who doesn't like to smile. She has dark, serious eyes, and a thin cloud of white hair.

"Jamie?"

Silence.

"Jamie, you ever think maybe Chloe belongs to Essence? She's the one that's got her all the time."

"You're an idiot."

"Well maybe she's hers."

"If Uncle Peter stuck his pecker in Essence's box to make a baby, you think it'd have white hair?"

"You're lying."

"You don't know you got a box between your legs for a pecker to make a baby? All the girls do."

"You're a liar, Jamie Palmer. *Liar, liar.*" Laura is suffocating, drenched in sweat. She stuffs her fingers in her ears, but she is too startled, too interested to think if she wants to cry.

1994. Wind gusts that pick up snow and streak the windshield with white: Laura drives carefully, tense, feeling the cold. She is ready for black ice, the invisible slick of frozen exhaust that surprises a car. But the lights of the approaching city, the shining half-arc on the top of the First Bank building distract her. She relaxes, feels her steadier self behind the wheel.

Breathing warm air from her mouth into her scarf, she hurries down the parking ramp stairs, crosses the street. It is not a gallery that she knows, this place where her cousin is mounting a show. Well, curating it, post-curating it—putting the imprimatur on the way it's hung and speaking about how it was brought together. This is what Chloe will do, if Laura understands. The show is of Civil War interiors—etchings and paintings collected by a descendant of General John Logan. Chloe has told her this in a letter.

Laura waits at the elevator. She is in an anonymous hall of gray marble or polished granite. (She does not always know the difference.)

There is a map of the country carved in the floor, and Laura examines it, standing on the Atlantic Ocean. There are no state boundaries and no river but the Mississippi, and she is sure she has never seen a map before with such a clear sense of where the Mississippi lies. In fact, she has never been so aware that a full two-thirds of the country lies to the Mississippi's west. She checks out the cities. As her children would say, random. San Antonio stands for all of Texas, and Kansas City and Anchorage are stunningly prominent. Minneapolis, etched in gold letters, is the center of the depicted universe.

A light goes on, and the elevator rings itself open.

In the hall outside the gallery, Laura stops under an unexpected chandelier and stuffs her gloves into her pocket, unbuttons her coat, lets her boots drip unavoidably on the green plush of an Oriental rug. People are coming through the door. A long mirror on the wall reflects a golden light the color of her hair, or of her hair come back fully to life.

"Chloe!" Laura reaches into the line and hugs her cousin.

"The hair?" Chloe says, and Laura laughs.

"Family I.D."

Laura shakes hands with the people Chloe introduces. She feels easy with the ease of Chloe, though the accent is missing. She realizes this. In the soft-faced, dark-eyed woman before her, it's the lazy, sweet southern sound that is gone.

1952. It is a swimming holiday. There is the ocean when Uncle Peter is free to take them there, and for the times when he is not, the pool up the street. Laura is allowed to walk there by herself, and she is glad of this because Jamie doesn't wait and she does not have to call to him that he should. He is always in a hurry to be somewhere and then somewhere else. On the train, he went through the cars—back and forth, up and down the aisles until the conductor said he'd walked half the distance to Savannah by himself. "He'll get there before the train does," he told their mother.

Laura has made two friends at the pool. Or girls who have talked to her and know she lives in Ohio and that it's her brother doing cannonballs off the diving board. Once she was asked to join in a bobbing game, and she held her breath the second longest. Mostly, though, she floats in the water, tries to sit on the bottom of the pool, makes sure she stays a long way from the deep end.

It is such an easy walk to the pool—her suit on and her towel and quarter in her hand—that she slips her sandals off and leaves them in the yard. Halfway down the block, she realizes how serious her mistake is. There is nowhere to walk but the pavement and the sand. They are burning hot from the noonday sun. She is stranded in heat—walking, running on a giant frying pan, hopping, leaping for the one tuft of black-green grass that has pushed up through the white sand.

In the late afternoon, this is the story she is bursting to tell her mother when she comes back from the pool, hurrying the length of her wet towel and then folding it over to walk on it again the way Jamie, holding on to the side of the pool, told her to do. The towel is grimy with sand. Knowing her aunt's neatness, she scrapes at it, beats it like a rug before she goes into the house.

Inside, it is so dark in the hall with the shades drawn in the dining room that it seems almost cool. She puts her towel on the sink in the powder room, leaves it with the cleanest part up. Her suit is all dry, dry enough to sit down in, and so she doesn't go into the bedroom to change, but looks quickly in the living room for her mother. Usually she is reading in the wing chair while Aunt Cecily rests in her room before dinner, but Laura sees the two of them through the window, sitting outside.

She hurries through the house. The screen door swings shut and she goes down the back steps and past the mulberries and tulip tree into the dark, moist perfume of the garden. Her aunt is dressed in white linen shorts and a blouse. She is on the chaise longue, nudging a tree branch with her foot. Laura's mother is in a chair, a book on her lap. Her dress is new, peach and blue plaid, but it is still like all the housedresses she wears at home.

Her aunt spots her first. "Honey, you have Essence get you some lemonade?"

"I didn't see her." Laura hangs on the arm of her mother's chair. She wants to tell about her feet, but she is certain all at once it will be impolite, that she will be a guest complaining.

"If she's not in the kitchen, look in Chloe's room. She'll get you some."

"Say thank you, Laura."

"Thank you."

Laura hesitates. She is the only person in her whole life she's ever known to have been almost on fire. But the saints had it worse. Boiled in oil. And, too, when her mother was small, the neighbor girl burned up, running from the kitchen in flames when she should have rolled herself up in a rug. Laura lets go of the chair arm. "Thank you, Aunt Cecily. I'll go ask her," she says.

She is standing in front of the refrigerator when she hears Essence in the hallway and her uncle coming in the front door, Essence speaking to him in a voice that travels quietly down the wall to the kitchen: "Thank you, Mr. Thomas, sir, for coming home early. I don't leave that baby with her. That's a promise still."

1994. If the accent is gone, the charm is not. As a group of them walks the block to dinner before the gallery talk, Laura can't remember anyone's name, but Chloe is shivering delicately and talking in complete, even witty sentences. To Laura, this seems all but impossible. She herself is grinding her teeth. She burrows into her scarf and coat, pushes against the harsh wind, tries to remember the number of seconds before exposed skin freezes enough to bring on a medical emergency. She pictures Chloe's perfect nose with a patch of frostbite. Maybe Chloe is running on adrenaline, a surfeit of blood to all her Georgia and California organs; maybe she doesn't realize just how cold it really is.

But in the restaurant, Chloe holds her fingers out and gets a laugh: "So what's the defrost time? Do you use a microwave?"

The waiters, scraping the floor, move two tables together. Laura eats a slice of baguette and watches Chloe. She has seen the slim dress, the good legs, but Chloe, though she could certainly pass for thirty-five, does not have her mother's silvered presence—that look which says she ought to be in pictures. She is engaging like her father, and smart, and she has the hint of a cast in her eye that in Laura's experience is drop-dead fascinating to men. Laura's daughter has it; her niece does.

"Chloe says you're an editor. Graywolf?" The bread catches in Laura's throat and she reaches for her water glass. "Coffee House?"

Laura shakes her head and swallows. "No." She turns halfway to the Yeltsin look-alike, the historical society fellow on her right. "Textbooks. Copyediting. I copyedit children's readers."

"Interesting. Must be a good way to relive your childhood."

"Actually it's not." Laura takes her glasses out to look at the menu, lets the ambiguity of her answer stand. She is not sure what her responsibility is in this situation, who she is here or even why she is here. She would like to say it is almost her birthday and that she does not want her husband in Bangkok and her son and daughter away at school and that, furthermore, she does not want to be reading children's books when she is forty-nine. Instead she scans the menu. *Coquilles St. Jacques à la Parisienne, Sole à la Normande, Crêpes d'épinards* . . . She takes her glasses off, tries to remember the French for grilled cheese.

1952. Laura studies her Mickey Mouse watch in the light from the streetlamp. Eleven o'clock. Almost. It's too hot to sleep and, anyway, lying on her comforter, she is wide awake. They have a babysitter for the night. Essence is gone and their mother and aunt and uncle are out for dinner and the symphony. The babysitter is a lifeguard from the pool, and Jamie's spent the whole night showing off for her, getting her diapers for Chloe and pouring her lemonade and telling her he's thirteen, which is a lie by a full two years, and stupid besides, since you can babysit if you're thirteen and you don't need any lifeguard from the swimming pool.

Jamie's awake, too. He's rolling around more than usual. He's been out to the living room half a dozen times until finally the babysitter said she was closing their door if he didn't stay put and she didn't care how hot it was. Laura wishes he'd lie still. She'd throw her pillow at him except the last night she did, he didn't give it back. She twists her finger in her pajama top, pushes her hair off her neck where it's damp.

Then Jamie's asleep. She can hear his breathing change, grow longer and smooth. And now she's really awake. She's worried about spiders and about people coming in the window. She's scared about bats. She holds her breath, pretending she's dead; she lies perfectly still, trying to be invisible. Finally, ages and ages later, there are lights in the driveway, and she hears car doors and then voices in the living room.

Her mother, though, doesn't come to bed. Uncle Peter checks on Chloe, but there's a conversation going on, and no Lucy Palmer walking down the hall. Laura gets up, untangling the sheet, and tries to listen from the door. She edges into the hallway. If anybody comes, she can say she's going to the bathroom. She moves farther down the hall. The voices have stopped, but the door to the living room is open partway. Laura sees the strip of light between the hinges and the arc of lamplight and the arm of the sofa that are visible through the doorway. She stands behind the door, leans over a little, squeezes her hands between her knees. Through the slit, she can just see the mirror next to the wing chair but that's all she needs. All three of them are there, all of them backward in the mirror. Her Aunt Cecily is lying down, her skirt a watery silk spilling over the edge of the sofa. The back of her hand is over her eyes. A headache, Laura thinks. Or maybe her aunt is listening to music in her head. Uncle Peter is fixing a drink. In the mirror, Laura sees the tongs in his hand. She hears the clink of ice cubes in a glass. Her mother has a program on her lap, but Laura can't tell if she's reading it. She's in the straight-backed chair, and she has her legs crossed.

"I think I'll go to bed," she says. Laura is ready to scurry down the hall, but her mother doesn't get up. "Cecily, can I get you an aspirin?"

A headache. Laura watches her aunt's hand wave in the air and go back to her eyes. She is wearing the gold locket and chain that is the family heirloom, her engagement present from Grandmother Thomas. Laura knows that she is, though she can't really see the locket in the mirror. She knows, too, that the locket was given to her, the rich southern belle, because it was the best thing Grandmother had to give.

The program slips off her mother's lap and she is leaning back against the chair. "No, Peter. Thank you, but no. Really, no."

"It's Chivas, Lucy. Try it. You'll find a taste for it." Laura can see the back of her uncle's head, the dark blond hair which is auburn in the mirror, the glass which he's holding out to her mother, and the starched white cuff of his shirt. His voice is raspy. His body sways to one side and then he hitches himself upward, rights himself.

It's a motion Laura recognizes with surprise. She steps back against the dark wall. Uncle Peter is drunk. She knows this because Carla Hubbell's father is a drunk. Once he broke the dishes in Carla's whole house and threw ketchup on the walls. Then he went outside and peed in the street and walked back inside like he was going to fall over, though he managed to keep jerking himself straight. The kids in the neighborhood were watching from their bikes, and, afterward, Laura's parents wouldn't let her play with Carla anymore.

"When in Rome, Lucy. Or in Georgia. Palmer's not here to say anything. You're a free woman for the time you're with us."

"It's nothing to do with him."

"God, Peter, leave her alone."

"So I'll drink the Chivas myself. No sacrifice. What about crème de menthe? It's sweet, Lucy. You can try your sweet tooth on it."

Laura is back at the crack in the door. Her uncle takes a bottle from the cabinet by the fireplace and holds it up to the light. It is a beautiful dark green and it has all the shapes of roundness. With great and careful slowness, he starts to pour, rubs a spilled drop from the table with his thumb, and fills a small stemmed glass. Now the glass, too, is green. Laura, watching, shivers with surprise.

Her mother is shaking her head. "No, Peter. I'm going to bed. It was a wonderful evening. I loved the symphony."

"Could I then? Taste it?" Laura walks on her tiptoes into the living room, blinks her eyes in the full light. Aunt Cecily drops her hand, sits halfway up on the sofa, and then leans back. Uncle Peter looks puzzled. It is Lucy Palmer, though, who is out of her chair and across the room.

"You aren't asleep?" Her mother does not smell of scent like Aunt Cecily, but of herself, of her hair and skin. She takes Laura's hand and they go down the hall, and the next thing Laura knows it is morning, and Jamie is up, gone, and her mother's bed is made. Laura is sweaty hot, hungry for breakfast.

1994. Put her in the guest room. Show her the rack of immaculate and unused quilts that is part of the decor. Show her the prints that are Zack's choice and the swirled snow and leaf painting that you love. Let the color catch her eye as it does yours each time you stand in the doorway—the slate blue and Chinese red of the walls, the flat black of the slatted chair . . .

Already done. The quick house tour. The picture of David and Mollie in the silver frame that was the anniversary present. Twenty-five years.

Laura fills the teakettle with water and puts it on the stove. At the stairs, she hears the bath running. The cat bumps her and she picks him up and carries him with her into the study to listen to her phone messages. One from David—"Hi, Mom. You're out and I'm going out. Happy birthday. Call you tomorrow." One with background noise from Mollie—"Mom, nobody on my floor believes you're that old. Did my card get there? If you can't tell, that's Andy and Jeff singing 'Happy Birthday.' "

One hang-up. Nothing yet from Zack.

Laura goes back to the kitchen. She looks at a magazine article on headaches and another one on juniper trees until the water boils. "I was just deciding," she says when Chloe comes in. "What would you like? Tea? Evian? There's white zin and you can look in the liquor cabinet. A hot toddy?"

"If it's as good as the bath." Chloe's in a robe. She's drying the ends of her hair with a towel. "I didn't know it could get this cold."

"Bud Grant weather." Laura reads the cookbook with her half-glasses, measures out brandy shots for two mugs. She hands Chloe hers. "Officially that's an impaled lemon slice studded with three cloves, but I only had one left. Is it too strong?"

Chloe takes a sip and holds her cup out for more water. She sips again. "Good. Perfect."

In the living room, they talk about Chloe's show, about how she stumbled into the bulk of the work while tracking down prints for another project, about how the interiors seemed as if they were hers—her mother's big southern family, her father from the North—how they had the Civil War right at home, not the all-out battles, but the politics, the inside positioning, how when her parents divorced, her mother called it the secession that took.

They talk of the last time they saw each other, decide that Chloe was twelve. Chloe tells Laura she didn't go to California to become an actress, but just to go. Laura says she meant to play the violin but lost her nerve, that she started as a copy editor because she could do it at home when the children were little, and then they were older and it was what she knew how to do.

Laura gets up, makes them both another half-drink, and brings the thought she left with back from the kitchen. She pushes a sofa pillow behind her head. "It always surprised me your parents split up." She can feel the warm spot on her forehead that the brandy has made. She goes on. "They were so iconic—these beautiful people . . ."

"Shock of the obvious for me." Chloe's feet are tucked under her. "But your parents had the perfect marriage. And now you—twenty-five years."

Laura nods and Mary Sue Clintock, hands on hips, voice accusing, is standing in her brain: *Well was it a trial separation?* Laura takes a sip of her drink. She's had it sorted out for herself for a very long time. Her parents were about boundaries, about who they were alone more than who they were together. And who they were alone meant that, close as they often seemed, their marriage had still been one long trial of separation.

"You never married," she says to Chloe.

"No."

"Gun shy?" The words are out before Laura can catch them, hold back the spin in her head.

"If you mean did the divorce scare me off, no. Neither do men." Chloe runs her finger along the rim of her mug, picks at the clove. "My father said he couldn't leave me alone with my mother for years after I was born, that my birth unbalanced her. I've always thought I wouldn't like my children. I thought that even before he told me."

Laura looks at her drink. An unexpected piece for a puzzle she knows can never be finished. She flashes on Uncle Peter waiting for Essence while they waited for him. "I remember Essence took care of you. But you'd like your children."

"You miss yours."

"Not anymore." Laura laughs. "Sometimes I forget that I don't."

"And your husband's in Bangkok."

"Yes."

"Funny name I always thought. Bangkok."

"Brought to you by the people who named Lahore. Pakistan."

"What?"

Laura shakes her head.

"You didn't want him to go?"

"It's fine. It's business. It's fine." Laura turns her head, reaches her hand along the back of the sofa.

Chloe waits, then stretches and unwinds her feet. She puts her drink on the end table. "Long day. Early morning tomorrow. This is great. California time I can go to bed at nine thirty. I should write it down."

"I'll get you a heavier blanket." Laura picks up the mugs and carries them out to the kitchen, puts the soap in the dishwasher, and starts it running. She goes down the hall. Chloe is brushing her teeth. Laura takes a blanket from the linen closet and leaves it on the chair in the guest room, pulls the door to so the cat won't get in.

1952. Sunday morning in a great white church. While the bells ring, Laura walks down the steps, swings her patent leather purse that matches her shoes. She is wearing her white hat with the turned-up brim and her yellow dress that is her father's favorite, though she doesn't like yellow herself. But it reminds her of him. She misses his whiskers. He is the one who tells her to hold her skirt down if the wind blows and, when she kisses him good night, if she's too impetuous he tells her he'd rather be kicked by a mule.

Jamie is already at the car. Their mother is at the top of the steps holding Chloe. She has fixed her hat with a new veil that she got from Aunt Cecily. The stain in her suit skirt is gone. Laura knows that the fabric pilled, but to see it, you have to look close. Uncle Peter and Aunt Cecily are standing next to her, talking to their friends. Uncle Peter is very handsome, and people look at Aunt Cecily. She is wearing a white dress with jet buttons and black lapels. She has on a black hat that Jamie says looks like a skinny, upside-down rowboat, but Laura knows that it's very smart.

She waits at the bottom of the steps.

They are going to a fort. This is an amazing fact. Laura thinks it is traveling through time, going to a place that existed in a war—the Civil War—with real soldiers and real guns. Her father was in a war, but it was a world war in the Pacific Ocean, and Mary Sue Clintock's father was never in a war at all. Laura and Jamie are under strict instructions from their mother not to whistle "Marching through Georgia," which is not a song Laura knows but one that Jamie says is about the Civil War and General Sherman and pillage. *Pillage.* Laura does know that the Civil War is what makes the difference between being from the South like Aunt Cecily and being from the North the way all the Palmers and Thomases are.

They ride in Uncle Peter's white Chrysler with the windows down. Chloe is on Aunt Cecily's shoulder in the front seat, and Jamie makes faces at her and she stares at him and then spits up all over the back of the seat and Aunt Cecily's shoulder. This is an emergency. Aunt Cecily jerks forward in the seat and holds Chloe away from her all in one motion. "Stop the car! God, Peter, I'm going to reek of this baby. Did it get in my hair?"

Jamie is squirmed in a knot trying not to laugh, but Laura sees her mother's calm, a sureness which is surprising. Lucy Palmer hands Chloe out to Uncle Peter at the curb and then mops up the seat with a baby towel from the diaper bag. She pushes her own lace handkerchief inside the shoulder of Aunt Cecily's dress and digs out a washcloth from the bag to dab the fabric clean, powders it fresh and almost dry. Laura is fascinated. Her mother is better at this since the chocolate on the train.

"Can we still go to the fort?" Jamie leans forward, pulls on the back of Uncle Peter's seat when he's behind the wheel again.

"Cecily?" Uncle Peter looks at her across Chloe, who's lying on the seat, and Laura waits. For a moment there's no answer. Then Aunt Cecily takes her cologne out of her purse and sprays it on her shoulder.

"I guess I can stand in the breeze. If there is one."

Jamie punches Laura's thigh and his own, too.

The fort, when she sees it, stops all of Laura's words. It is not logs put together like Jamie's Lincoln Logs, but something white, full of big spaces and black cannons, and open to the air and sea. Uncle Peter lifts her up on the wall. She listens to the waves crash in. Jamie is running from cannon to cannon, *rat-a-tat-tatting* a war and roaring out booms.

"How many people died here?" he asks Uncle Peter, and Uncle Peter says no one, that Savannah saved itself by letting Sherman in.

"That's Vichy water out there," he says, and Laura sees her mother glance quickly at Aunt Cecily to see if she's listening, which she's not. She's on a blanket, sleeping with Chloe.

1994. Laura is reading in bed when Chloe knocks at her door. She sets her book and her glasses down on Zack's side of the bed.

Chloe sticks her head in the door. "I've got a photograph for you of one of the show etchings."

"Come on in." Laura moves over, and Chloe sits down on the edge of the bed. Laura picks her glasses up again. She studies the picture that Chloe hands her—the flood of sunshine on the ceiling and on one wall, the twelve-light windows, the trunks and the rocker and Major Anderson alone at his desk at Fort Sumter, his back to the room. It's the picture she liked the very best in the whole show.

"I always wonder what he was thinking just then, what he was planning to do," Chloe says. "What is it men do while they're waiting to be shelled?"

This is a question Laura has thought about—her father in the Pacific and Zack in Vietnam before she met him. What did they do? What did Zack do? It is a part of him she doesn't know, has never known. The Asian part.

"If you like it, you can have it," Chloe says. "I brought it for you. And this." She reaches into the pocket of her robe and lifts out a small leather box. "Remember this?" She opens the box lid and Laura sees a locket, its etched pattern of leaves and flowers worn almost smooth—the locket she touched long ago on her Aunt Cecily's neck, knowing, as she did, that it gained in loveliness because her aunt was wearing it.

Laura takes it from the box, holds it up by the chain. "Grandmother Thomas's," she says. "And your mother's."

"Not hers. Not really. It was a trinket for her, Laura. Take it. No, really. You're the proper line of succession."

Laura feels the weight of the chain on her fingers, holds the locket in her hand. "It reminds me of your mother," she says. "If I keep it, Chloe, that's why."

"Deal." Chloe gets up, smiles. She is like Mollie, Laura thinks, like Mollie will be in twenty years. It pleases her she's pleased that she thinks so.

1952. For their last full day of vacation, Laura and Jamie can pick what they want to do. They are awake at six, but their mother says it is too early to go to a restaurant for waffles with Georgia pecans, so they shoot marbles on Jamie's comforter while she goes back to sleep. At eight o'clock Essence is shelling peas at the kitchen sink, and Uncle Peter, who has the day off from work, is at the table in his terry robe reading the paper and smoking. Laura and Jamie wait in the doorway so he'll know they're all dressed.

"Your mother ready?" he asks them over the paper. They shake their heads.

"Neither is your Aunt Cecily. Tell you what. If you can wait five minutes for me to shave, we'll go just the three of us."

Jamie pinches Laura and she uncrosses her fingers behind her back.

They ride in the front seat of Uncle Peter's car. Laura thinks she can smell where Chloe spit up, but she doesn't say so. Jamie counts Chevys and Fords. At the restaurant he orders for himself, and Uncle Peter orders Laura a large glass of milk and a waffle heaped in the center with pecans. She pours the syrup carefully, filling every square in the waffle. Then she spreads out pecans from the center. She eats for a very long time. Uncle Peter's arm is stretched across the back of the booth. He has on a white shirt with the collar open.

When they get back to the house, Laura finds her mother busy in the sewing room with the suitcases open on the daybed. She's folding Laura's yellow dress that Essence ironed.

Laura rocks in the rocker by the window. She holds her feet out in front of her. "I think I'm growing," she says.

"Could be," her mother says. She turns around with one of Jamie's shirts in her hands and looks at Laura over her glasses. She laughs. "Could be your waffle was too big."

Laura rocks off the chair and goes down the hall to find Jamie.

It is a waiting sort of morning. They are going to the beach, everybody's promised, but Aunt Cecily's in bed late with a headache, and Essence doesn't have their picnic ready. Uncle Peter is talking to his office on the phone, and then he calls their father in Ohio about the train reservations, which is the only time Laura has ever heard a long-distance call except when Grandmother Thomas died and her mother called Uncle Peter to let him know. Laura thinks about their arrival home, about her mother's suit and her hat veil and the green bags the porter will lift down from the metal train steps and how their father will be there to hug them and kiss their mother hard on the lips the way he does when he's been away.

Finally they're ready to go. Essence holds Chloe in the driveway and helps her wave good-bye. Jamie makes the same face that made her spit up, but this time it doesn't work and she's just a baby in a pinafore, all clean while Essence holds her and Uncle Peter backs out the drive.

Then they're back at the ocean. Laura runs with her towel along the beach. She can smell the sea air on her lips, feel the sand pushing in between her toes. The gulls call and she makes a small cry in her own throat she thinks is an answer back. She tosses her towel on the sand and wades into the water. Jamie is ahead of her. He is doing somersaults into the waves. There are swimmers out by the buoys, other children in the shallow water next to the cracks in the tidal flats.

Laura turns back toward the shore. They are all going swimming, Uncle Peter with his boxer's hairy chest and Aunt Cecily in her aqua two-piece and Lucy Palmer in her short swim dress that does not cover the blue veins of her legs. Laura sits back, kicks her feet up, and floats. She sees a strip of green trees, the long, curling stretch of white sand, the water that is green on her suit but blue from the sky. Laura sculls, trails her hand along the sandy bottom. She does not care if Jamie bumps her, dares her; she does not care if there are children smaller than she is paddling out toward the buoys. Uncle Peter and Aunt Cecily swim in long strokes far out in the water and then turn, floating their way back, Aunt Cecily's head on Uncle Peter's shoulder. Laura's mother, uncertain without her glasses, tries to float but she can't.

Laura closes her eyes. She sees the sun white beneath her eyelids. She hears voices around her. She is floating blind in a crowd, and she thinks shark first when it happens. And she thinks second that there are no sharks here but only Jamie's sharks at night in Ohio when they all play shadowgraph and make hand monsters behind a sheet with a flashlight. Yet it was like a shark, she thinks, like a shark moving by in silence, the stroking fin that smoothed the fabric between her legs. Somebody's hand.

1994. She has them then, these gifts from Chloe who is sleeping down the hall: a picture of a man embarking on civil war and a locket for remembering, delivered with the unstruck gong of her fiftieth year. Laura rolls over in the dark, watches a headlight striping the window blinds. She has not been asleep. Or she has been floating in a half sleep of long grasses, green and alluring. Asia. Not one night in Bangkok, but a deeper surprise as when the glass turned green, and not fear, but mystery as when the shark fin passed. Laura closes her eyes. She feels a whiteness, the kind of blinding light that sears her eyes when she makes love.

Things

It was not a surprise to Laura that her mother was back. It was awkward to explain perhaps, so often she left the obvious unstated: she had her mother's things and her father had remarried because eight years ago her mother had died.

Her father's new wife was not a problem. When her mother returned, the wife receded to a presence in another state. A letter to be expected at Christmas. A part of the general snowfall of cards. She had no standing as wife, in fact, was not wife to any man, though it was known that for a part of the death she had been, understandably and legally, spouse.

Yet if the wife was not an issue, what had belonged to Laura's mother—the vast wander of things—really was. It was not that her mother begrudged her having these things. Her mother had no opinion. She gave no show of pleasure that much was in use, no sign of dismay that her clothes were gone. As it was, without clothes, she always was clothed.

The problem, Laura recognized, was her own and not her mother's. To her, it seemed her mother should have need of what Laura herself had kept or had dispersed first to the battered women's shelter, then to friends and children, finally even to refuse and breakage. The crumbling flower of turquoise in a silver band. The thinning white silk purchased in Okinawa by Laura's father after the war. The sweet junk, like the gilded angels that were salt and pepper shakers.

She'll notice that, she thought, deeply guilty, holding a plate that had either chipped in the dishwasher or had grown so clean in its first washing in eight years, that the chip which had gone into storage gleamed new. And she thought this: her mother should have the whole pantry of clean glassware arranged in the house she didn't have so she was ready for her bridge club, for the card game she played badly through the middle strip of eyeglasses that no longer were.

Laura did not recall precisely when her mother had returned. Her presence, as always, was unassuming, undemanding, and, on a given night, the thought simply occurred: her mother was back; she no longer was dead.

She made introductions as needed, to local friends, to friends from abroad: this is my mother. If there seems a gap, some lack of knowledge of current events, it is only that she was dead for a while. For eight years in fact. Now she is back.

Her friends, from kindness, did not speak about it. They attended their brandy, examined their thighs for bruises or cellulite. But at night, when her mother had gone with Laura's father to catch up, to live in the house that was sold and to sit on the air of its furniture, Laura, found herself weeping over pans, the bent edge of a sauce pan the lid didn't fit, the tipsy, round bottom of a frying pan, weeping because she did not use these pans her mother had used, had bought from a salesman who'd convinced her, as a bride, to buy on credit for once in her life because Club Aluminum would last and it had.

Yet when her mother was present, the pans were in no way an issue. Laura cooked in her own skillet of iron and stained porcelain, brown from curries and heated oil, and her mother ate or did not eat the food without comment, though, from precedent, the assumption was that she approved the food, tasted or not. Laura thought perhaps her mother would rummage in the cabinets for the pans or say outright that she needed them in order to cook. But she did not hunt or ask. In fact, it was not clear that she cooked. The one day Laura thought she heard her rolling the lid of the frying pan across the floor, turning it with the empty spool Laura's father had made into a handle when its plastic one broke, she found the neighbor's child she was caring for pushing the lid instead.

If the pans troubled her, Laura felt more torment over the furniture. What she had kept she had settled among her own things, and as she moved from room to room, eyeing the beauty of what she had arranged, she felt a dark sense of loss. Damage had been done: a ring marked a table leaf; a drawer front was scarred. There were subtler insults, too: frames robbed from pictures and inseparable pieces now separated. Even the table that she loved, placed with its chairs facing beneath a window as her mother had always placed it, caused her distress, rekindling the shame she had felt at twenty-four when, seated in the farther chair and swollen with her own future, brazenly she had asked her mother just what it was she had done with her life and heard her reply: "The best thing, I suppose, was raising you."

She should offer the table back, she thought, offer to return it to the sunny window that had disappeared into the sun, although when her mother passed idly from the kitchen to the dining room, carrying not even a dish towel, the furniture—table and all—disappeared from Laura's thoughts. She was back to the dishes again, and glassware. She counted, noting the odd numbers in sets: nine dinner plates, twelve soups. Had she lost something or had they come to her lost? What glassware was crystal, what a variety of bottle glass? Why were there nineteen punch cups? *Nineteen.*

This inventory, Laura knew, had nothing to do with her mother's return. It had started because of a wedding. She had offered her house and garden to friends who, lacking the presence of their homes in Buenos Aires and London, had considered City Hall in Minneapolis or a giant plaster fish in Wisconsin as places to be married. She had insisted quickly—suddenly her mother's daughter (perhaps then it had been after her mother's return, although perhaps before)—that she would give them a wedding, a generosity that startled her and astonished Zack and then nagged at her when the friends accepted and she was stuck. She knew she would clean everything, search through her own things and the things of her mother's she'd never touched. She would find what was needed for a wedding it would never have occurred to her to try even on her own daughter.

On an afternoon when the daunting stock of pantry china she was eyeing for the wedding had immobilized her, and when her mother was napping or not napping, Laura knelt by the cedar chest. For a half hour she stared vacantly. Finally, she shifted from her knees and drew out the bag of wrinkled linens that was the remnant of her mother's household trousseau. She touched the fabric, wincing at each broken thread, each thinned strain or yellowed mark. She asked herself questions which were questions for her mother, although later, in her mother's company, they did not come up. What is tatting? Why is the embroidered figure on the day-of-the-week tea towels a girl instead of a woman—why a child set to wash, iron, and sew, market, clean, bake, and go with a dog to church? Should the scalloped blue trim on the torn pillowcases be saved? Why call dresser scarves scarves? What are the names of the stitches?

But though it was a wedding which was the proximate occasion for taking stock, Laura did not look for the sole and relevant garment in the chest: her grandmother's wedding blouse—so small with its lace and buttons, its eyelet and shirring. The blouse was organdy and, for decades, had been assumed too worn to be worn. Laura shrank from the thought of more disintegration. There was no need to look again, she told herself. The bride would find a suitable dress. And even if the blouse were whole, the bride was surely too large-boned for such a garment, although she was not unusually large. She might, in fact, be regarded as small, Laura thought, by those who had not formed their notions of the English from the more diminutive, unfleshed sort.

Laura considered the bride, the groom—framed them in her mind. They were an unexpected couple—the groom with a certain doltish sweetness and the bride with a zaniness and candor that could feel puzzling, as she was no longer really young. As a couple they were awkward in the impression they made of an aimless good cheer, conveyed through a medium of sparring accents. Simply put, they were her friends and, as most friends, accidentally met. She did not need to analyze them more, or wonder if they were the right scale for her house or why they lacked the smiling, untouched delicacy of her parents in the wedding picture in which her mother's train was held in her hand and on the arm of Laura's father as, newly married, they descended the church steps.

Laura had stretched out on the bed, which was not her parents' but Zack's and her own bed, strewn now with linens from the chest. She held the picture of her parents she had slipped from her mirror. Her father had hair. The crown of her mother's veil was heart-shaped and her gown had a Peter Pan collar. In the picture, which was small, her mother's flowers were too tiny to have a name.

On the day of the wedding, Laura's garden bloomed with blue and ivory hydrangea and the rooms of her house were pungent with roses. The bride, to honor her husband's homeland, carried pampas grass. Laura was not sure where the vows were said. She had pruned the ivy on the porch bower and placed the chairs in a fan shape below it, out of the sun, but no one seemed to sit and, from the kitchen, she heard no processional. The bride and groom mingled among the guests, and the judge and trio wandered after them. Laura kept refilling the punch bowl and putting more trays of canapés and truffles on the dining room table. From the periphery, she sensed that the wedding ceremony was being parceled out in phrases, in a traveling sequence of hugs and promises so that each guest received a part of it, but not the whole. She did not know if her mother would understand or, in fact, if she did herself. The groom drank from a bottle of champagne he carried under his arm, and the bride, who wore a gown which was part peasant blouse and part sheer skirt over spandex shorts, kept swooping to kiss the hands of the guests.

"Of course we're already married," she told Laura on a sweep through the dining room. "We did the troth thing at Mystic Lake with the slot machines humming. So indigenous—a money buzz and a Native American casino. But this is awesome. And bloody official."

Laura nodded. "Does the Wedgwood feel English?" she asked. "Hardy or the country scene in *The Winter's Tale*? It seemed so to me with the garland of wheat and the wildflowers. You must meet my mother again. The Wedgwood is hers."

She felt she was babbling. Retreating through the pantry, she carried a Wedgwood cup with its permanent sprigged face and wished fervently for her children, for Mollie and David, who were away in their own lives. Loyally, Zack mixed drinks. Laura's father sat near the garden fence, his plate balanced on his knees. She was not sure about her mother. Since it was Saturday, perhaps she had headed off to market as the towel in the kitchen prodded, though Laura was certain she had seen the hem of her mother's skirt, heard her voice.

The Angelus belled noon from the Cathedral on the hill and Laura clanged through the utensil drawer to find an egg whisk, not a French one but her mother's, which she preferred to her own. She had one sauce left to make. She beat the egg yolks in her own stainless steel bowl, metal on metal the main sound of all the sounds that collided in her kitchen: cars passing, a Bach sonata, planes high on a new flight path northeast, laughter and voices, a bird chirping through the window screen. The neighbor child sat on the kitchen floor and pulled at Laura's skirt while she whisked. To Laura, adrift in the wedding she had dreamed into being, the tug felt right. She picked up the child. Whirled her into laughter. Held her solid, sweet, talcumed softness in her arms.

She thought she was a frightful hostess. She had barely met the guests. Most of them she did not recognize, these friends of her friends and their friends. There was a chiropractor, and a stockbroker, and a woman who had spent New Year's Eve barhopping with her boyfriend and with a writer who'd once worked on *Northern Exposure*. One man had arrived with a riding stock and boots and an actual horse. She had trusted them all with so many things. The horse might step on a caned chair that her mother had inherited through three generations. Someone might steal the guest towels which sixty years ago her mother's neighbor had embroidered as a bridal gift. And the china. The silver and crystal. Already she had rescued a fork from her kitchen garden and seen a candlestick used on the tap of a volunteer beer keg. Every set of everything she held as steward had been disbursed. Would her mother understand? Could her mother forgive her? Where was she?

Settling the child on its father's shoulders and drizzling butter into the heating yolks, Laura was impatient. She sweetened the sauce, finished it. With her apron strings undone, she made her way through her thronged house, her swarmed garden, to look for her mother.

She asked her father if he knew where she was, and he simply looked toward the front of the garden. He was chewing carefully on a strip of marinated beef and, though it was not cold out, he had zipped the sweater he was wearing under his jacket all the way to his throat. He seemed huddled into his plate. Laura pulled a table next to him and filled his water glass.

"She can't have gone far," she said. "Even if she was marketing, she must be back." She edged her way around the people who were drinking coffee by the table that held the cake stand. She had ordered a hundred petit fours and mounted them in tiers, but she could see that the petit four she had placed strategically over the chip that had not been in the cake stand on her sixth birthday had already been removed. The half-inch wound that distorted the glass curve above the pedestal was clearly visible. Laura pinched a begonia bloom from a garden pot and covered it. She did not see her mother.

"I'm hunting for a woman, older, in a shantung dress with purple flowers on it. She might answer to Lucy, though she seems not to," she told the man she thought was an airline pilot. He shook his head but seemed ready to talk. Laura moved away and thought again that it was odd her mother was wearing the same dress today she had described as her very first formal gown. Laura had not seen it before. She was sure it had not been in the things she had given away. Tripping on a rise in the ground, she righted herself, felt herself swimming up to the sky.

From the corner of her eye she saw her grandmother's wedding blouse draped on a tree, but when she turned there was only a man in a white shirt, his arms akimbo as he drew a harmonic—long and eerily high—from his violin.

Laura took her apron off and left it near the bush. As she walked, she was not quite on her feet. The bride and groom were standing next to the gift table, the walnut heirloom she had not meant to bring outside and that was so laden now that its feet had sunk into the earth though there had been no rain all week. Someone had found the basket of dresser scarves she had pushed to the back of a closet, and the neighbor's child, seated in a ruffle on the grass, was pulling them from the basket the way a magician takes scarves from a hat.

A woman with a camera took Laura's picture. She pushed her hair back from her eyes in the wake of the flash. "A lady with purple flowers on her dress?" she asked. "She's not very tall. Her hair was a lovely red once, but I'm not sure about today. She used to wear glasses."

The headshake again. Laura tugged at the sleeve of a frail young man who could not clear his chest and repeated her query. From the back of the garden to the front she greeted each guest with her question, but her mother was not outside. A sparrow, a streamer of crepe paper in its beak, blundered into the sky.

Inside, she caught her own breath and followed voices down the long hall. A couple was seated on her bed. In the hall, a girl leaned against the curve of the banister, a man talking earnestly beside her. The door to the bath was open, and the bathroom was empty. Laura moved toward the dining room. She wanted punch, but there was someone ahead of her. On the buffet wall, in the long mirror, she saw the reflection, a face that had grown small, a face whose features shifted in the wave of the glass. In the mirror, Laura was not sure of the purple flowers. She thought she saw silk.

"Mother," she said. She watched the punch cup touch the lips and then the unexpected slow motion in which it fell away, the golden splash of liquid rising first toward the ceiling and then muffling the crash on the floor. Laura stared at the bits of glass, the shattered prisms of purple light that speared the floor and moistened rug. By itself, the flat handle of the cup lay in one piece.

"It's all right," Laura said. "Is it all right? They were an odd number, of course."

But her voice had nowhere to go. The face in the mirror was undisturbed. More than that, it seemed indifferent. Laura, as the house stood silent around her, backed away.

In the evening, not yet exhausted and refusing help, Laura washed and counted each set back together. Tea towels and guest towels lay in a basket, waiting with lace placemats to be ironed. The pantry filled up, each crystal glass and sherbet dish, each china plate safely returned. The silverware, nesting, added up. For as long as she could stave off washing the punch set, she did. At midnight, when it was the only thing left, Laura braced her elbows into her sides, and lifted the bowl into the sink. Slipping her hands underwater, she ran her fingers around the heavy glass circles that ringed and shaped the bowl. She washed it. She rinsed it and dried it. She washed the platter and ladle with its flared scoop and ribbed handle. Then she washed and dried each cup.

While she worked, she did not count. But when she had restored the whole set to its place on the lower shelf of the buffet, sitting cross-legged on the rug, she did. She got to six and stopped. She pivoted the platter on its base. She counted to twelve. She turned the platter again and, stealing herself, counted upward from thirteen. At eighteen, she stopped counting and looked at the remaining cup. Then she started over again with one. Three times she counted. Four times and then five. Sometime after one o'clock Zack called to her to come to bed. She counted once more. *Nineteen*.

The number would not change. The nineteenth cup was intact. In the dream-haunted night and slow morning when she pulled her own lace curtains open and cried for no reason at all, it was that fact and the appearance at Sunday brunch of the extra wife from another state, which persuaded Laura of a new and unyielding idea. Once again—this time like the final, tight slam of a door—her mother was dead.

IV

SWIMMING

Swimming

In the frozen winter of his illness, as his cancer spread and he began to die, Edward's pale eyes shone a luminous brown. Stilled in her private weather, Nora looked at herself, at her own eyes puffy with elephant skin. Ridgy. Gray. She pulled at her face, looked to see if her teeth had moved in their bones.

Six years earlier she had married Edward. Quietly. Simply. He was steady—the absorbed face she saw when she looked through the glass windows of her office and realized she was thirty-six: past the optimum window for marriage, past the years of ready, casual relationships. She wanted a home. A husband to touch in sleep. A child.

On their wedding trip to Spain, she had tried not to think whether she was in love, though certainly she thought she could love Edward. She loved easily: she loved her cat, she'd loved teachers, she loved her friends. But in Sevilla, city of a thousand wedding dresses and as many dogs, while Edward walked the winding streets of the Jewish Quarter, guidebook in hand, one eye alerted to *caca*, Nora's mind wandered to daydreams of passionate Moors. When motor scooters rocketed by, she held her ground and Edward pressed his back against buildings. In restaurants he was solicitous, oversolicitous. As formal as the Spanish waiters in their black tuxedos, he chose dishes for her until she put her spoon in the *sopa castellana* and its raw egg yolk flooded her bowl. She ordered for herself then, and Edward, without comment, withdrew a distance into himself as though something more fragile than the egg had broken. Nora, for the first time, thought she had married selfishly.

There was sex but no child. As careful in lovemaking as he was at his work editing math-crammed economics texts, Edward never failed to make her come. But he had a studiedness to his movements, a certain roteness that made Nora feel she might read along: *For variety, manipulate clitoris with opposite hand while trailing lead hand between breasts. In beginning thrusts, set a slow pace much like a two-beat kick in swimming.* More than a marriage, she had entered a depression, she thought, though she kept the secret, guiltily praising Edward's kindness until it was legendary with her father: "A little stuffy, we thought at first, but he's been real good to our Nora."

And always no child. Never a child. No flutter of hope but the clock-beat regularity of each month's small stain of red death. Eventually, reluctantly, they had consulted doctors. Nora had been tested and prodded, laparascoped and advised she could be optimistic. Edward, on his third visit, was routed abruptly to an oncologist. Pancreatic cancer, they were told. Certainly fatal. Probably fast.

When he could no longer talk, Edward caught at her clothes, looked at her with the urgency of speech. Nora brought him his laptop, placed his hands on the keys as though he were an autistic child to uncode.

Nothing. Staring eyes.

She offered him soup. Wrapped him in goose down comforters and cashmere mufflers that did not scratch. Played the limping Caruso records that had been his father's. Read to him from the *Tales of the Alhambra* which he'd loved from the day she'd bought it in Granada, and which she'd always found stiff and tedious.

"Washington Irving is wrong," she said. "The towers of the Alhambra aren't ruddy at all." She had told Edward this on the Costa del Sol where she'd left the book facedown on the sand and watched him swim his even strokes in the cold February sea, said it when he came out of the water to dry off and kissed her readily as though he had gotten used to it. Said it now, though she did not think that he heard her.

In the morning sunlight, she watched him sleep, saw him miss a rattled breath and grow still. She sat quietly, hands in her lap. Thought *what if he's dead, he is dead, is that what it smells like death, his eyelids are cold and that's death.*

She ran. In the kitchen, the fall of her footsteps on cold tile, she listened to see if the water was running. She tore at the drawer, found the phone book, fumbled the stunned pages of calling areas and numbers for repairs. She leaned into the wall and dialed "O."

"I think he's dead. My husband." This was her voice. Sound in a bottle. "What should I do? Is there something now I should do?"

A funeral. A cremation. Nora carried light ashes home in a box.

At work she resumed a full schedule, asked that Edward's last project carry his name, selected the typestyle herself. She dressed carefully. Soft blouses, tailored suits. She brushed her hair sleek and fastened it back in a clip, smoothed her makeup over her cheeks and etched her lips clearly with liner. She kept her in-basket clean, walked with an invisible book on her head.

"Stop doing this," her secretary said. "You're in shock. Scream. Nobody will care if you cry. Everybody would really like it if you did."

On the stairs, her boss stopped her, touched her on the elbow. "Take some time off," he said.

She moved his hand, answered him. "I already have."

The weather grew milder, but she did not feel the thaw, barely noticed the snow shrink. On Saturday, in jeans and a flannel shirt and Edward's one baggy sweater, she sorted. Methodically, she filled boxes, labeling them, extracting her life from Edward's life, his life from hers. His music and books and the collection of pipes he had never smoked all went into the corner of the living room next to his chair. She pulled his suits out of the closet and found the clothes she had pushed to the back wall. They were hers—dated and too big for her. Pre-Edward clothes. Pre-size 8. She held a jacket in front of her and looked in the mirror and for a blurred second did not know herself. She dropped the jacket and went into the kitchen. She piled fruit on the counter: white-rotted grapes, apples and oranges, a hard pear. She found a peach and gnawed it down to the pit.

The doorbell rang and she let her father in. "You're not moving," he said tentatively, looking around. "They say to wait a year."

Nora held out an apple. "Maybe I've waited forty years. No, I'm not moving." She pressed the apple into his hand, wouldn't let him talk.

She gave him lunch and sent him home with a carton full of tissues, paper towels, toilet paper. "Edward stockpiled. Not me. Take it," she insisted, suddenly hurried, suddenly panicked.

Her calendar in front of her and leaning on her hands, Nora sat on the hassock by the window. She ran her finger down the Saturdays. Counting the days, it was two weeks since Edward had died: two weeks since his death and almost six weeks since her last period. Nora spread her hand open on the calendar, felt the draggy smoothness of its paper. She knew the likelihood: a hormonal screwup from stress and fatigue. She knew the stranger possibility: a baby.

She leaned on her side against the couch, let the calendar roll over itself and onto the floor. A month ago they had slipped into grayness, into the clouded world of deathwatch. Yet Edward had managed full arousal one last time and she had helped, scared the whole time they would kill him.

"I want this," he'd said. He was feverish to the touch, his breathing uneven, and Nora wondered seriously if the cancer had moved into his brain.

"But what if it hurts?"

"The morphine . . ." Edward closed his eyes and Nora thought he had drifted back into sleep. She had seen this kind of deep tiredness in her grandparents when they were very old, but it still startled her in Edward. She could not separate the sense of it from age. She turned the lamps off, clicked on the night-lights her father had bought the day after Edward had fallen against the dresser on his way to the bathroom. She picked up the water jug from the nightstand and took it out to the kitchen for more ice. When she came back, Edward was awake and looking at her, his face a filmy blue in the dim light. "An aquarium," he said.

She looked at him puzzled, then understood. "I'm blue, too? We look like we're in an aquarium? Maybe one of the big ones in Chicago."

He was fumbling at the covers, his fingers scratching against the sheet as he tried to push it down.

"Oh, I don't think so," she said quickly, speaking even before his eyes tightened, a sudden pain riding his body.

When his body relaxed, she unclenched her hands and sat down on the bed. "Are you OK?" she said. She was aware of how pointless the question was, but how important. For her. She longed for his words, his explanation of all the ways he was sad at dying and the way he knew he was alive because he could feel pain and the way he wanted to be alive from pleasure even in his jagged, skeletal body.

She touched his cheek. "We can do this if you really want," she said, surprised at her own words, certain, as she said them, that she was right.

She helped him with the sheet. She touched him and stroked him. He wanted her clothes off. Everything but her open, silky blouse that cooled his hands, made her eyes green. She could tell these things. Knew that he wanted the Barber cello concerto on, wanted it turned low so the *fortes* were muted.

She lay on the bed, still stroking him, smelled the papery skin odor that had grown over the quiet scent of him that always lingered on the pillowcases and in his shirts. "What's going to work here?" she said, trying to sound cheerful. "What should I do?"

His eyes were filled with the room's light. He touched her breast and she thought she felt a fingernail, then knew it was the bone of his fingertip. She saw the light in the wisps of his chest hair. She rolled over, moved a leg across him without making contact. She touched his face, kissed him. Her weight was on one elbow and her knees, and she lowered herself so she could feel him just beneath her.

"You all right?" she whispered.

"Keep going," he said. She rubbed against him. He had closed his eyes. She could feel the slow, slow stiffening, the pulse of blood. Finally, with her fingertips she pressed him carefully into her, hoped for a point of weightless contact. Wondered if his dying was this death, too: of sex.

His orgasm, when it came, was a muffled gasp. He shivered his semen into her and then lay flinching with pain. Nora slipped off him and lay quiet, tried helplessly for something to say. The scent in her nostrils was unmistakable. Marron. A seminal odor like the pungent flower of a Spanish chestnut tree.

Edward's hands twitched against the sheets. "Garden of earthly delights," he mumbled.

Nora wanted to cry, wanted to know if death, with its narrowing eye, had taught him bitterness as life never had. And now a baby from this sorrowful lovemaking? She did not want a baby. This baby. This theoretical baby, product of an aging egg and the irradiated sperm of a father who'd not lived to be loved. Or to stick up for himself. She could not imagine this nightmare child.

Nora picked up the calendar, lobbed it into Edward's books. In her study, she ransacked her desk, searched for her French tapes, found them and stood tapping her fingers, frowning at the rush of sounds, the muffled smear and swallow of syllables she couldn't understand. She tried reading the manuscript she'd brought home from work, then opened the piano and practiced the *Goldberg Variations* she'd intended as a gift for Edward but accepted now as a gift to herself. She concentrated on time, studied each measure as a synergy of rhythm and math.

In the night, thunder cracked. She stood at the bedroom window and saw not the pummel of rain but snow sheening from dark silver to white as lightning flashed across it. She touched her nightgown for blood. She found none.

Dreaming and awake, she perceived herself as a container, a full cup to balance to prevent a spill, though she knew she could not allow this child—child?—to grow to full term.

Yet wide awake at 4:00 a.m., she was wild with hope. She could pretend. She did pretend. She closed her eyes and held her baby: squirming and moist-lipped, perfectly sound, perfectly smart. A smiler. A baby who laughed. She divided up features: Edward's small ears and gray-brown eyes; her mouth, her chin; a perfect nose from the ancestral heap. A bubble-blowing, beautiful baby.

In the morning, rain shooting down the windshield like tracers from a firecracker, she drove to their club. It was Edward's place more than hers. She was a runner and had been since they married and Edward had asked her what she did for an exercise program.

The rain dripping down her face, she hunted in her purse for her membership card while the girl at the desk waited. She went through pockets, through her wallet cardholder.

"Here," she said, remembering the zippered pouch in her duffel bag. She pulled out the card, handed it over, bar-code side up.

The girl read the name, slid the card through the scanner, and smiled when she handed it back. "The teachers always point out Mr. Luca's strokes. Such good mechanics. I haven't seen him in a while." She looked over Nora's shoulder toward the parking lot.

Nora fumbled the card into her purse. "He's not coming. He's been very ill. Actually, he had cancer and died."

She picked up her duffel bag, saw the girl's face turn a blotchy red, saw her open and close her mouth, felt the shady power, the pulled trigger of her own knowledge.

"I can tell them to change you." The girl was talking over the music for the aerobics class. "I'm terribly sorry, Mrs. Luca. To the reduced rate. They'll give you the lower rate. How awful. His stroke mechanics were really the best."

Nora nodded, shouldered her bag. "I've forgotten my goggles. Later. Thanks. Maybe I'll come back later."

In the car she held on to the steering wheel, blinked the baby into a second of nonexistence. She wanted to smile, wanted to tell Edward he'd made a conquest of an eighteen-year-old with sweet, round glasses, wanted very much to tell him that.

At her office on Monday, she poured her coffee down the water cooler and turned down an offer of drinks after work. She took the exit from the building that skirted the smokers' corridor and got on the interstate. Fifteen miles later, she spotted a drugstore she'd never been to where she could look for a kit for a pregnancy test. With the motor idling in a strip mall lot, she sat in her car and listened to an aged writer tell a radio interviewer he'd not just written books but had told stories to his wife at night, that if he fell asleep before he finished, she woke him up, pulling him back to consciousness so she could learn what happened.

This was what wives did, Nora thought. They didn't worry a man's conscience, but rather his consciousness. And they brought him back, when necessary, so his voice could grow perilously old. And beautiful. This was what they did.

She shifted into reverse, pulled onto the freeway and drove with the glistening, blued lights of twilight back into the city.

In her neighborhood the streets had disappeared, jackhammered open since morning. She made detours until she found a route into her own driveway. Inside her living room, she glanced at the boxes, decided once more she'd decide later what to do with them. She ate a banana. She ate a bowl of cereal and got out her swimsuit and did her own pregnancy check: still no blood.

At the club desk there was a new girl, and Nora went to the locker room anonymously. She'd mocked Edward for his swimmer's faith. "Right. The perfect exercise. No heat stress. Low impact. I'll put it on your gravestone," she'd said before he got sick, but here she was. She was ready for the exercise that didn't jar anything loose.

She made her way through bodies, all with their signature mark of triangle fuzz. She remembered this familiar thing—that women out of their clothes surprised her. The matter-of-factness of their shapes and movements. The way their bones and muscle and fat molded perfect shapes or big-haunched, saggy ones. The way long thighs and low-curled breasts and a thick pad of stomach could look very sexy. Once, on a morning when she'd come with Edward to use the exercise machines, she'd told him that.

"Your theory is the ones that look like they'd look the best don't?" He had lifted their duffel bags from the back of the car, and he held on to them waiting for her answer—teasing, not letting her off the hook.

"Something like that." She'd laughed a little, half-defensive, half-embarrassed. "It's just there's all this variety—more than fat and thin—and we pretend there's not. Like *Schindler's List*. We're supposed to believe no Jewish women have cellulite? A little flesh maybe looks good. Lived in. I don't know. Disturbing. Like a woman had something to do with making her own body."

"Write an article. Take a camera to all the health clubs and Ys."

"Right," she'd said and said now, half out loud, soaping herself in the shower. She saw the surprised look on the face of the naked woman next to her, wanted to say she was talking to her husband the swimmer who'd died with perfect joints, that this was how she did it.

The pool was almost empty. Nora stretched her arms, her legs, tugged her swim cap on, and adjusted her goggles, realized she was nervous. On their trips to Florida or Aruba, she'd paddled a little, floated next to the shore while she watched Edward swim against the waves. But basically, she didn't swim. Basically, water frightened her very much.

She put her feet in the pool, slid carefully down the side until she could stand up. She eased her shoulders under water. OK. She was doing OK.

"If you can run, you can swim," Edward always said, and she tried that now. Tried running in the water until she had pushed herself off the bottom and was kicking, kicking, her body tensed, her face in water that pushed in her nose and her ears, scissored her neck, pulled her sideways. She flailed up, exploded air, felt her heart beating. With the shock of chlorine, she inhaled her first real breath in weeks.

In a coffeehouse with tall ceilings and potted palms, Nora was drinking coffee with her friend Liz. She'd ordered decaf.

"Can't sleep?" Liz asked. Her saucer eyes, which were dark like her hair, were full-bore on Nora.

"No. Just decaf. I can sleep. Well not exactly, but it's not that."

"Are you OK? Are you doing OK? God, Nora, you worry me. You're so contained with all this. You should go ahead and fall apart if you need to. I'll catch. Everybody will. You've got friends."

"You cut your hair."

Liz pulled at an earlobe length curl and turned her head. "Is it fuller? I hate it when it looks stringy. Argh. An attack frond." She ducked, pushed away the fringy palm hand that had swished over her neck when she moved. "Don't try to distract me. I'm not kidding about this. Have you got somebody to talk to? I'd have been crazy without my shrink when Steve and I split."

"Maybe I need more than a shrink."

"What?"

"Maybe I'm pregnant."

Liz juggled her cup two-handed onto the table. She looked at Nora. "This is possible?"

Nora nodded.

"It does explain the decaf."

"I was thinking maybe it's stress."

"It could be stress. Right. Or hysterical pregnancy. Didn't you always hear about that when you were a kid?" Liz drummed the table, stuck her finger in her coffee. "If it's for real—God, what do you do from here?"

"I don't know. The crazy part of me keeps seeing this perfect baby that shakes off the radiation and chemo and doesn't mind being fatherless and passes amniocentesis for aging moms with flying colors."

"You're not that old for a mother these days. You'd be almost a baby of a mom in Italy. But you don't really know."

"I don't know a thing. You don't either."

"Right. I can do that. I don't know a thing." Liz was shredding her napkin, pulling at the earlobe curl again.

"Are we ready to go?" Nora reached for her coat.

Liz looked at the clock. "Sure. Right. I can catch a bus in three minutes." She stuck her napkin in her coffee mug and slid her own coat off of the chair.

Outside, Nora pulled her gloves on, pushed the fabric into the webs of her fingers. The weather was chilly, uncertain, lodged in the fault line between winter and spring.

"I miss Edward," Liz said. "You had the perfect man. Smart and cultured. Fit. Devoted. One in a million. Clean."

"Clean?

"Is that like saying somebody's earnest? He just always struck me as clean. It was a comfortable clean. You know, clean."

"And you know I love you even though you're nuts." Nora felt the wind whip up, roll down from the height of the buildings. A neon sign had blinked Liz's face blue, and Nora reached over and grasped her hand. "I've been scared. That I'm not me anymore. That I'm this Nora St. Clair Luca person who turned into the other bookend to Edward. And the most awful part is for the last years of Edward's life what he had was me wanting something else. Excitement. Babies. I don't even know what all. I cheated him."

"Never." Liz looked at her, hugged her. "Loony girl. He was crazy in love with you. That was the cleanness. A sort of transparency of love. But you've got the bookend thing. You were in sync. A real out-of-body experience for me watching that."

"Here's your bus."

"Get one of those kits. Let me know. I'll call you if you don't call me. Are you going home?"

Nora shook her head, reaffirming her own decision. "Swimming," she said. She buttoned her collar, stepped back from the curb and the air hiss of the bus's brakes, opened and closed her hand good-bye.

At the pool, she was ready for the water. Before work, she'd sat at the kitchen table reading one of Edward's swimming books. Brushing toast crumbs from the pages, she'd memorized a list of basic skills. Now, with a picture in her mind of Johnny Weissmuller in a loincloth, she felt purposeful. She adjusted her goggles, snugged them under her eyes. "Learning to swim, baby," she whispered.

Releasing the side of the pool, she dunked herself. She tried a bob. Another bob. She exhaled and inhaled until she'd pockmarked the water with gurgles of air, and then bobbed some more. She kept jumping and bobbing, counting and bobbing, water swishing down her shoulders as she emerged, water enveloping her when she z-ed her body back below the surface. Then she pushed herself over, jellyfished, felt the water buoy and hold her as her arms hung down, felt it move beneath her like the swift, sudden curve of a manatee.

Her father was waiting on the front steps when she got home. "You don't have your key?" she asked.

"I didn't want to scare you. Somebody inside when you got here. It's not that cold out." He was shivering a little, small in his jacket.

Nora opened the door. "That's me." Her father pointed at the blinking answering machine light. "I called before I came over. Your mother told me I should."

Nora nodded, then kissed him swiftly and hung up his jacket. "Got a new picture?" she said. He was unrolling a pebbly sheet of drawing paper.

"I did it off the wedding photograph of you and Edward. I thought you needed a real picture of him."

Nora looked at the sketch her father was holding. It was smudgy with charcoal, innocently drawn in her father's self-taught style. But it had something of Edward. His own innocence perhaps. His near-youth. His health.

"You made him very handsome," she said, looking at the fine features, the intelligent eyes.

"He was a handsome man."

"You think so?" She looked at her father and back at the picture. "I was never quite sure."

"The smartest person I ever knew and very handsome. The sickness wasted him." Her father cleared his throat. "I figured you'd want the picture of the man you fell in love with. So you remember things right after all this sorrow."

Nora felt the drawing paper rolling back against her hand, creasing itself against her fingernails. Her hair was still wet against her neck, clingy like a newborn's. She let the picture curl itself shut. "I'm learning how to swim," she said.

When her father left, she clicked the television on and off and sat in Edward's chair and read about body roll, about Bernoulli's Theorem and laminar flow, about the principles of lift and drag in the water. She wanted a name for how the water carried her, and that was an Edward thing to want, but she wanted it anyway. She hunted for his Barber CDs, and put on the first movement of the cello concerto, saw herself swimming, moving in the snaking currents of its sound, holding to its steady tempo despite the syncopation, the rhythmic edge.

She fed herself a tangerine, made a bowl of Cream of Wheat, and ate a cold spear of broccoli. She went to bed.

No blood.

The night compressed itself around her. Nora pushed her cupped hand through its space. Edward hadn't made stories for her, but he had read to her, had floated her into the surface of sleep. Her mind was full of partial tales, theories: she knew that the perception of reality changes with the amount of information possessed, but she didn't know who had said so or the proof offered. She knew a shampoo of urine was the aphrodisiac of somebody's culture, but not whose. She knew there was a case for the slugging average as a measurement in baseball, but she wasn't clear what it was. She knew that Liberace, J. Edgar Hoover, and Barney Frank had all had chauffeurs, but she didn't know to what extent. And she knew all these things in Edward's voice, but she could not find it now to make her sleep.

There were shadows on her ceiling, a starchy newness to the sheets. She was wide awake.

She squinted at the dial on her alarm clock, waited for the minute to switch and then held her pulse until it switched again. Seventy-two. She'd lifted her head, so she should start again, though what did it matter? Edward, before he was ill, Edward unsedated and facing oral surgery was a fifty-two in a dentist's chair. He had a pulse like Pelé's, a pulse that you waited for like waiting for the other shoe to drop, and yet before he died, he was in the 100's, his body burning itself up.

Nora hunched herself into her pillow. If she slept, *when* she slept, she would dream a new baby. This had started to happen.

On Thursday, Liz called her at work during a morning production meeting. Nora took the phone, cradled it while she fanned out color samples. "Not these. Green for a book on pulmonary disease?"

"It fits. The whole green thing," Liz said in her ear.

"This is a bad time."

"OK, but did you get the kit? I left two messages on your machine."

Nora shook off more colors. "I'll call you later."

"Can you meet me for lunch? Twelve thirty?"

"Probably. You can check with my secretary." Nora pushed an extension button and handed the phone off to the art director. "This is about breathing. We want the color of water and air. Understand? You do understand? We need blue," she said.

She left the room. She shut the door hard and leaned against it, her body tense, reaching for the motion of the butterfly stroke she'd read about at breakfast. She could almost feel it in her nerves: the pulse of the wave through her body, the tuck of her chin as her head forced the surface and down.

At lunch, Liz was curious. "What's with this swimming thing? I thought you hated swimming."

"No, I'm just afraid of the water." Nora spooned an ice cube out of her glass. "And I'm too old to be afraid of things."

"Then this won't scare you." Liz reached down on the bench and set a paper bag on the table. "I got you a kit. You can find out now instead of driving yourself crazy."

"I should take this as a friendly gesture?" Nora paused. "Maybe I'll be crazier if I find out."

"You'll know what you're dealing with so you can make a decision. No baby and, if you really want it, maybe you can have one anyway. All you need is a doctor to have sperm shipped to. Some of the stuff is from really smart guys. Or good looking if you'd rather. You can even do it yourself. Well maybe some ovulation shots."

"And you are certifiably crazy. This is something you've tried?"

"No. You're older than I am. Don't shake your head. You are. Six months. I haven't panicked yet. And, anyway, I'm not sure I've got this baby thing you do. What if the kid got my hair? But there's this other business. You have to go through these stages and I don't think you're doing so well. The grief thing. I've got a book at home. You have to do all of them—denial and apathy. Anger. Resolution. Maybe there're more, but that's what I remember. You're like somewhere between weird guilt and smooth sailing. I think that's a problem."

"Maybe I'm ahead of schedule."

"I don't see that."

"Well I know Edward is dead and I'm not inert and I'm not angry at him that he's dead. It's more like I'm angry he was ever alive. You have that on your list?"

"That could be anger."

"Right. Here's this perfectly admirable man who was forty before he ever really learned irony, and for six years I'm his wife and I'm not single anymore—not really. I'm this altered thing, except older."

"Maybe this is like opera."

"Explain?"

"The thing Shaw said. That an opera's just a tenor and soprano wanting to make love, but they get stopped by the baritone. Wait, Nora. I've got this figured out. Edward is the tenor and you're the soprano, but this *idea* of something got in the way of your understanding you really were in love. And that's the baritone."

"Edward was a baritone."

"We're talking metaphor. Anyway, Nora, he did learn irony. Doesn't that count?"

"Maybe," Nora told herself, but it was later when she was driving to the pool after work. She'd gotten new goggles and when she put them on in front of the locker room mirror, she thought she looked like a Martian. Two little black girls, smooth and dry as stones, pointed at her and whispered while they wriggled their suits on.

In the water, Nora stood with a kickboard and measured the pool length with her eyes. She knew she had the start of a decent kick. When she'd held the pool side and stroked her legs against the water, she'd felt a current move across her soles and insteps. She settled her goggles now, slicked the strap ends away from her eyes. She gripped the board and pushed off the wall, started the slap of her feet through the surface, aimed herself down the pool toward deep water.

She gulped, spit out water, gripped the kickboard harder, felt the hard give of the Styrofoam. Stale water had caught her mouth—water like the foot smell of the locker room corridor. She could feel the tension in her thighs, the slow going, her breath high and choky in her lungs, but she wasn't going to stop, wouldn't stop, wouldn't. She was past the guard stand. Halfway. Past halfway. The stripe on the pool floor bent, dipped down, and there was more water to kick against, and she didn't know where her chin should be. But she was moving, the blue kickboard riding ahead of her. She could see the string of colored pennants coming at her, and she kicked harder, but it slowed her down. Their isosceles colors went stationary, stayed hanging out of reach. And then she was moving after all, a snail's kick until at last the pennants were over her, past her and she stretched out, stretched until the board nudged the pool wall, and she could grab on and fumble the board into the gutter, the trough, the thing it was that carried the water's spill and splash at this hard perimeter.

"Mrs. Luca." Nora heard the voice above her.

"Did you want some help?" It was the girl from the desk, the girl with the Edward crush leaning over her, hands on her knees. She had on a suit and a tank top that said LIFEGUARD.

"I'm OK."

"I mean with your kick. If you relax your ankles. Turn your toes in a little and bend your knees on the downbeat. It's kick a ball, kick a ball, keep your foot loose. And follow through. But loosen your ankles. That's the main part. It's using your muscles but not pumped."

Nora nodded. "Thanks," she said, but she waited at the wall until the girl had moved away, waited until the girl had whistled the children from the locker room to walk not run, waited until she was starting over with her heartbeat.

Kick a ball, kick a ball. She grasped the kickboard and let go of the pool edge. She was pushing through panic, and then she caught herself, let her feet go floppy. First her right foot. Then her left. The hiccoughy Barber *pizzicato* was playing in her brain and she was going faster. Going almost fast.

At mid-pool, safe in the shallow water, she popped the board free and tried one whirl of her arms, her shoulders powering up and out and her tucked chin pulling her face below the surface. When she came up for air, she wanted to shout and the shout stayed bursting inside her even when she went out to the parking lot. In the darkness, the streets still gone, she drove the parallel universe of alleyways, skinnying her car by the backsides of buildings, the canted views, the sets of BMWs and Toyotas parked next to each other on cement slabs. When she'd found a parking spot, she carried her duffel bag up to her door and turned the key. There was a message from Liz on the answering machine, and Nora knew she wouldn't call her back, wouldn't tell her she'd left the pregnancy kit locked in her trunk on purpose, that in this matter of discovery, she'd settled on the same laissez-faire approach she'd adopted for the boxes in her living room.

She'd showered at the pool, but she started a bath anyway, wrapped herself in a terry robe and waited for the tub to fill. At

Christmas, Edward had given her bath beads in a high-necked bottle with a gold leaf label and satin tie. Translucent. Peach. She knew when he'd bought them. On Christmas Eve, he'd gone out alone, determined, happy she thought, though he came home exhausted and shivering. She'd pulled him out of his coat and scarf, the hat and gloves, clothes. She'd piled blankets and hot water bottles on him until his trembling had almost stopped.

"Don't look in my jacket pocket," he said, catching her hand, pulling himself back from sleep, and she nodded her promise.

She reached for the bottle now, taking it from the shelf above the bath. Untying the ribbon, she held the open neck to her nose. Sandalwood maybe, talcum, a hint of tangerine, a penetrating and exotic scent of sensual perfume that Edward with his blasted senses could hardly have smelled.

She pried out the first bead, a second, and dropped them under the streaming water, watched them ride their own foam. Even before she stepped into the water she could smell the scent on her skin.

She soaked in the water, rubbed at her toes. Carefully, she worked the loofah sponge over her body, examined her fingernails, and pushed the cuticles back. She brushed her hair from her forehead and ran the hot water, watched the bubbles pop and disappear. The scent clung, powdery, layered: even her thoughts bore its code. A genie scent. Odor from a bottle that had slipped through time and, because her breathing was no longer tight or resistant, gave her Edward. His presence. His desire. A hint of all the things he knew, which she'd boxed up, banished, she'd thought, to the living room.

The phone rang, stopped after two rings when the answering machine intercepted it. Another message from Liz. Or maybe a discreet hang-up from her mother who bore her worries quietly, who offered help but who suggested with her familiar body language that there really wasn't any.

Nora pushed the handle to let the water out. She stepped onto the bath mat. No blood. She dried the wet ends of her hair with a towel, tried rubbing the scent from her skin, kept rubbing, realized even as her eyes stung that the scent wouldn't go away, wouldn't. She put on her nightgown and crawled into bed. For a still moment, Edward was there. In the perfumed air, she could feel the rocking motion of his voice.

When she slept, she dreamed a dream of many infants, a tawny one like a black man she'd faced in the split time of a revolving door—something private and spare, inexplicable and alluring in his manner. Another baby that was twins, each infant motion telegraphed in duplicate. A baby with a dental bridge of smiling white teeth, and one that came with a pedigree of a Nobel Laureate, one fathered through a wet suit by a deep sea demolitions expert. A last one did perfect flip turns inside its amniotic sac.

Exhausted mother that she was, she turned to Edward for help. And this was what surprised her: in spite of howling infants, the man she observed commanded her full schoolgirl attention (she, a teenage mother with round glasses). He was motion picture large. She took the slow, camera's-eye tour of each feature, each muscle group, until the lens reversed and Edward was looking at her with such fearless scrutiny she could not look back but opened the eyes of her dream and knew she had dreamed a true thing: Edward a year ago in a cold Prague bar, more brown eyed than gray in his suede jacket, preoccupied until the instant she looked at him and he looked back, and she startled with love. A familiar thing. A thing as true as the scent on her skin, and she had forgotten it.

In the morning her father surprised her, walking up the steps out of a blue sky when she went outside to get the paper. "Is something wrong?" she asked.

"You didn't answer your messages. Your mother was worried."

Nora picked up the newspaper and held the door for him to follow her inside. "So, what were my messages?"

"Just about how are you?"

Her father stopped in the living room and in the middle of Liz talking on the answering machine: . . . *and it says, too, you should speak to someone about sex. Use it or lose it. Call me, OK?*

"You need to pick that up?" her father asked and Nora shook her head and then laughed. "You have time for tea before I leave for work?"

"I got time, yes. But maybe no. Nora, your mother and I were talking about this. If you're grieving over two deaths, Edward—and you know, family plans—your mother and I want to be all the family we can."

"I know. I do know," she said thinking maybe, just maybe he was getting close.

At work she left a flower and a note for the art director saying aqua was a good compromise, he was right to keep that much green. She worked through lunch, eating a sandwich at her desk. At four-thirty she was out the door, headed toward the pool. She'd studied the schedule and there was an hour between Masters' Swim and a water aerobics class. In fact, she had the pool to herself except for the lifeguard.

"Excuse me," Nora said. She'd recognized the Edward fan, though she looked different with a new spiky haircut and no glasses. "I don't know your name. Would you mind watching my stroke and telling me what I'm doing worst?"

"Tree, but T-r-i," the girl said, pulling her chair closer to the pool edge. "Short for Triumph. I've got five older brothers. Sure, I'll watch."

"Tri," Nora said. She started out, started running into her kick, started streamlining her body, the way she'd read to do in the swimming book, and then reached her arms crablike into the water. She swam with her face down.

When she came up for air and turned around, Tri was standing on the pool deck. "Not bad. Relax, though. You're tight and you need to lift your left arm out of the water more. Your kick is better. Can you follow your arm back with your head and catch a breath? It's all in one motion. Watch." She pulled her tank top off and made an easy, shallow dive into the pool. Nora saw the Edward smoothness of her stroke, the easy rhythm as she swam half the pool and back to her.

"See the air pocket at my shoulder? Face the wall first. Just your breathing and arms. Blow all your air out underwater."

Nora tried planting her feet while she pulled her arms through the water and rotated her head to the side and back. She felt like a ventriloquist's dummy, but she was catching the breath. She was getting it.

"Great," Tri said. "Now try it with the kick."

Nora nodded. She resettled her goggles. Counted to three. Pushed off the wall. She was kicking too hard, her dead-in-the-water kick was back, but the arm pull felt close and she was getting air. She was probably swimming. Twelve strokes down the pool, she thought *deep water ahead* and swallowed a mouthful and came up sputtering.

Tri laughed. "You were doing it. But you're tense. Are you scared?"

"Of the deep end."

"Try just hanging in the water like you're lying over a table."

"The jellyfish?"

"Right. Do it and relax every muscle you've got."

Inhaling, Nora tried to remember the water moving to hold her as she hung below the surface, thought of the manatee. "Relax," she heard in her ear, and then she felt the tight grasp of her wrist and her body rolling over, her face up, and she was being drawn through the water, flying as though she were pulled by a harness of dolphins.

"Unbelievable," she said when Tri transferred her hand to the pool wall.

"You can let go," Tri said. "Be an arrow and drop."

"You sure?"

"Hands at your side. I'm here."

Nora thought about that and let go. She was underwater, the whole five feet six of her, and for the first time in her memory with nothing solid to touch, nothing, and she was frightened, but not really panicked. She looked at the blue walls, blew her breath out and then kicked herself up. She was a body's length from the pool end, and she swam to it.

"See? The water holds you. And you've got the lungs. Uh-oh. Kid alert. Back to work." Tri was off down the pool in a flash of heels.

"And maybe I'm dreaming this," Nora said aloud to herself. She leaned back in the water, stared at the ceiling lights, traced their curved rims with her eyes. She rolled over and in the deep water tried a surface dive, not quite afraid but curious at the slight sensation of pressure in her lungs. She practiced her strokes off the wall, her half strokes, and maybe the start of a whip kick. Marveled that she'd never before craved this rhythmic suspension. Made a perfect somersault and came up with water in her nose but didn't care. Swam three solid strokes out, three strokes back, three out, three back. Hung with her shoulders pressed against the side of the pool, her legs in front of her. Saw the gluey balloon of blood on the water: tiny blown filament of blood, impossible parachute. Thought *this is death, is this death, is this death too?*

She swam. Her arms thrashed, flailed. She sucked in water instead of air. She'd lost the sense of how her legs should work. Yet she was not drowning, and knew that she was not. The sway of the water lifted her up, forcing her afloat and into Edward's words from an old beach in their life, that you didn't wrestle Poseidon but ignored him and he went away.

She chopped her way down the water, her goggles steamy, fogged. Had she swum a body out of her body? Had she bridged a span of primordial liquids? And if this choking well of tears and the hollowness tunneling through her were grief at last—the unhealing of what was messily healed—had Edward, Edward for whom she grieved, left a medium to hold her?

In the locker room, she spent twenty-five cents for a tampon, and closed herself inside a changing booth. She sat on the bench in her suit, held her shoulders. Wondered that wracking sobs, a sea of crying, could be so quiet. She dragged her duffel bag between her feet, leaned against the partition, felt its cold metal against her cheek.

A lone black foot, perfect and miniature, appeared beneath the curtain. She looked. A second foot followed, snagged in a pink and yellow swimsuit. Nora sensed a topple even before the curtain gave and a small bottom grazed her legs. She heard the startled *oh*, felt the warm body against her. A red barrette like a shiny jawbreaker bobbed upright on a black braid.

Nora heard the squirmy breaths. "My sister won't. Can you get me into my suit?" The child was intent, righting herself, her face squeezed tight as she kept on tugging.

"I'll try." Nora nodded. "Yes, of course," she answered, surprised into calm, into usefulness. She untwisted straps, smoothed the suit across the round stomach, held the arm loops and settled them firmly, snugly, the quiet snap on soft shoulder bones.

ACKNOWLEDGMENTS

Version of stories in this collection have appeared in *Prairie Schooner* ("The Temple of Amun"), *North American Review* ("Swimming"), *Third Coast* ("Eleven Days to China"), *Florida Review* ("Birdman"), *Crania* ("American Snapshot, 1993"), *Pikestaff Forum* ("Treasures"), *The House on Via Gombito* ("Journeys in the Hidden World"), *Stand* ("Watching Oksana"), and *The Second Penguin Book of Modern Women's Short Stories* ("Watching Oksana").